JANETTE OKE
& T. DAVIS BUNN

The Birthright

BETHANY HOUSE PUBLISHERS
MINNEAPOLIS, MINNESOTA 55438

By Janette Oke

Celebrating the Inner Beauty of Woman
Janette Oke's Reflections on the Christmas Story
The Matchmakers
Nana's Gift
The Red Geranium

CANADIAN WEST

When Calls the Heart
When Comes the Spring
Beyond the Gathering Storm

When Breaks the Dawn
When Hope Springs New

LOVE COMES SOFTLY

Love Comes Softly
Love's Enduring Promise
Love's Long Journey
Love's Abiding Joy

Love's Unending Legacy
Love's Unfolding Dream
Love Takes Wing
Love Finds a Home

A PRAIRIE LEGACY

The Tender Years
A Searching Heart

A Quiet Strength
Like Gold Refined

SEASONS OF THE HEART

Once Upon a Summer
The Winds of Autumn

Winter Is Not Forever
Spring's Gentle Promise

WOMEN OF THE WEST

The Calling of Emily Evans
Julia's Last Hope
Roses for Mama
A Woman Named Damaris
They Called Her Mrs. Doc
The Measure of a Heart

A Bride for Donnigan
Heart of the Wilderness
Too Long a Stranger
The Bluebird and the Sparrow
A Gown of Spanish Lace
Drums of Change

Janette Oke: A Heart for the Prairie
Biography of Janette Oke by Laurel Oke Logan

The Birthright
Copyright © 2001
Janette Oke & T. Davis Bunn

Cover by Dan Thornberg

Published by Bethany House Publishers
A Ministry of Bethany Fellowship International
11400 Hampshire Avenue South
Bloomington, Minnesota 55438
www.bethanyhouse.com

Printed in the United States of America by
Bethany Press International, Bloomington, Minnesota 55438

ISBN 0–7642–2229–5 (Trade Paper)
ISBN 0–7642–2230–9 (Hardcover)
ISBN 0–7642–2232–5 (Large Print)
ISBN 0–7642–2231–7 (Audio)

The Library of Congress has catalogued the Hard cover edition as follows:

Oke, Janette, 1935–
    The birthright © by Janette Oke & T. Davis Bunn.
        p. cm. — (Song of Acadia ; 3)
Sequel to: The sacred shore.
    ISBN 0–7642–2230–9
    ISBN 0–7642–2229–5 (pbk.)
      1. Great Britain—History—George III, 1760–1820—Fiction.
2. Canada—History—1763–1791—Fiction. 3. Inheritance and succession—Fiction. 4. Canadians—England—Fiction. 5. Acadians—Fiction. 6. Sisters—Fiction. 7. England—Fiction. 8. Acadia—Fiction.
I. Bunn, T. Davis, 1952– II. Title.
    PR9199.3.)38 B55 2001
    813'.54—dc21

                                    00-011950

I call to remembrance my song in the night;
  I commune with mine own heart,
  and my spirit made diligent search. . . .
Thy way is in the sea,
  and thy path in the great waters,
  and thy footsteps are not known.

Psalm 77:6, 19

T. DAVIS BUNN, a native of North Carolina, is a former international business executive whose career has taken him to over forty countries in Europe, Africa, and the Middle East. With topics as diverse as romance, history, and intrigue, Bunn's books continue to reach readers of all ages and interests. He and his wife, Isabella, reside near Oxford, England.

JANETTE OKE was born in Champion, Alberta, during the depression years, to a Canadian prairie farmer and his wife. She is a graduate of Mountain View Bible College in Didsbury, Alberta, where she met her husband, Edward. They were married in May of 1957 and went on to pastor churches in Indiana as well as Calgary and Edmonton, Canada.

The Okes have three sons and one daughter and are enjoying the addition of grandchildren to the family. Edward and Janette have both been active in their local church, serving in various capacities as Sunday school teachers and board members. They make their home near Calgary, Alberta.

Prologue

Catherine stood in the tiny second bedroom of her daughter Anne's home. She could hear the sounds of departure beyond the closed door. But Catherine was not good at leave-takings. There had been far too many in her life already. She was determined to be strong this day, but to do so she needed a moment alone. Time to sit by the window and watch the last of autumn's finery carpet the small front garden, time to pray to the Lord for strength.

So much had happened in these past months. She felt as though her memories were a swirl of autumn colors, caught in the winds of time. The previous summer, Sir Charles Harrow, eighth earl of Sutton, had come to Halifax in search of his brother, Catherine's husband. Unable to have children of his own, Charles required an heir to carry on the Harrow legacy and to secure his vast landholdings in England—the only need great enough to force him to renew contact with his estranged brother. But Charles had discovered that the child Andrew and Catherine had raised was not theirs by birth.

Though not by bloodline, Anne was as close to Catherine's heart as any child could be. As she sat by the window, Catherine felt nearly overwhelmed by the wonder of great events and small beginnings. Simple friendship with an Acadian family had blossomed into both heartache and joy. Though Catherine had lost her daughter and raised an Acadian baby as her own, in fact she had received gifts beyond measure. Now she called both these lovely young women her daughters. Nicole, the child raised by Louise and Henri Robichaud in the Louisiana bayous, and Anne, the girl she and Andrew had cherished these eighteen years.

Now Anne was wed, and as Catherine sat with her eyes half-closed against the sun's warming rays, she inwardly heard once more the joyful sounds of those wedding-day bells. Andrew's brother had arranged for a ship to bring Henri and Louise to Nova Scotia for the marriage. This had been the gesture of a man transformed, both heart and mind, through the hardship and discovery of his voyage. Charles was not only a man now at peace with himself and his brother's family, but a living testimony to the power of God. As Catherine prepared herself for yet another departure, she gave silent thanks for this brother-in-law who had become a friend.

Before his return to England, Charles had presented two bolts of finest silk as a wedding gift. Catherine did not even try to guess at the cost. She and Louise and Nicole all had worn new gowns. Her own was lavender in color, and Catherine could not help stroking its softness. The other bolt had been a creamy pastel silk, taken from the hour before sunrise, and they had used almost all of it for Anne's wedding dress. When Anne had emerged through the church's front doors, a collective sigh of wonderment had risen from the congregation. Anne's betrothed, a fine young doctor by the name of Cyril Mann, had watched his bride's approach with something akin to awe. Catherine had sat and held Louise's hand through the entire ceremony, both of them trying not to weep. Anne, this precious one who was daughter to them both, this fragile girl whom they both loved, had looked radiant that day. Nicole had stood beside her "sister" as bridesmaid, together at last.

Now it was Nicole who knocked and opened Catherine's door. "We're ready, Mama."

"Then so am I." She rose and held out her hand to her daughter. "I was thinking about Anne's wedding day."

"So much joy," Nicole agreed, the words accented by her native French. "A good thing to remember at this time."

"Yes." Catherine stood holding her daughter's hand, studying the strong, lovely features. The wedding was a month and more behind them now, and the time had come for yet another parting.

"Is something the matter, Mama?"

"I just wish I could hold on to the good moments longer," Catherine said. She took a deep breath. "Come, let us be off."

But as she followed Nicole out to where the others waited, it was not just this day's parting that pierced her heart. She looked ahead and saw the future with a mother's wisdom and prayed for strength to endure what she sensed might lie ahead.

Chapter One

The day was gentled by a wind far too warm for early October in Halifax. Out over the slate gray sea, light rimmed the horizon. Above was only cloud, so thick it appeared more like twilight than midmorning. Anne reached out with both hands, one taking hold of her husband, Cyril, the other gripping Nicole. She drew strength from these two fine people and knew with utter certainty that were it not for them here beside her, heartbreak and tears most certainly would overwhelm her.

Henri and Louise Robichaud made their way about the gathering, holding each person in turn, saying their good-byes. Two months they had been reunited here in what was once known as Acadia and was now called Nova Scotia. Though this particular day graced them with the comfort of a gentle autumn, already the landscape was dotted with the remnants of two early snows.

Three times Henri and Louise had postponed their departure, not wanting to leave behind their precious daughters. Now they had no choice.

Still, when Henri released his brother Guy and turned to Andrew, he waved Nicole over to translate a final apology. "They say this will be the last ship of the season heading south."

"With the troubles rising," Andrew replied, "I have no doubt. Some are even calling it war."

"May God grant that it not come to that, not now, not ever." Henri spoke with quiet fervor in his native French, but Nicole's English translation was so subdued, so tragic sounding, that Anne turned away.

The sky seemed grayer still, the wind softer, the sliver of light on the horizon more golden than ever. It was a curious sort of day, the world darkened and brooding, yet with a crown of brilliant light shimmering in the distance, countless miles away. Anne clung to the light with the desperate hope that this was indeed a sign for her, a promise that if she held on through this heartrending moment, there would be joy again.

The time with Louise and Henri had been unlike anything she could have ever

14

expected. Their reunion was branded upon her heart. It took place here at the quayside, on this very spot where they now stood holding one another. Catherine had waited beside her then, with Andrew, Nicole, and Cyril. Just like now. Only different. For her body had not been wrenched by sorrow as now. Then Anne had seen the impossible come to life, the dreams of years. And had experienced joy so great her heart could scarcely contain all she had felt. The boat drew near, and the two figures rose up above the gunnel and waved and shouted and laughed and wept. The three of them—Andrew, Catherine, and Nicole—had replied with tears and cries of their own.

Anne had suddenly found herself blinded, as though her heart's only defense was to wash the day in tears, leaving her unable to see a thing. No matter that she could no longer see, as the boat had scraped against the rocky quay, and the cries and the footsteps came nearer. No matter that she had no memory even today of what the newcomers said, for her sobs had drowned out everything else. No, it had not mattered at all. When first the rough, sinewy man's and then the softer woman's arms had wrapped around her, Anne had felt her heart growing, expanding in her chest.

Re-forming so as to create enough room for these new folks she could now call her parents.

Anne was drawn back to the present moment as Louise stepped in front of her. Now it seemed to Anne that Louise understood exactly what she was feeling. She stepped before her daughter and said, "Never shall I be able to think of this place on Earth without knowing the joy of lifelong dreams come true and the sorrow of this day."

Anne struggled to draw a fraction of breath, enough to whisper, "Momma."

Then a hand caressed her cheek. "Look at what this day has brought. The dream that woke me in the night, year after hopeless year, has now become real. What joy I feel in hearing you speak that word. What impossible joy."

"Oh, Momma. I cannot let you go."

"You never shall, my daughter. Whatever this strange thing called life may bring, we shall never be parted from one another's hearts." It was Louise's turn to struggle for breath. "It is the only thing which grants me the strength to endure this day."

A second figure stepped up alongside her mother, stockier and grayer, with a strength that reminded her of a great oak tree, able to endure the harshest winds, bending and creaking but remaining ever steadfast and sheltering. "Oh, Father."

"There is no man wealthier upon this earth," Henri whispered as he held her close. Then lowering his voice for her ear alone, he added, "Or sadder."

Louise fitted herself into their embrace, and the three of them held together as one. "I came with one daughter and one hope," her mother said. "I leave with two daughters and the wonder of seeing miracles come alive with my own eyes."

Strangely, Louise's hardest farewell was not with the daughter she had borne, Anne, but rather with Nicole, the daughter she had raised as her own. Or perhaps not so strange at all. During their two months together in Acadia, Louise had come to see her daughter as the adult she now was. No longer viewing her with protective eyes had also meant accepting the choices, even the mistakes, her daughter might make.

Her adventurous young lady with the fiery gaze hungered for all the experiences life had to offer. So unaware of her beauty and its effect on others, she paid no mind to the young men who stumbled in their haste to grace her with whatever caught her eye. But since severing the relationship with Jean, her first love, life held too great an appeal for Nicole to give further thought to romance.

It was a mother's wisdom that colored Louise's expression now and filled her heart with fear. She feared all the dangers and mysteries that such a life of yearning, of searching, might bring to Nicole.

But when Louise finally released her embrace of Anne, her dear sweet Anne, it was to Catherine that she turned. Louise gave her dearest friend yet another hug, murmuring words neither of them truly heard. Then Andrew, then Henri's brother Guy and his wife. Until finally there was no one left but the baby who had become her own. This reality ran against all the logic of this Earth, yet was so right that Louise could imagine no other truth than to be mother to this willful, wonderful woman.

"You will take care, won't you?" Louise whispered, her eyes imploring.

"Of course, Mama." Nicole gripped her mother's hands with both of hers. "What a question."

"It is only, well . . ." Louise had spoken

several times of this, but still there was the sense of leaving too many things unsaid. "I know how much you want from life. And I know the cost—"

"Please, Mama, not here. You've already told me all this."

"I know, I know. It's just . . ." Louise bit her lip. "You are my precious daughter. And I would do anything to be the one to carry your burdens. But I cannot. So all I can ask is that you take care, daughter. Please. Take great care. The world can be so harsh, especially to lovely young women with the desire to know all there is to life."

Nicole started to deny her longings. Louise could see it in her daughter's eyes. And for the first time in her life, understanding Nicole so well brought its own sadness as Louise looked into her jade green eyes and saw all the mysteries yet to be unfolded. All the future possibilities, all the challenges, all the dangers. And now there was nothing she could do except pray.

To her surprise, Nicole did not speak, did not dispute Louise's words. Instead, she gave a fraction of a smile, the first anyone had shown that gray and dismal day. "You have always known me better than I know myself."

"Sign of a mother's love at work,"

Louise replied. "Now promise you will take great care. And above all else, that you will be honest with yourself and honest with your God."

The smile trembled, then completely melted. A single tear escaped to trace its way down one cheek. The sight threatened both Louise's heart and the day itself. Nicole whispered, "I wish . . ."

Louise yearned to have her daughter finish the sentence as she wanted, that Nicole would agree to come home with them, to return to the life they knew, the world they had shaped and claimed as their own. But though she willed it with every shred of her being, still Louise knew it was not to be. Whatever future was open to her daughter, Louise knew Nicole's explorations—within herself and without to a vast, unknown world—were not yet over. In fact, she realized with an awareness that pierced her heart, Nicole's own quest had barely begun.

This time it was her husband's hand that reached up and lifted the tear from his daughter's cheek. "The most precious jewel in all the world, here in my poor hand."

"Oh, Papa." Nicole allowed herself to be a little girl again, flinging herself into Henri's embrace with a force that rocked the strong man back on his heels. "Don't go. Please, I beg you."

"I must, my darling daughter. Just as you must stay. No, no, don't speak. Let us not cloud this day even more with words we both know mean nothing. Here and now, let us only hold the truth between us. Yes?"

Nicole released her grasp on him just enough to search his seamed features and piercing dark eyes. Though it cost her to have her sorrow and indecision revealed, still she needed to draw from his strength and drink in the furrowed face once more. "You are right."

"The gift of truth, then. You are searching for your destiny. This restlessness is your greatest strength. And yet it is also your greatest risk, my beloved daughter, for it can blind you if you allow. Do not enter your future blindly, my precious one. Do not."

"I will pray, Papa." She gave her face an impatient wipe, clearing her eyes. "I promise."

"And you will study the Word and seek to do His will and not your own."

"I promise," she quietly repeated. "And I will seek to know Him as you do."

"Ah, what praise, what folly." Henri attempted to smile. "Know Him better than that, daughter. Rise above my own poor limits. Make me proud."

"I will miss you so," she said and couldn't help but let go another tear as she turned back to Louise. "Both of you."

"Let us join together in prayer, then. Will you ask Catherine and Andrew to translate?" Henri waited till all had come together, an assembly tightly bound by sorrow and faith. "Dear gracious Lord, we give solemn thanks for all the wonders of our lives. Even here, even now, in the midst of the hardest farewells we have ever known, still we place our lives and our hopes upon your altar. Grace us with your presence and shelter us from all life's storms. Be with our daughters, both of them. . . ." Henri stopped and drew a deep breath, taking comfort from the arms and hearts that surrounded him. "Be with both these precious young women and grant them the joy of knowing you and living in your will. Be with Louise and me as we travel home. Be with all of us as we face life's journeys. In Jesus' holy name I pray, amen."

Louise found she couldn't focus on the figures gathered at the quayside. The boat rocked and strained against the waves as they were rowed ever farther from the rock-lined harbor wall. The scent of salt and the voyage ahead filled her senses, and her heart keened a forlorn cry. So Louise turned away. Just for a moment, long enough to gather herself. She had to. But the vision of those slate gray waters and the ship ready to take them away offered no comfort at all.

A breath of salt-laden wind kissed Louise's face, and a gull swept in to hover alongside the boat, so close Louise could have reached up and caressed the bird's white wings. It hung there riding the wind, drawing a chuckle from the seamen. Its dark eyes fastened on Louise. For some reason, she found comfort in this strange moment, as if the bird were a reminder of the possibilities of her life—a herald of tomorrow's hopes. There was no making sense of her thoughts, yet Louise found herself now turning and peering out at the figures growing smaller on the quayside. She rose up to her tiptoes, waved a final time, and called across the waves, "I love you all!"

"I love you, too, Mama! Farewell, Papa!" Nicole allowed her arm to drop to her side. Her heart felt squeezed, and it hurt to breathe. It was not just sorrow she felt but aching guilt. How could she permit her parents to leave without her? She knew it was selfish to give in yet again to her desire for a life beyond the borders of her Louisiana world. Nevertheless, as she had prayed over and over during the nine weeks of their visit, Nicole had felt a sense of being called in two directions. Or perhaps even more than that. As though the choice was hers now. She could go, or she could stay. Or . . . what?

Nicole's face lifted to the ship waiting at anchor, and with a sudden jolt, she felt a new realization that took her beyond the confusion and sorrow. It was as if words were being whispered to her mind and heart there on the quayside, words suddenly more clear than the screeching gulls overhead.

She raised her arm and waved once more, this time wishing them a safe journey with all her heart . . . yet held also by a new conviction, one that left her shaken and transported beyond her sadness.

Though she couldn't explain why or how, Nicole was certain she would be leaving as well. She would go to England. And she would leave with the coming of spring.

Chapter Two

The unseasonable warmth lasted six full days, long enough to have the entire region talking. Halifax's older ladies gathered each evening as was their habit, and while they knitted they recalled hard winters gone by and the one yet to come.

Then, on the seventh day, Anne woke up to find the day lost behind drifting veils. The world beyond her front porch lay cloaked in fog. The surrounding trees, now robbed of the last of their fall colors, were transformed to dark etchings against the misty dawn.

Cyril called to her from inside the house, "Anne? What on earth are you doing?"

She smiled but could not bring herself to turn around. She was too busy impressing the morning on her memory. "Enjoying the sunrise."

"Don't be silly, my dear. There is not any daybreak to enjoy." Cyril emerged already dressed for his morning rounds, all except his frock coat and boots. His house slippers slapped across the holystoned planks as he strode to the open front door. "Come back inside. You might catch a chill."

"In just a moment." Anne inhaled another lungful of the biting air. She tried to hold it in, wishing she could also hold everything she was feeling with perfect clarity. The whole day seemed surrounded by a special luminescence. The dark shadowy trees were burnished with a glow only she could see. The haze itself was not gray but silver, which sparkled with the light of her joy. Anne strained with all her might to retain every last detail. She wanted to look back on this morning with such vividness she would be able to close her eyes and see again how everything had been, captured by the sparkling hush that filled her heart. She shivered with the delight of it all.

"There, you see?" Cyril walked up beside her and slipped a wrap about her shoulders. "Cold and trembling already."

She reached up and clasped his hand. "You are such a good, dear man."

While drawing her inside, Cyril halted and looked down upon her face. "You're a funny little robin this morning."

Anne held her husband's hand tighter still, thinking how remarkable it was that just the week before she had been inconsolable in her grief over Louise and Henri's departure. Her heart had felt so heavy she questioned whether she might ever recover. Yet here she was, receiving the day with joyous fervor. She was not someone given to great swings of emotion, but there was so much happiness to this dawn, so much goodness in this day, she wanted to dance and sing her way down the lane. She turned her head, kissed Cyril's hand as it rested on her shoulder, then said, "I don't deserve you."

"Ah, my darling Anne." Normally Cyril did not express his feelings in public. And any show of sentiment on her part where others might see, even within their family, was met with frowning displeasure. But not this time. Perhaps it was because of the way the mist clung so tightly they could hardly see their front fence, or perhaps because of how she had moped her way about the house since the Robichauds' departure, or perhaps because he now sensed the exultation that caused Anne's heart to overflow. Whatever the reason, Cyril leaned in close and, with his free hand, stroked her fine, dark hair. "It is good to see you returning to your old self, lass."

She slid around in his arms, bundling in close, knowing it was time to share the news. "I have something to tell you."

"And I you, my dear." He made a show of pulling his father's watch from his vest pocket. "I am late for my rounds."

"They will have to wait a bit longer." She took another breath, once more caught by the need to hold this memory close. This was her husband's face the day she shared the news, the way he looked, the love he held in his eyes, the way his arms felt around her. When she released her breath, it was to say, "Cyril, we are going to have a baby."

The news catapulted him back until he was stopped by the doorjamb. "Y-you are . . ."

"With child," Anne finished for him, when it was clear he couldn't do so himself.

"M-my dear . . ." He straightened himself, then reached out. "Look at me. I deal with such matters a dozen times a day, yet now I am trembling like a leaf."

"But you're happy?"

"Happy? My dear darling Anne, I am beside myself with joy."

She smiled, knowing to him it would

look like she was behaving calmly, while in truth she was preoccupied by the need to capture the moment, the impact the happy news had on him. Tears of joy flashed in his eyes, and his body shook with delight as he looked on her with awe. Yes, all of these things needed to be experienced so deeply that she could reflect back at the end of their long and glorious life together and re-member with crystal clarity this resplendent moment. "I am so glad."

"You . . . you seem so . . . well, serene."

"I've had time to come to terms with this."

"How long?" he asked.

"A few days now." She watched as he stepped over to her and then drew her close. She felt the strength in his embrace, and the love. "I wish I could have been certain ear-lier and told Louise and Henri before their departure."

Cyril did not slacken his hold on her when he replied, "But think of what your news will mean coming later on. Instead of a letter describing your sorrow over their departure, you will give them reason to cel-ebrate and be glad for you."

"For us," she said, wondering how it was that one heart could hold such joy, such love, and still remain intact. "Glad for us, my husband."

Nicole heard the horse-drawn cart long before she saw it. Cyril and Anne always used the wagon with the harness that jangled like bells for the journey to Georgetown. Catherine had been poised at the window for two days now, knowing they were coming, though not exactly when. Knowing too it would be the last journey Anne could make this winter. Anne remained a delicate figure and prone to the grippe during the winter months. Therefore, a two-day journey over snowbound trails would be impossible for her. Weather permitting, Nicole and Catherine and Andrew would travel to Halifax once Andrew had delivered his Christmas sermon. Even so, this was to be their final time together for three months, and Catherine had been beside herself with excitement. Nicole heard Catherine's little cry of delight as the cart rounded the last turn and finally came into view.

Through the window Nicole saw Catherine and Andrew greeting the young couple with welcoming embraces. She felt no resentment over their closeness, nor jealousy. No, she held back because it was at such times that she felt most acutely her own lack of roots. Returning to Acadia, or Nova Scotia as it was now called, had been a most satisfying experience. She remained certain she had made the right choice by staying behind when Henri and Louise sailed back to Louisiana. But there was nothing she could do about her feelings of isolation. She carried this deep inside her, probably would the rest of her days. Coming to know the Father had comforted her greatly, yet there was this mystery to her makeup, this legacy from her early days upon hard and bitter roads.

The kitchen window looked out over the front garden. Other than a few scattered turnips and potatoes, the garden now lay brown and bare. Nicole kneaded a piecrust into its tin while watching Andrew and Catherine erupt into cries of delight. She guessed at the news and smiled in shared pleasure. Anne and Cyril would make wonderful parents. Nicole smiled even brighter when she raised her flour-covered hand to return Anne's enthusiastic wave. No, she was not jealous, but the family's joy over this most natural of events seemed to heighten her sense of wondering where she belonged.

Journeying to Nova Scotia, discovering her family, settling into their routine, and now learning English had all proven to be valuable lessons. More precious still had been the sense of binding herself to her Lord. Yet for every answer she gained, for every lesson learned, even more questions sprang to her mind. What was to be her own lot in life? Would she ever find a man and settle down? Was she to have a family, a home, a place that was hers and hers alone?

"Nicole, look at you!" Anne bustled in, as happy now as she had been sad the last time they saw each other, the day Henri and Louise left. "You have more flour on yourself than you do in the pan."

Nicole accepted the slighter woman's embrace and then gazed into her fragile porcelain features, noticing right away the new flush, the bright joy that shone about her. There was no question now. "Tell me the news."

"Wash your hands and come with me."

"Tell me first."

"I won't. This is *my* news, and I want to tell it *my* way." Anne laughed and grabbed Nicole's arm. "Hurry or I will burst!"

Catherine came through the door as Nicole was wiping the flour off her hands. "Would you like a cup of hot cider to take away the chill of the road?"

"Thank you, Momma, but first Nicole and I are going out to the point. That is, if this sluggish lady can hasten her step."

Catherine gave them a fond look. "My two fine daughters, look at you."

Anne's impatience only made Nicole move more slowly. "Perhaps I should brew you a cup of tea. You look all peaked," Nicole said.

"She does not," Catherine chided. "In fact, she looks marvelous."

"John Price has gone out for a walk," Nicole continued. "He'll be so glad to see you, perhaps you should wait—"

"Grandfather will be seated by the fire when we return," Anne broke in. "That is, if I can ever get you up and ready to *leave*."

"Sit a spell," Nicole teased. "Catch your breath and tell your mother about the journey. She has been spending her days waiting at the window—"

"And I have been waiting *weeks* for the chance to talk with you alone!" Anne found Nicole's cloak and flung it at her. "Now either come along or I will drag you!"

Hand in hand they emerged laughing

from the cottage. Cyril looked up from unpacking his cart—medicines for the village and Halifax goods for Andrew and Catherine—and grinned. "Hello, Nicole. Has she told you yet?"

"No, I haven't, and don't you say a word!" Anne gripped Nicole's hand tighter and tugged her out the front gate. "Cannot you move any faster than this?"

But Cyril had not finished. He hefted a cedar chest from the cart and cried, "Look what Charles has sent us, a chest full of spices!"

"Don't stop her now with such distractions," Anne pleaded. "I'll never get her started again!"

"Careful what you say," Nicole warned, caught by the smaller girl's joy. "I might race away and leave you in the dust."

"Not this time." Anne seemed to laugh even when speaking the simplest words. "For today I have wings all my very own!"

"Then show me these wings!" Nicole gathered her skirts and sprinted ahead, finally able to cast aside the melancholy and escape from all the unanswered questions.

The two girls ran together through the village, holding hands and laughing, spurred on by the smiles and fond greetings of those they passed by. All knew their story and shared in the mystery of their becoming friends.

Friends yet much more, for Anne was fast becoming the sister Nicole never had. They reached their spot at the cliffside, high above the point where the Bay of Fundy joined up with the Bay of Cobequid, then seated themselves on the massive old tree trunk. Anne took a long moment to find her breath while staring out over the waters of her home. "I used to come here when I was a little girl."

"You did not drag me out here to speak about your childhood," Nicole objected.

"No. But I was thinking about this on the journey." Anne kept her face turned toward the sea and its chilly breeze. "How I sat here through my growing-up years and wondered who this girl was, a girl my age, who had given up all this so that I might live."

Normally, thoughts of the early days and their hardships left Nicole feeling as though a shadow had been cast over the entire world. But not here, not now. Anne shone with a joy so profound, not even the darkest memories could touch Nicole. "Tell me."

Anne turned to her. "You already know, don't you?"

"You're with child?"

"Yes." Anne looked back to the sea, breathing in the air and the day both. "When I was little, I always thought it would be nice to know you. I hoped it would. But never in my wildest dreams did I imagine it would be this good, this . . ."

"Perfect," Nicole whispered, turning her own face seaward. "Perfect in every way."

"To have another woman my own age, one who knows my deepest secrets and my past, some parts even better than I know myself. It is a miracle. But as for perfect, I am not so sure." Anne reached over and took Nicole's hand. "I pray every night that you will soon find a young man of your own. Someone who will give you the kind of joy that I've found in Cyril."

Nicole said quietly, "Pray for the joy, but not the man."

"You don't want to marry?" Anne asked with an astonished look on her face.

"In truth, I don't know what I want. Some days it is one thing, others something else. I have always had a restless spirit."

"You aren't happy here?"

"I am happier than I've ever been in my life." And this was true. Despite the alien countryside, the harsh weather even in the height of summer, and the days of wind and rain that presaged even fiercer weather still to come, Nicole had found herself mostly content. "But I don't know if it is happiness because of the place and the people or from all the new things I am learning."

Anne nodded slowly. "I think I understand."

"Never mind me. This is your day and your news." Nicole squeezed her fingers, which were as slender and delicate as the rest of her. "I am so happy for you."

But Anne's face remained solemn, her gaze searching. "You're going to England, aren't you?"

Nicole found herself unable to respond.

"That's it, is it not? You're going to accept Charles's invitation?"

"I don't know. But I think . . ." She felt it impossible to complete the thought. Speaking it aloud would grant the words too strong a focus, too great a potency. "One thing I do know, and only one. If I decide to go, I'll need you with me when I tell our parents."

"Our parents," Anne whispered, tightening her hand over Nicole's. "Whatever will I do when the roads close and we are separated?"

"You will write, and you will pray. Just like me." Nicole's mind was suddenly filled with other partings. She no longer thought of the snowbound roads between them, but of the vast and desolate seas. "And don't you worry, not for an instant. I have not gained a sister and a family only to lose them again."

Chapter Three

Anne could not say what left her more distressed, the morning nausea that accompanied her pregnancy or the news that continually sifted in from every side. No one was able to decipher which of the rumors were true and which were not. Even so, it was disturbing to hear of the many battles and rising conflicts. She wished she could shut it all out, for she wanted to welcome her baby into a sane and wholesome world. War had already touched her life in far too many ways.

Had it not been for the warmth of her home, both in the fireplace and in Cyril's constant care for her and their coming baby, Anne may have deemed the winter too much to endure. But the excitement of the coming child and this new dimension to their life together made it impossible for her to feel dispirited for long. God had been good, had given them so much. Counting her blessings always began with the miraculous yet heart-wrenching way He had intervened in her own infancy.

Whenever such memories invaded her mind, Anne pressed a hand tightly to her abdomen. The very thought of giving up this little one filled her with a new understanding of what Catherine and Louise had suffered on her behalf. How did they live through the sorrow of losing a baby? Anne couldn't imagine the pain it would bring.

But God had been gracious in allowing them to be reunited. A miracle—that is what it was. Only a miracle of God could have brought them all back together again.

And Cyril? Anne felt that Cyril was another of God's miracles. She had thought her love to be complete the day she walked up the aisle to be joined to him as man and wife. She knew now her love was only a bud then, waiting to burst into full bloom with the passing of days and the binding of hearts. The child growing in her womb had meant a new intimacy, a new reason to cling to each other. To plan. To promise. To build a life and a home fit for such a gift from heaven.

She knew that Cyril felt similar stirrings. Anne sighed, then moved from her chair by the fireside to add another log to the hungry flames.

Cyril had been coming home so tired and worn. It had been weeks since he had managed a decent night's rest. Almost every night, as his head settled on his pillow, another pounding came on the heavy wooden door. Someone begging for the doctor to tend a desperately ill family member. Ailments always increased with the snow and cold of winter's fury. But a greater number were now coming down with grippe and inflamed chests. Cyril had already begun losing patients to the winter infirmities. This troubled him deeply. On such days he returned home with features stricken by the agony of failure. Anne hated to see the darkness in Cyril's eyes, the grim set to his jaw, the way his hand stole to the back of his neck as though the tension building there was almost too great to bear. With all of her heart she longed to shield him.

But she dared not leave the warmth and safety of their home. Cyril had forbidden it. Her husband had decreed that, for her own and the baby's sake, she mustn't expose herself to the winter illnesses. Even as Anne appreciated his concern and love, she chafed at the order. Over the months of working alongside him, she had learned much about caring for the sick. Now it seemed wrong that she was not using her skills to ease the burden Cyril carried. Yet Anne couldn't disregard his wishes, so she stayed at home and fed the fire and stitched little garments to add to the drawers where she caressingly placed the baby things.

And over and over she prayed. She prayed for the end of winter. For the world to turn to peace again. For all those who were ill. For the child she was carrying. But mostly for Cyril, that God would give him strength and rest and wisdom. That God would hold him close and assure him of her love. That God would grant her strong, capable husband safety as he made his way through storms and dark nights, caring for those who no longer could care for themselves.

The weather broke enough for Andrew, Catherine, and Nicole to make the trip to Halifax to join Cyril and Anne for a belated Christmas celebration. Nicole felt thankful for an opportunity to shake up the routine of her days. And until their arrival in Halifax, she would have no idea how Anne was faring that winter.

Tears streaked down Anne's face as she opened the door to greet them. "You've come!" was all she was able to say, and then she flung herself into three pairs of arms all at once.

The ladies were hustled into the house and over to the warmth of the fire. While Andrew went to care for the team, Anne set the kettle on the hearth, promising to serve everyone just as soon as he came in from the cold.

"I thought Grandfather might agree to come," Anne said, joining her mother. Her excitement kept her on her feet.

"We pleaded, but he said no. He does not find the cold agreeable," Catherine said. "Besides, he said he'd manage the fires while we are gone."

Nicole rubbed chilled hands together, scooping up heat from the open flames. Everyone knew it was important to have someone to care for the fires when the winter winds threatened to glaze the window-panes with patterns of heavy frost. In a matter of hours, everything within a home could be frozen solid. Had it not been for Nicole's own restlessness and the intense desire to see Anne again, she would have remained there with him. The trip down had been freezing.

Nicole turned back to her sister. "How have you been keeping?"

Anne looked down at her still-slender waistline. "Confined. How else could I be when Cyril hardly lets me lift a hand? And he won't let me out beyond the doors. He's so afraid I might come down with the grippe."

"And rightly so." Catherine extended her feet toward the orange-red flames. A crackling log sent out snapping sparks, making her withdraw again. "The season has been beastly. I think it has been one of the most miserable winters I remember. One day brings more cold and snow, then a milder snap but with a horrid damp. Then a wind that goes right through. A body can wrap up to hold off the cold, but not the dampness and the wind that drives to your marrow. I fear that is why so many have been ill. No number of layers of clothing seem to help."

"I suppose," agreed Anne, her face slightly shadowed.

Nicole felt that she gave little thought to the words. "Your nausea has eased?"

Anne laughed. It was a soft, awkward sound that prompted Nicole to think she may have had little to laugh about over the preceding weeks. "Finally," Anne replied. "It probably did not last as long as it seemed at the time. Some days I thought I'd never be able to eat another breakfast. But I have a voracious appetite now. Cyril teases me."

The door was pushed open, and then Andrew appeared. He shook snow from his fur cap and brushed it from his shoulders. "It's snowing," he announced needlessly. "I fear we made it just in time."

Anne helped him with his wraps. "I have the kettle on. Tea will soon be ready. Get close to the fire and thaw out your bones."

Andrew stomped his feet thoroughly on the heavy woven mat by the door and moved to do as Anne had directed.

"Met a fellow out on the road. Said the war to the south seems to have picked up momentum."

Nicole saw Anne freeze midstep. Her face went pale. "There are always rumors," Anne replied, "but no one knows the truth of the matter."

"Well, this man said there are those who continue to flood into Halifax bearing tales of a coming conflict."

Nicole watched as Anne's hand went

unconsciously to her aproned front, but she did not speak.

"I'll get the tea," Anne finally said. "Have a seat, Father." Then she quickly left the room and disappeared into the small kitchen at the rear of the house.

Andrew and Catherine exchanged glances. "Perhaps the news of war disturbs her," Catherine said in a soft voice.

"News of war disturbs us all." Andrew crossed to the offered chair and lowered himself with a deep sigh.

"This is not a good time to be worrying her with what cannot be helped," Catherine went on. "With God's grace this present conflict will not touch us where we are."

Andrew ran a hand over his grayed beard. "Every conflict the world over touches us in some way."

There was no further mention of war, however, during the remaining days of their visit. Talk was of cheerier things, like the baby, springtime, and the summer sun. By the time they had to say another temporary good-bye, Anne was laughing quite naturally again. The shadows seemed to have left her eyes, and her spirits lifted as she counted off the weeks before their home would be graced with a new little life. "I do hope the sun will have cared for the winter ills," she said rather wistfully. "I want Cyril to have time to enjoy his new son."

"Son?" Andrew raised a teasing brow.

Anne laughed again, a merry laugh that bubbled up with joy she felt deep in her heart. "We say *son*," she admitted. "We've even named him—John, after Grandfather Price. Cyril says he's sure it's going to be a boy. And he is the doctor," she laughed.

"More than one doctor has been wrong on that score," Andrew chuckled, picking up on Anne's lighthearted mood.

"Well, should Cyril be wrong, there will be no grieving in this house," Anne said. "A daughter would be just as wonderful."

Nicole moved for her turn to embrace Anne as they said their good-byes. Inwardly she had to admit that, though she was thankful they had made the trip, she was also glad their visit had come to an end. It had been rather depressing to be in Halifax, sharing Anne and Cyril's home, being reminded daily of their great affection for each other. And the intensity with which they looked forward to the baby's coming became hard to bear. For some reason it had planted a longing in Nicole's soul, but a longing she couldn't identify nor express, not even in her prayers.

She had intended to have a talk with her

father and mother during the days of leisure with Anne and Cyril—days away from the demands of the village parish and household chores. But the time had never seemed right. She wondered now if they had already guessed what her answer would be to her uncle Charles. If so, they had said nothing. Now as Andrew led them to the waiting team, and Anne called one last good-bye from the open door, Nicole felt a strangeness within her being. Sadness and uncertainty and a longing for closure regarding God's leading all in one. She forced a smile and turned to wave to Anne standing in the doorway, bundled in a heavy shawl against the damp cold of the day.

Back in Georgetown, Nicole found it easy to take up her familiar routine. The weather held stubbornly to its lower temperature, encasing the East Coast in an icy grip. Cold sea winds blew off the frigid water and pulled at the sleeves and hems of cumbersome coats, whipping the ends of scarves used to protect faces and ears from frostbite. The cold fought its way through the heaviest of woolen shawls draped over hunched shoulders.

There were days when Nicole felt she did little else but feed the ever-hungry fireplace. But in truth she did much more. Increasingly she was able to help Andrew with his parish duties. As much as she had come to appreciate the time spent with her mother, she enjoyed getting out and stirring about the village. As the days grew longer and warmer she was even taking the horse and sleigh now to visit her uncle Guy and the other Acadians in their newfound settlement that lay a half day's ride down the road. Nicole enjoyed expressing herself once again in flowing French, rather than stumbling around for the proper English word. She always returned after a few days' visit feeling reinvigorated.

Andrew joined Nicole on one visit to see Uncle Guy and found himself so warmly welcomed that he encouraged Catherine to make the trip, also. Soon they were all traveling from Georgetown at least once every month. Nicole was thrilled by their coming along with her, for she felt her two worlds were at last beginning to blend. Even as she translated for her English and French families, the old and the new gradually melded, making her feel she now belonged to this homeland she'd come to love. She felt more whole, more at peace with who she was. Perhaps soon God would show her how the past was to be played out in her future. Surely there was some purpose for the events of her life, some way that they would benefit her, and others, in the days to come. If she could just discover what that might be, she knew she could make peace with her past.

She took every opportunity to improve her halting English. Catherine helped her add words to her vocabulary. In their daily Bible study together, they bent their heads over the Book and read and talked and learned. But it was more than Bible and language study; it was also a wonderful opportunity to bond as mother and daughter. It soon became Nicole's favorite time of the day, and when she looked at Catherine's glowing eyes, she felt her mother shared the feeling.

Catherine prayed in English, her words slow and deliberate. Nicole knew this was for her sake, not the Lord's, who understood perfectly every language on the face of the Earth. Nicole knew it was Catherine's way of helping her become at ease in talking with her heavenly Father in her mother tongue.

In these shared times together, Nicole struggled to say her prayers in English. But she believed that God was an understanding God. In her private times of prayer, she went back to the familiarity of the French, pouring her heart out with abandon.

She still treasured the worn French Bible given to her by Louise and Henri, yet she was equally touched by the new English edition from Catherine and Andrew. It was another indication to Nicole that she had been richly blessed to have two sets of loving parents.

It had been many months since they had heard from Henri and Louise. Their last letter said they had returned to Louisiana safely, but the news of unrest had met them at every port. They were much relieved to be home once again. But since then, Nicole had received nothing.

Surprisingly her uncle Charles's letters had not been delayed by the threat of war. A fresh bundle of post arrived with each ship that pulled into the Halifax harbor. They were family letters, written to inquire about family affairs. Though Charles never pressed Nicole for an answer, he shared newsy items about English life and continually assured her that he was praying God would lead in the matter. In one such missive he was bold enough to request that, should she consider his offer, she not come for a short term but remain at least two years. *It takes time to adapt to something so totally new,* he reminded her.

Nicole continued to pray for God's guidance, but in her heart she felt she'd already been given her answer. To refuse to go, she felt strongly, would be denying what God had been gently urging her to do. One day she would agree with the plan, her body tingling with excitement, then the next day she would draw back, fearing the unknown. But in her heart she did not waver in her decision. She would go in obedience. Still, she couldn't bring herself to discuss it with Andrew and Catherine. Nicole dreaded the thought of fighting through another decision that would rend herself from the family she loved.

Chapter Four

After nine days of wind and pelting rain, the morning was shocking in its silence. Nicole made her way out to the point, walking the now-familiar trail through a frozen world. To everyone's surprise the early March storm had been warm—warm, that is, for winter in this northern world. No matter what she might have thought while living in the bayou country, March in Acadia was certainly not a month of spring.

After the winter she had just endured, the early morning freeze was almost pleasant. At least now the air was still and dry. In fact, she had come to cherish such times. The winter winds could be unbelievably powerful, sweeping in from the Atlantic and gathering immense force in their journey. They could transform flakes of snow into stinging bullets and make a walk from one house to the next a deadly trek for the weak and elderly. The winter storms imprisoned all but the hale and hardy and seemed to last forever. The cottage's front room became like a cage then. And the patient manner in which Andrew and Catherine sat by the fire, reading Scriptures or talking silently or just watching the flames, only added fuel to Nicole's irritation over being shut inside.

But in spite of the harsh weather, she had come to dearly love this place and the people who inhabited it. There was no logic to these thoughts, and if she had been asked to describe herself, she would have said she was a child of warm days and soft green waters. Even so, along with the adverse weather and shorter days, she had come to feel a deep appreciation for these people and the world they had made for themselves. In the depths of the winter now passing, when the storms raged and the darkness settled at midafternoon, Nicole had found herself astonished at how the villagers had not merely endured but prospered. She would have thought it easier to carve homesteads from solid stone.

And then there were mornings like this one, when frozen silence captured the essence of the tempest now past. Every leaf was transformed to a work of jewel-like precision. Every blade of grass shined. The sunrise appeared impossibly long, the hours before dawn so gradual that when the sun finally revealed itself, it then rose triumphant, as though not night had been vanquished, but winter itself.

Now, with thirty minutes or more before sunrise, all the world was a soft silver. A mist swept about her feet and ankles, lying close to the earth. Her footsteps stirred up delicate tendrils that danced in the gentle light, then disappeared.

Nicole emerged from the woods and halted. The squat tree trunk looked like a frozen throne in the mist, sparkling its welcome. The little meadow was a royal chamber in white and crystal, walled not with trees but with ice. Icicles and frost clung to every branch, trapped in reverent stillness as if waiting for the dawn. She held her breath as she walked over and sat down. Beyond the frozen point, the world dropped off and then vanished altogether. The sea was utterly masked by the low-lying fog.

The sound of crunching footsteps whirled her around. It was too early for Grandfather Price to be up and about. When the weather was cold he rarely got out of bed before the sun was high in the heavens. To her amazement, Andrew emerged from the wooded trail. He took a long, slow look around, then whispered, "Mind if I join you?"

"Of course not."

He treaded quietly over and lowered himself to the trunk. "It has been far too long since I last enjoyed a sunrise like this."

"But you are always up before dawn."

"And always with something to fill my hands." Although their voices were scarcely more than whispers, their conversation sounded loud to Nicole's ears. "Anne will be so glad to know you are enjoying her favorite spot."

"At times like this, I feel that God is almost close enough to touch."

Andrew nodded slowly. The predawn light softened the weathered features and eased the years of strain that lined his brow. He wore a well-patched greatcoat and a fur hat so old it was no longer possible to tell its color. From beneath its rim his hair was lightened with strands of gray. Yet there was a strength to the man, an authority and wisdom that left him ageless in Nicole's eyes.

"It's good to know places and times where words aren't the only bridge to God," Andrew said, "where prayer would only hold God at bay."

They sat together in silence for a while, their breath soft plumes that drifted out to mingle with the rising mist. The rim of the earth turned orange, then fiery gold. Down below, the fogbound sea became a billowing realm, a reflection of divine light. Then the sun's upper edge peeked above the unseen horizon, and Nicole was forced to turn away. The light was too pure, too powerful. She studied how the world reflected the sun's beauty, how every tree limb was now a prism. How the mist was infused with color, with life.

"Glory, glory," Andrew murmured beside her. "All the world reflects God's glory."

They sat there till the dawn became day

and the cold filtered so deep Nicole could feel it in her bones. When she shivered a second time, Andrew stood with her, and together they started back. On the way, he asked, "Do you miss your home?"

Perhaps because the sunrise was still freshly impressed on her senses, Nicole was able to respond to the question with honesty and ease. "I don't know where my home is anymore."

Andrew's voice came quietly from behind her as they walked the trail. "Did you ever?"

She stopped and faced him. "What a strange thing for you to say."

"I've observed you and loved you through an Acadian winter," Andrew replied. His words were spoken softly, but they still had the power to rock her. "And I see that you have been given a restless spirit as a gift. One which thirsts for the new and the challenges of the unknown."

"I don't know," Nicole confessed, "if I would call that a gift."

"In another it might not be," Andrew agreed. "In someone who does not have your strength and your confidence, it could be a terrible burden."

"But I don't feel strong at all." The

confessions came easier now. "I feel confused and lost."

"No one who has been found by God," Andrew replied, "can ever count themselves as lost."

"Then why does the answer elude me?"

"Oh, I think you have come upon your answer." He smiled, but it quickly faded with the knowledge of what he was to say next. "I think you have known for months now."

Nicole opened her mouth, shut it, then tried again. But the words wouldn't come.

"Did you think we would not notice? Did you think we, your parents, couldn't see what direction you would probably seek?"

Finally she found the strength to ask, "Catherine knows, as well?"

"Of course she does. She saw it before I did."

Nicole felt the rising swell of confusion about to surface. "It all seems so impossible to me!"

Andrew crossed his arms. "Tell me what distresses you."

"Everything." She cast a worried glance about her. Sunlight now entered the forest glen, filling the world with light, though its warmth could not penetrate the season's cold. Nicole was reminded of the passage of days and seasons, counting down toward another time of change in her life. "The Acadians are starting a school, and they want me to teach. I am French and I know the English. I *am* English. I could help them come to know the people, as well as the language."

"It seems a natural fit. Your English has improved more than I would have thought possible. But this new work may not be enough to grant you fulfillment, am I correct?" When she did not respond, Andrew continued, "So you have prayed about this. I know you have. I have seen the worry and the fervor with which you have turned to God."

The dripping world seemed louder now, so clamorous she felt propelled toward what she couldn't see. "Then why has God not answered me?"

"Oh, I think He has."

She studied the lean, reserved man, saw both the strength and weakness of his sorrow. She hurt because she was the one causing him pain. "But what if I don't want to go?"

"God's gentle response may be because of your indecision," he said. "You are a believer now. You are a member of His family.

Of this I have no doubt. Perhaps He's willing to let you decide, knowing that you will serve Him wherever you are."

She heard a different cadence to the morning now, a dripping sound like that of tears, as though the day were weeping softly. She seemed to hear Acadia crying because she would need to leave. Strange how all the world knew what she had not yet accepted: that she would depart for England.

Then Andrew said, "But God has granted you wondrous gifts, of beauty and strength, and also this restlessness. You will find your greatest fulfillment in putting these to use for His glory."

Nicole found herself thinking of Henri Robichaud and the wisdom he showed in such impossible times. "How can you speak to me like this and release me so easily?"

"It is *not* easy and it will be harder when the day arrives." Andrew's eyes held a mixture of peace and sorrow. "But God's gentle voice has been speaking to me. And to Catherine, too. And He has made it clear what is to be our next challenge."

"What challenge?"

Andrew reached over and took hold of Nicole's quivering fingers, then whispered, "Letting you go."

The last Tuesday in April was very much an English sort of day, with low scudding clouds and a cold wind so heavy with moisture it seemed to carry an invisible rain. Lord Charles, the eighth earl of Sutton, paced impatiently near the manor's front gates. The carefully tended gardens that flanked either side were ringed by cedars planted by his great-grandfather, grown now until they stood taller than the manor. Their narrow fingers bobbed and weaved, tracing the clouds' swift flight. The distant fields—already knee-high with grass and ready for the yearlings to gambol and graze—looked as windswept as a stormy sea. The meadow flattened and shimmered, reflecting the impatient energy that found Charles the hour after sunrise striding back and forth between his great stone gates.

His ear caught the faint sound of a horse clip-clopping along the cobblestone lane. As soon as the horse and young rider came into view, Charles broke into a run. "Any news?"

"Aye, m'lord."

The rider was the youngest son of the married couple who essentially ran

Charles's home. Gaylord Days was the chief butler, and his wife, Maisy, was in charge of the kitchen and scullery. Will was their youngest of six and everyone's favorite, a bright lad with a laugh that seemed to chime louder than the Sabbath bells.

Will waved a newspaper over his head and shouted, "A battle, sir! A big one as well, over a thousand of the rebels against our brave redcoats! Someplace called Bunker Hill."

"Never mind that." Charles rushed up to where Will had reined in the dappled gray mare. The boy exercised two of Charles's favorite horses. In exchange, he rode out to meet the mail coach making the semiweekly run from London and Southampton. Charles gripped the stirrup and demanded, "Any letters from the colonies?"

"Aye, m'lord. From Nova Scotia." Will unslung the leather pouch that he carried under his oilskin. "A new hand this time. A fair one."

"New?" Charles bit down hard on his sudden surge of hope. But he couldn't completely stifle his trembling fingers as he fumbled with the straps. "This knot is impossible!"

"Allow me, m'lord." Will made swift

work of the straps and then handed Charles the packet of mail.

"You're a good lad, young Will." Charles flipped through the mail until his eyes froze on a letter. In his haste to unfold his pocketknife and slit open the wax seal, he dropped the remaining post. Charles did not even bother to look up. Will slid from the horse and began gathering the post. The wind picked up one piece and flung it back toward the stone gates. Will pounced on it. Charles did not see a thing.

"Here you are, m'lord. I think I found them all."

But Charles was captivated by the words inscribed on the page. He reread the short letter a third time, then clenched his hands together and raised his face toward the storm-tossed sky. "Thank you, Father. Oh, thank you!"

"Good news, m'lord?"

"Not good, young Will, but excellent news! Outstanding news!" Charles searched his waistcoat pockets and extracted a pair of silver farthings. "Here you are, my boy. Celebrate with me!"

"Thank you, sir!"

"Now ride home and tell your father to air out the front rooms and have the curtains and coverlets replaced. And we will need new paint—the finest of everything."

Will bounded back into the saddle. "There's to be company, sir?"

"Not company. Family!"

Will's face lit up. All in the manor knew of Charles's fervent hopes. "Then she's coming?"

"She is indeed. She might well be on the high seas by now. Hurry, my boy."

"Like the wind, m'lord!" Will whipped the reins and spurred the horse into a gallop.

Charles laughed as he watched the lad raise a cloud of dust in his race to the manor. Then his eyes fell back on the letter. It was the first written entirely by Nicole. In the past, she had only penned a few words at the bottom of Andrew and Catherine's letters. Nicole had always written in French because of her struggle with written English, which she was learning at a much slower rate than spoken English. Yet now she was writing with as fair a hand as Charles had ever seen, expressing words that gave him inexpressible joy.

My dear uncle, Nicole wrote, *I write this letter with my own hand to show you that my English is much improved. But still I make mistakes. I know this, and know also I will make greater mistakes even than this when I arrive. But if you will still have me, then I shall come, and agree to your condition. I shall give you two years of my life in your fair England. I have also decided to return to my given name, and be the Harrow that I was at birth. Yet my French heritage can not and must not be denied. So with your permission I shall be known as Nicole Harrow. I shall do my best to make you proud. Fondly, Nicole.*

Charles laughed heartily as he turned back toward the manor. "Make me proud? By all that's good, my dear, you will do more than that!" He did not care how his words might sound to anyone who might hear. It was either speak his thoughts out loud or burst. "You will do far more than give me pride! Of that I am—"

He stopped. The familiar pain whispered to him, which was good, for it granted him a moment to reach the gate and use it for support. Sometimes there was this first faint hint before the real pain struck. Other times it attacked without warning, and that was worse by far. But this time was bad enough. Charles held the pillar with one hand and his chest with the other. The pain made him wheeze. Again he was grateful that so far the pain had only struck where he was able to find a private corner.

He fought the pain, waiting for some relief. Gradually it subsided, and he was able to rise from his crouched position and walk slowly back to the manor. In truth, Nicole's coming was not a moment too soon. The matter of his legacy had to be resolved while there was still time.

Chapter Five

Nicole walked streets that felt both familiar and alien. Halifax was a town transformed.

She had moved in with Cyril and Anne to spend the final weeks with them before her departure for England. Anne had not been feeling well. Anne was a delicate woman, and carrying the baby through the long winter had been hard on her. Many winter illnesses were still rampant in the area, and Cyril continued to shoulder a tremendous burden. Therefore, Nicole's offer to help around the house until her sailing off to England was accepted with relief from Anne and Cyril alike.

Another reason for her visit was that Nicole's presence was required to help find a vessel. Securing a berth bound for England was proving to be extremely difficult. Cyril had initially thought they could merely contact one of the local shipping agents, pay the money, and thereby book the voyage. But with the troubles to the south, all the ships headed for England had been booked for weeks and even months in advance.

There was a third reason, not discussed yet known by all. Catherine both knew Nicole's departure was coming and had accepted it long before the discussion was over. But after the matter was out in the open, a shadow coalesced about Catherine. The daily strain of waiting to hear that a berth had been found and Nicole must leave had been hard on them all, but far worse on Catherine. Then late one night, Nicole had entered the front parlor and overheard Catherine speaking to Andrew in their bedroom. Nicole had heard her murmur how each day that went by was only adding to the hardship of saying farewell. It was then Nicole had known that, for Catherine's sake, she must make a clean break and get herself to Halifax. When Andrew received the letter that stated Nicole's only chance for acquiring a berth on a ship was for her to be near the Halifax port—so at a moment's notice she might take the place of someone who had failed to show—they had all been very sorry, but also a little relieved.

Yet since her arrival, Nicole had discovered that Halifax was no longer the town she had once known. During the four months since Christmas, it had changed dramatically. The advent of spring had brought many new arrivals: soldiers by the boatload, horses, and Loyalists from the southern colonies. New noises rang out everywhere. All the talk was concerning the impending war and most of it was bad. In winter-clad Georgetown, Nicole had heard none of this, so her walking around the Canadian colonies' most significant Atlantic port had been quite a shock.

She gripped her basket with both hands and hurried back from the market, keeping to the raised plank sidewalks that fronted the main streets. It was not the most direct way home, and her basket was heavy. Yet she did not dare use the side streets. Soldiers spilled from the taverns at all hours of the day and night, noisy and dangerous. The constabularies were overwhelmed. The locals had come to refer to all the changes as simply "The Troubles." Nicole had never heard a more apt description in all her life.

As Nicole was about to cross a street, she suddenly had to stop and wait for a trio of clanking artillery pieces to trundle by. The horses drawing the cannon seemed as dusty and tired as the soldiers who escorted the weaponry. She tried to muffle her ears to the discourse of war that went swirling through the streets.

There was news about another attack aimed at Quebec, others at forts along the Saint Lawrence River. One man spoke of the defeats that were growing in number, another of the victories, which were almost as troubling as the defeats. Nicole strived not to give thought to her own conflicting loyalties. All she knew was that there was little fighting in Louisiana and none in Nova Scotia. Her two homes were safe for now.

Watching the warships cram the harbor and the soldiers march on the streets evoked old memories for Nicole. She couldn't help but recall the adversity her family had endured. What other young mothers would be facing the fear and upheaval of war? No, she wanted nothing to do with English soldiers and this war brewing to the south.

The troubles all around her seemed to bring out the confusion Nicole felt within. In the eleven days since she had arrived in Halifax, she had come no closer to feeling at peace about going to England. Somehow it was not enough that in her heart and in her prayers she had felt her decision to be the right one. Or that Andrew and

Catherine's prayer time had confirmed the same direction. The sense of harmony with her newly found parents and her God only heightened Nicole's bafflement. She wanted to go, but she also wanted to stay. She felt a great sense of loss in having to leave this wild, harsh land she had come to love, yet was excited about what lay ahead. It hit her like a pang of hunger. She grew impatient with finding a ship and berth. Still, all the while she was half hoping it would all turn out to be infeasible.

Nicole arrived finally to the end of the raised sidewalk and continued on along the path that led from town toward the western hills. Halifax was an unpredictable sort of town, thriving and bustling one moment and totally quiet the next. This far from the central market and the harbor, all the houses had fenced-in yards that held geese, chickens, goats, and pigs. Once the last traces of winter departed, a vegetable garden would be grown in many of the yards. Now everything was snow patched and muddy, except for a few irises blooming from porch boxes—the first sign of a season Nicole was destined not to share.

She pushed through the kitchen door and called, "Anne?"

"We're in the front room."

Nicole set down her basket and pulled off her mud-caked boots. She then stepped into a pair of house slippers and proceeded to walk to the parlor. She was halted by the sight of an unfamiliar young man seated nervously at the edge of his chair.

In response to Nicole's questioning glance, Anne said, "Nicole, this is Harold Younger. Mr. Younger works for the bank Uncle Charles does business with."

He sprang to his feet and gave an awkward bow. "Your servant, ma'am."

Anne's features formed a pinched cast. She had not been particularly well these past few days. Although she complained very little, one could see she was in considerable pain by the way she held herself. Even seated as she was, the baby looked huge on her slender frame, bulging mightily underneath the beaded housedress. It was incredible to think she had almost two months left to go.

"Mr. Younger has come with very good news," Anne said.

"Indeed, Miss Harrow. I am happy to report that space has been found for you upon a vessel departing for England."

The news, though not unexpected, pushed Nicole down into the seat beside Anne. "When?"

"Four days from now," he said.

She exchanged a glance with Anne. "So soon."

"Our parents are expected this evening, tomorrow at the latest," Anne replied as she shifted slightly in her seat. Her face tightened and then relaxed. "Four days will be fine."

"Here, let me get you another cushion." Nicole rose and plucked a cushion from Cyril's rocker, helped Anne to lean forward, and slipped it down beside her. While she watched Anne lean back and nod that things were better, she said, "I should stay and help you through the final days."

"Nonsense."

"Stay?" The man's nervous hands fluttered his beaver-skin hat as he spoke. "If you will excuse me for saying, Miss Harrow, but this berth we've managed to obtain is a treasure. A veritable treasure, ma'am. It was only through our chairman's direct intervention that we found you space at all, meeting as he did personally with the ship's owners. I cannot say if another berth will be found."

"Later in the summer, perhaps," Nicole pleaded.

"Not this season, ma'am. And especially not a vessel where the captain's own wife is on board. This was a remarkable turn of events. It means you will travel with a proper chaperone."

"It sounds like a miracle," Anne agreed.

The thought of Nicole declining had Mr. Younger twirling his hat like a top now. "Again, if you'll excuse me for saying, ma'am, but if you refuse, I hate to think what the chairman might say. After all his trouble, I expect he might think I've mishandled my mission here and hand me my walking papers."

"There, you see?" Anne tried to be firm, but her voice lacked sufficient strength. Clearly something was disturbing her. "It's all settled then."

"Nothing—" Nicole held back her objection at the sound of boots on the front steps. She waited as Cyril entered and greeted his wife and was introduced to Mr. Younger.

After the news was passed on, Cyril said firmly, "You must go."

"But Anne needs me." The thought of leaving so soon, while all the quandaries remained unsettled, left her in a panic. "I cannot just leave her—"

"You must. If need be, we can ask Catherine to come and stay with us for the duration." Cyril had adopted his doctor's voice, stern and brooking no argument. "Listen to me, Nicole. The situation here is becoming more serious by the day."

Anne demanded anxiously, "You have news?"

"Nothing worth discussing. But I hear things. Two of my patients are generals. The situation is not nearly what people here are surmising. It is worse. Both these generals are convinced that war is coming. They are not certain as to when. Perhaps this year or the next, but no later than that. But it *is* coming. The greatest question they are facing at this point is whether Nova Scotia will get caught up in the fighting."

"Surely there is hope," Anne protested.

Cyril glanced at his wife and started to speak, then turned back to Nicole and said, "My other concern is this grippe that continues to attack the people here. I lost another patient this very afternoon."

"Oh no," Anne cried. "Who?"

"Old man Townsend."

"Oh, his poor family. I must go—"

"You will go nowhere, my dear." His tone grew sterner still. "Widow Townsend and their eldest son both show every sign of coming down with the same wet chest. This illness is a terror, and there is little I can do besides apply my poultices and pray."

"But they need me," Anne said.

"Your baby needs you more," Nicole answered.

"She is right, my dear. You must harbor your strength and keep yourself from danger." Cyril looked back to Nicole. "As should you."

The day was a gift. Nicole had heard the words three times on her walk to the quayside. A *gift*. And perhaps for others it was so, with the sudden summertime warmth, the kind breeze, the clear sky, and the chirping birds. Even the gulls sounded welcoming as their little group approached the harbor. Sailors' voices carried across the water, chanting their songs of the sea as they flitted up rope ladders and scrambled along the crossties. Rope halyards beat gentle time against the masts, metal clanged, and bare feet drummed staccato melodies on the main deck. Even the officers' orders carried a note of excitement and adventure.

As they passed the sentries now permanently stationed at the harbor entrance, a signal gun boomed, and then all heads turned to watch a magnificent ship unfurl its square white wings and slowly, gracefully take flight across the blue water. A soldier jostled by them, saying to his shipmate, "Bound for Boston and the battles."

"Give my right arm to be sailing with her, I would," he replied.

One of the sentries pointed with his musket to where Nicole and her family stood. "Here, you lot. Get a move on. There's important business afoot."

The order spurred Andrew forward. "Come, we are blocking the entrance."

The four of them hurried toward the ship moored at the quayside. Andrew carried Nicole's chest, which contained all of her things except for what she had packed in her cloth trundle bag. Cyril had on his shoulder a second chest that had arrived just two days earlier from England. It was marked for Nicole. Because of her rush to get ready, she had done nothing more than quickly glance over the different items in the trunk. She found that they consisted mostly of extravagant dresses and mantles and shoes—things she would never dream of wearing.

Anne had been unable to join them, as the sudden change of weather caused her to become extremely fatigued. And so Cyril bore the distracted look of one whose mind was elsewhere.

Nicole's farewell with Anne had been tinged by a slight jealousy over how grand the couple seemed together, despite their worries and the long hard winter. As they left the house that morning, Nicole found herself wondering if she would ever find such contentment. And in the jarring honesty that goes with leaving behind family and a place that had become home, she felt confused again about whether she in fact wanted this for herself. Nicole felt more torn than ever between staying and building lifelong ties, bonds to people and place that meant no more farewells like this one, and a life full of adventure and new beginnings.

Nicole and Catherine approached the ship hand in hand. The one blessing of this day of good-byes had been the early-morning talk she'd had with her mother. It still felt strange using the word *mother* to refer to anyone but Louise. Yet on this day it came more comfortably than ever before. Their conversation had begun with talking about Andrew, Anne and Cyril, the baby coming, the winter just past, and the Acadian school where Catherine had agreed to help teach.

Then as they heard the first sounds that announced the house was coming to life,

Catherine, who knew they would be joined by everyone soon, suddenly said, "Nicole, I want to thank you."

"There is no need."

"There is every need. For making the journey to Georgetown. For answering my prayers so wonderfully. For growing into the beautiful woman that you are. In spite of all the nightmares and the yearnings and the regrets, God has faithfully helped me to see that what we did was right. Thank you also for giving me this wonderful winter and . . ." Catherine's voice became shaky, so she stopped and used the edge of her housecoat to dab the corners of her eyes. "No tears. I promised Andrew and myself before we left Georgetown that there would be no tears."

"Oh, Mama." It was then that Nicole had felt the impressions come together into a kind of revelation. No matter what the natural course might be or how it was for the rest of the world, she did not have one mother but two. This was not mere feeling, for when she reached over and took hold of Catherine's hands, she knew it to be truth. "I love you so much."

"My darling Nicole. I think I knew the instant you arrived that you would be leaving. And hard as this morning is, I also think knowing this time would come has made the days we have shared all the more precious."

Nicole leaned back in her seat and confessed what she had difficulty speaking of, even to herself. "I feel as if I am being pulled apart inside."

"I understand."

"How is that possible, when I hardly comprehend it myself?"

"Because I see you with a mother's love." Catherine's smile was sweetened by a sorrow beyond tears, beyond time. "I don't know if you were born with a restless spirit or if perhaps you breathed this in with the shipboard air during your first voyage. But I saw the way you would sit at Anne's favorite spot and stare out over the Bay of Fundy. With Anne, it was a place to reflect on things and see God's answers written in the clouds and sky. With you, it was a place to yearn."

Having someone understand her so well and hearing the words spoken with such undemanding love left Nicole feeling as though her heart had been branded. She could only nod in response.

"You must follow the direction God has placed within you." Catherine seemed unaware of the tear that had escaped and trickled its way down her cheek. "I hope and pray that you shall keep your eyes fastened not on the splendor and the mystery but rather upon the divine."

The harbor market's bustle swept them up and deposited them in a relatively calm space between the ship's two gangplanks. A steady stream of cargo handlers and bleating animals pushed up the two platforms and into the vessel. They stood encircled by the clamor and excitement of a seaborne voyage. Nicole took a deep breath and tasted the flavors of sea and far-flung lands and found herself suddenly elated by what was about to begin. She felt impatient to get on board, yet heartsick over having to say farewell to those she loved.

Cyril dropped his case, extended his arms, and offered her a quick kiss on both cheeks. "Anne made me promise I would give you those at shipside."

"I will pray every day for her and the baby's safety," Nicole said.

"Thank you from the bottom of my heart." He then allowed his worry to show through a little. "I can hardly wait for all this to be behind us. The one positive note to this whole affair is that Catherine has agreed to stay and help Anne through the coming weeks."

"I could not do otherwise," Catherine responded. "Shame on you for not letting me know earlier how she was doing."

"Anne would not permit me," Cyril said.

"I cannot see much positive in this day," Andrew sighed. "For I am losing not one lady of my life but two now."

"Only for a time, my husband," Catherine said. She held her smile tightly, and her eyes shined. But no tears.

Nicole found it easier to turn to Andrew than to draw her newfound mother into an embrace. "Good-bye, Papa. I will pray and I will write."

"Give my love to Charles," he said, loud enough for all to hear. He wrapped her into a fierce hug and moaned, "O Lord . . . give me strength."

There was nothing left for Nicole to do now but face Catherine. The moment seemed to pierce her, and in the brilliant sunlight, Nicole saw more clearly than ever before the lined features and the silver gray strands threading through her mother's hair. The hard-earned wisdom that shone in her eyes spoke to her of time's passage, of harder farewells still to come. "Oh, Mama . . ."

"Shah, my child." Catherine's grip was as strong as her husband's and longer lasting. Nicole clung to her as well, so tightly there was no room for either woman to draw a breath. They finally released each other, permitting enough space for their eyes to meet once again. "You carry my love with you. You always have; you always will."

Nicole bit her lip and nodded. *No tears.*

"Andrew, will you bind us with prayer?"

"Let us join together." The four of them laced their arms around one another, and they drew so close that their foreheads touched. They stood this way for a while, waiting for Andrew to pray. Finally he confessed softly, "My heart is so full. I fear the words will not come."

"Then I shall speak for us all," Catherine said. "Dear Father in heaven, be where we cannot be. Sail with our darling daughter across the great sea. Let her hear your blessed voice where she cannot hear our own. Embrace her when our own arms cannot hold her. Fill her with your love, and ours. And when she kneels at night and speaks with you, let her hear our response

81

with your own. In the miracles that are yours and yours alone to bestow, let her know that we are with her still."

Chapter Six

Nicole stood at the landward railing and waved and waved. Long after the three figures had been blocked by the ships lying at anchor, still she stood. At every tack, as the ship threaded its way carefully among the merchant vessels and the men-of-war, she raced to the opposite rail. There she craned and searched, desperate for one more glimpse of the family she had found and was now leaving behind.

Only after they had cleared the harbor mouth and the rocky promontory blocked her view entirely did Nicole release her hold on the railing. Even then she did not turn away, for she now found herself caught up in a surging wave of regret and sorrow. She watched as each rise and fall of the ship, each slapping wave and mark of the bosun's whistle drew her ever farther from the place she loved. Now that it was too late, now that she had given in to what she thought she wanted, she felt desperate to return again to her Acadian home.

"Begging your pardon, Miss Harrow."

"Yes?" She used the excuse of wind-flung hair to sweep away the gathering tears. Only then did she turn around.

"Andrew Potter at your service, ma'am." The midshipman was fair-haired and freckled and appeared younger than she. Her inspection caused him to blush a little. "The captain's compliments. Perhaps you'd like me to show you your quarters."

"Thank you. My things . . ."

"They've already been stowed, miss. This way, if you please."

Nicole followed him across the deck, now rising and falling with greater intensity as they headed out into the deep-ocean swells. "My father's name is Andrew, also."

A deeper crimson traveled up his cleanly shaven face now, starting from his neck. He adjusted his stiff uniform and said, "Everyone on board calls me Andy, ma'am. That is, save the captain."

She felt as much as saw the eyes upon her, directed from every station on the ship. "And what name does the captain use?"

"Lad, when he's pleased, Potter, when I am slow. I am his nephew; my mum's his baby sister." He hesitated at the stairway leading into the aft hold, turned back, and gave her an impish grin. "But when I've mussed my navigation and put the ship somewhere off Madagascar, he has some right names for me. I dare not tell you what I am called then."

A voice from the quarterdeck blasted out, "Look lively, you lot! This is not some ladies' Sunday tea! Bosun, take the names of every sailor on the mizzen there. And you, Potter, what are you hanging about for?"

The grin vanished in a flash, and young Potter clattered down the staircase. Nicole risked a glance up and found her gaze met by a scowling older gentleman. His weathered face was framed by white muttonchop sideburns, so bushy they protruded almost a hand's width from his face. His sharp gray eyes swept over Nicole as though taking in every aspect, seen and unseen, and finding little that met with his approval. Nicole shifted her eyes toward the deck planking and then she sped down the stairs after Potter.

She found him waiting for her at the end of a long, narrow passageway. Slightly out of breath now, she whispered, "Your captain is . . . remarkable."

"Remarkable is the word, ma'am. You best step lively about him and mind your p's and q's."

Nicole liked the young man with his playful, mischievous look. "Should I salute, do you think?"

"Oh, ma'am, I beg you . . ." Then Potter realized she was jesting and rewarded her with another of his animated smiles. "If you do, pray allow me to be around to watch the fireworks."

He rapped on the door, and at the sound of a woman's voice from within, he opened it and announced, "Miss Harrow, if you please, ma'am."

"Very good, Andy. Show her in."

The woman who rose to greet Nicole was gray haired, very slender, and held herself rigidly erect. Though she wore a dress of violet rather than black, Nicole had the immediate impression of standing in the presence of someone recently bereaved. Her eyes were red rimmed, and her lips were pressed so tightly together that the skin wrinkled around her mouth. Her right hand clutched a crumpled handkerchief. "Good day to you, Miss Harrow. I am Emily Madden. Captain Madden is my husband."

"An honor to meet you, Mrs. Madden." Nicole gave a low curtsy, more than anything to hide her dismay over having to spend weeks in this grieving woman's company.

"Andy, perhaps you would be so good as to have Benson serve tea."

"I'd be happy to do it myself, ma'am." Before she could object he hastily offered a quick bow and backed out of the room.

"I see you have already smitten one of James's officers. No doubt you shall have them all under your charm before the day is out."

Nicole wondered if Mrs. Madden was displeased with her, just as the captain had seemed to be earlier. "I beg your pardon, madame, but I wish to be no bother to any-one."

"No, of course not." She then noticed the direction of Nicole's wandering eyes. "Rather impressive, is it not?"

Nicole took this as permission to give herself over to enjoying the ambiance of the room. "It is positively stunning!" Built into the rear of the cabin was a swath of glass panels through which she could view the sea streaming out behind the ship.

"Yes, I imagine the captain's great room would make for marvelous accommodations in which to enjoy one's first voyage across the sea."

"I have been to sea before, madame." In the distance she could still see the tall hills near Halifax and two of the town's higher steeples.

"Oh? And when was that?"

"Once as a young child. Then again the summer before this."

"Do my ears not detect a French accent?"

The hills gradually turned a soft bluish gray as the distance and the sea mist grew between ship and shore. "Indeed so, madame."

"But I thought my husband mentioned something about an English connection."

Nicole sighed and looked away. Watching the hills disappear beyond the horizon only made matters worse. "That is correct."

"Then you must be from the Quebec region. No doubt you elected to avoid the coming battles." The thought of war turned her tone bitter. "Such wisdom in one so young."

Before Nicole could correct the woman, there came a knock on the door. Andy Potter reappeared with a silver tray and tea service. He set it down and said, "With your permission, ma'am."

"Oh, very well, you may pour. But then you really must be off. I won't have the captain coming down on me for allowing you to shirk your duties over this young lady."

The crimson flush appeared again, creeping up from Potter's collar. "No, ma'am."

Emily Madden pointed at the seat beside her. "Do sit down, my dear. You can turn your chair to take in the view."

Dejectedly, Nicole lowered herself onto the seat. She struggled to understand how such excitement and eagerness could come from the same heart as all the regret. "No, thank you, but I have seen enough."

Emily accepted her teacup and said, "Our young guest is from the province of Quebec, Andy. She has traveled here by sea."

"Excuse me, madame. But I am not Québecois. In fact, I have never been farther west than Halifax."

Potter and Mrs. Madden glanced at each other, then at Nicole. "But your accent . . ." Emily said with a quizzical look on her face.

Nicole accepted her tea from Andy, secretly detesting how her privacy was being quickly eroded. But she had no choice. "I was raised in Louisiana."

The news appeared to upset Emily. "But Louisiana is not involved in the conflict."

"No, madame."

"Then, why . . ." Emily became silent for a long moment. She set down her cup, folded her hands, and said with a sternness that seemed modeled after her husband, "Young lady, I fear you have boarded this vessel under false pretenses. When in Halifax my husband was specifically ordered to make room on this ship for a very important *English* guest. Yet now I discover you are from Louisiana. Or at least you say you are."

Nicole kept her eyes focused on the cup in her lap. "Everything I have told you is the truth."

"You will forgive me if I find that somewhat difficult to believe. If you have been at sea before, how is it you never saw a captain's great room?"

"Because I was not invited." Nicole found herself forced to have to meet the older woman's gaze and reveal yet more of her secrets. "I was separated from my parents at birth and raised in southern Acadia—what you may know as Cajun territory. Last year I sailed north and was reunited with my family."

Emily's mouth opened, but her mind remained blocked by too many questions seeking to be asked all at once. Finally she settled on, "But why England?"

Nicole shook her head at the question. Why indeed? Was she allowing her adventurous spirit to speak to her so loudly she failed to hear her Lord's quieter request? If she had truly followed His will in embarking on this voyage, why then was she now awash in remorse?

Nicole realized the room waited for her reply. She couldn't think of anything to say but the truth. "My uncle is childless and has asked that I come to be his heir."

"And who, pray tell, is this uncle?"

"Sir Charles Harrow."

The silence that met her answer was so deafening, Nicole could hear the water rushing beneath the stern and the dull footfalls of sailors overhead. She had no choice but to lift her head once more. In any other setting, the pair of expressions she saw would have seemed comical. Both the young midshipman and the captain's wife stared at her in round-eyed shock.

"Lord Charles, the earl of Sutton?" Mrs. Madden managed to say.

"Yes, madame."

"He is one of the wealthiest men in the realm," added Andy.

Emily had completely forgotten the young man was still there. She looked at him and said, "That will do, Mr. Potter. You may go now."

"But . . . yes, ma'am." He bowed to them both, but more earnestly to Nicole this time. "Your servant, Miss Harrow."

When the door had closed behind him, it was Emily's turn to peer out over the flowing waters. "You must excuse my abruptness," she said.

"No apologies are necessary, madame."

"Indeed they are." The handkerchief was retrieved from where it had been stowed up her left sleeve. She bundled it tightly in her hands and said as if to the sea that churned outside the glass, "I made this journey with my husband, because my two daughters, our only children, live in the southern colonies. One is in Boston, the other is farther down the coast in New York. I implored them both to leave. We are not without means in England, and so we could have offered their husbands proper situations. Think of the grandchildren, I begged them. Think of what it would be like to have them surrounded by war. . . ."

Then Emily's voice became unsteady. She clamped her mouth shut and sat there, immobilized by the effort to contain her grief and her worry.

Nicole's heart went out to the mother.

"They would not agree, madame?"

"Would not even let me finish. Come what may, they told me, their place was with the colonists and their grievances. Come what may." The fist clenching the handkerchief beat against her thigh. "I regret to say my daughters have inherited their father's stubborn nature. I cannot help but feel that I failed in my duties as a mother and grandmother. Had I spoken the right words, used the proper tone, perhaps I could have them here with me now. Safe and sound."

"I do not know what is right for them," Nicole confessed, "but I admire their ability to know what is their proper place and station. And I admire you for permitting them to stay."

Emily's countenance seemed overly bright as she turned toward the younger woman. "You do?"

"I have just watched my own mother letting me go." Suddenly the cabin's air seemed filled with tiny needles, and it hurt to breathe. "Such a difficult act I could never imagine doing myself, no matter how right the deed."

"My dear young lady . . ." Emily paused long enough to dab at her eyes with the kerchief. She then forced herself to pick up her teacup and offer Nicole a smile. "I do believe you are going to prove a veritable tonic."

A few minutes later, Potter returned to announce, "Captain's compliments, ma'am. He requests the pleasure of your company at dinner."

"Very well," Emily replied. "You may tell him we shall be delighted to attend him."

After they were alone again, Emily explained the accommodations to Nicole as she gestured toward the different rooms. "This chamber is in effect the master's dining room and great room. His office is through that door, which he has rigged into a sleeping cabin. We are to use his bedroom through there." Her smile came easier now. "These are quite exceptional quarters for a trading vessel, though I assume you are used to far more luxurious surroundings. But Captain Madden is also part owner of the trading company and rarely puts to sea anymore. He made this journey mostly on my account. He was fairly certain from the outset that our daughters would not return. Their husbands are both very active and prosperous. One is a representative for the upstart Colonial Congress, or whatever they have chosen to call themselves."

"I must be honest with you, madame,"

Nicole decided aloud. "I may be related to the earl, but it is something I learned only a few months ago. As for these surroundings, I spent most of my last journey at sea wedged into the central hold, praying to survive a terrible storm."

Emily's eyes seemed to gain a new light. "Everything you say raises a thousand questions, my dear. So many I scarcely know what to ask next."

Perhaps it was her conflicting emotions or the vastness of the sea out the back portals or the richly burnished cabin that enclosed them so comfortably. Whatever the reason, Nicole suddenly felt ready to disclose her secrets to a woman she had known but a few hours. "My beginnings were among the very poor, madame. The Acadians were expelled from our homeland when I was only a few months old, so I made my first sea voyage before my first birthday. After that, my family lived in a lean-to that was attached to a cowshed. When the Spanish opened Louisiana to Acadian settlement, we walked there from Charleston. That journey took us over a year."

Emily was silent for a while, gazing behind Nicole at the westering sun. She then pulled a pocket watch from the belt around her middle, opened it, and said, "My goodness, we must begin our preparations. You will find my husband is a stickler for punctuality. We must be ready in time to permit the duty-men to fit this cabin out for dinner." She rose to her feet. "Which trunk will hold your finer dresses?"

"I am afraid I have nothing better than what you see before you."

Emily cast a doubtful glance over Nicole's dress, coming to rest on the dirty hem left by her crossing the market and harbor square. "The captain requires all his guests to dress rather formally for dinner, my dear. And your figure is so much fuller than mine, I fear nothing I have will fit you. Surely you must have brought something finer."

"Nothing. Perhaps I should just decline . . ." Nicole halted, thinking for the first time since her departure of Charles's trunk. "Well, perhaps there is something."

"Yes?"

She moved to the newer trunk and unfastened the straps. "My uncle sent this from England. It arrived just as I was preparing to leave."

"You haven't even looked?"

"I looked, but I did not pay it much mind." What little she had seen of the trunk's contents had somewhat frightened

her, for it seemed in the haste of final preparations to be a harbinger of the unknown
that awaited her in England. Nicole flipped
open the trunk, peeled back the layers of
wrapping blankets, and lifted the edge of
the first garment.

Emily gasped. "Oh my!"

Nicole stood slowly with the garment in
hand. It was a full-length gown of finest
satin. The bodice and body were a brilliant
blue that shimmered in the softening sunlight. The half sleeves and flounced shoulders were decorated with tiny flowers sewn
with gold thread. This same floral pattern
traced its way down both sides, broadening
to become glowing gardens about the wide
hem. The dress possessed a swooping dé-
colletage, kept to a fitting modesty by a
sheath of white silk that buttoned around
the neck and was embroidered with sky blue
flowers to match the hem.

Emily bent over the chest and retrieved
the note that had dropped from the dress
when Nicole unfolded it. She read it aloud.
" 'My dear Nicole, in hopes that you shall
deign to join me in England, I have taken
the liberty of ordering up a few items to
help with your journey. You will find a vis-
countess-to-be is expected to dress the part,
even on board a ship. I do hope they are of

a proper fit. Yours ever, Charles.' "

"I cannot wear this," Nicole murmured.

Emily's gaze shifted from the dress to the young woman and back. "Whyever not?"

"Because until last summer, all my clothes were homespun! Until I was thirteen, my only shoes were deerskin moccasins sewn together by my father."

"But you just said you did not meet your father till this very year."

"I mean my French father." Nicole dropped her arms, bunching the dress together at her waist. "Whatever am I to do?"

For some reason, Nicole's distress brought a cheerful light to Emily's face. "A veritable tonic," she repeated.

Chapter Seven

Emily Madden insisted they not take in the air on the quarterdeck as was customary, while the great room was being fitted for the evening meal. Instead, she retired with Nicole in the captain's bedchamber, in what was now to be their sleeping quarters. There she helped Nicole unpack and stow her meager belongings and inspect the rest of Charles's gifts. Everything they unpacked brought soft cries of delight from Emily, who said she wanted to "keep the prize a secret" for the moment. Emily's excitement was enough to ease even Nicole's pall of worry.

The chest contained two more dresses: a cotton-and-silk frock of delicate coral and a heavier, more wintry affair of midnight blue. There was also a shawl of wool, so soft Emily continued to stroke it long after they had put it aside. Below the shawl sat three pairs of kidskin shoes, one for each of the dresses. Though the shoes were a tight fit, the leather was soft enough that, with the tiny gold buckles fastened at the widest position, Nicole felt she could manage. And manage would be all she could do, for she felt as though perched on a tower with a hard wooden base. The shoes had a "fashionable tilt," as Emily explained, with underpinnings of proper calf and cork. All Nicole knew was that they were positively the strangest things she had ever worn.

But that was before Emily ordered her into the dress. Emily had already dressed and then helped Nicole pin her hair into something she said befitted a young lady attending the master's table. There was only a tiny hand mirror in the cabin, yet what little Nicole could see of herself and her new hair left her decidedly uncomfortable, particularly after Emily discovered the paper-wrapped bundle of satin ribbons—two for each dress. Emily tied the ribbons into her hair with the bows dangling down over one shoulder.

Finally, there was nothing more to unpack, nor any excuse to prevent her from fitting into the dress that lay on the bed as if taunting her. The noises from the other room pressed her, as did Emily's frequent glances at the pocket watch now lying beside the dress. So Nicole admitted defeat and raised her hands, thereby allowing Emily to slip the dress up and over her head.

Emily helped her do up the buttons at the back, took as far a step away as the cramped cabin allowed, then whispered, "Turn around."

She did so. Emily's not saying anything caused Nicole to demand in a hushed voice, "Well, is it awful?"

"Awful? My dear . . ."

Then a knock came at the door, and a gruff voice said, "The captain is descending, ma'am."

"We are ready." To Nicole, she said, "Slip on your shoes. No, not those. The light blue ones there by the bed."

They were the same type as the darker blue that she had already tried on, but when she pushed her feet into this pair, her right foot made contact with something bundled into the shoe's toe. Nicole removed her foot, lifted the shoe, and pulled out yet another paper-wrapped package. "Not more ribbons."

As she opened the paper both ladies gasped in unison. In Nicole's hand lay a slender gold necklace from which hung a pendant and large square-cut green stone surrounded by tiny diamonds.

Again Emily unfolded the note and read it. " 'This belonged to my mother. I am certain she would be delighted to see you enjoy it.' "

"This is not for me," Nicole protested.

Emily lifted the necklace from Nicole's trembling fingers. "Turn around," she said.

"I cannot possibly—"

But she was silenced by a second knock on the door, sharper this time. "Hurry, dear," Emily said. "We mustn't keep the ship's company waiting."

Before Nicole knew it, Emily had strung the necklace, and her hands were plucking at Nicole's shoulders, straightening a strand of hair, pulling at a sleeve. Then she quickly opened the door and started pushing her forward.

Nicole had no choice but to enter a great room now filled with officers in glittery uniforms and lit by more than a dozen candles. In the flickering light she caught sight of a stranger, looking at her from across the room where a silver platter was mounted on the wall. The plate was polished to such a brilliant finish that it reflected better than any common mirror. The stranger was bedecked in the finery of fables, a dress of softest blue, with cascading hair and eyes green as the glimmering pendant hanging around her neck.

It was only when her hand reached up to touch the gem that Nicole realized she was looking at herself.

In a voice full of pride and excitement, Emily Madden announced, "Gentlemen, may I present to you the Lady Harrow, viscountess of Sutton."

Chapter Eight

Nicole climbed two of the stairs leading to the quarterdeck. She spread out what had once been her best shawl and then settled herself on top of the hogshead lashed to the stair's railing. The great oak barrel was two-thirds her height and broad as a table. Its top made a perfect stool from which to look out over the sea, read, and reflect.

Two weeks into the voyage, the days had fallen into a carefully structured routine. Mornings she spent taking lessons with the midshipmen. These four lads were aged anywhere from fourteen to her own nineteen and were generally drawn from the families of officers and their close friends. Most vessels carried two to six middies, who had learned navigation and sailing lore while serving as cabin boys. The sailors called them "dogsbodies," for there was no duty too low for a middy. And Mrs. Madden had taken it upon herself to teach them what she referred to as "proper parlor etiquette." Nicole was only too happy to attend, though the rules seemed absurd and the lessons endless: Sit up straight and at the edge of the chair, feet and ankles and knees always touching, chin just so, never allowing oneself to rest against the back of the chair. And there were the table manners and the proper use of cutlery.

"Your pardon, Miss Harrow. A word, if you please."

Nicole turned with a start and found the captain poised on the third stair, his head a little higher than her own. She began to rise from her perch. "Most certainly, sir."

"No, no, stay where you are. This won't take long." But the captain seemed unable to find his course. Then his eye caught the volume in her lap. "Ah, reading, I see. French or English?"

She held it out. "English, sir."

"Ah. The Bible. Most noteworthy of you, Miss Harrow."

"I cling to it, sir," she said quietly.

"And why is that, pray tell?"

"It is the only time when I am certain God is with me still, and that I have not strayed too far from His will for me."

For some reason, her words seemed to relax the captain a bit. He leaned against the stair's top pillar and cocked his hat slightly back on his forehead. His working uniform was salt stained and patched in several places. The gold on his shoulders looked faded, the seams frayed. Even so, the dark blue added to his austere presence.

"A woman who can speak straight. Good. Very good. I shall try to match you with my own words. I have observed you closely these weeks, Miss Harrow, and have come to the conclusion you are cut from an uncommon fine cloth."

"Why, sir—"

"No, no, pray let me finish. You are neither flighty nor a flirt. You do not use your station to offer querulous demands. Nor do you use your remarkable beauty to stir up my crew. I have spoken with my wife, whose judgment I hold in great esteem, and she feels the same way. So I have come to ask if I might offer you a few words of advice."

"Most certainly, sir."

"Very well, then." He took a great breath and launched with, "You are clearly worried over what you shall face upon your arrival in England."

"Terrified," she admitted.

"I would therefore urge you to use this time on board to, shall we say, hone your tactics. Take the measure of your saber. Practice your thrust and parry."

"I . . . I am sorry, Captain, but I don't understand."

"You rarely speak at dinner. You hold yourself like a little mouse trying to squeeze into the tiniest of holes. I have observed how you shrink whenever one of my gentlemen offers you a kind word. You have difficulty speaking even with the ship's surgeon, who is the meekest man who ever walked a foredeck."

Nicole hung her head. "I am so very afraid of making a mistake."

"Don't be. It's utterly natural, but not necessary. Those not already smitten have nonetheless found you acceptable. They would be honored to be of service, if not beg for your . . . no, no. Let no more be said upon that." When she did not respond, he went on, "My advice, Miss Harrow, is this: Do not hide yourself, nor show such shame here on board. My wife has shared with me a bit of your story. It is, if you will permit me to say, marvelous. Learn to deal with society through these people who already think well of you."

The evening routine was now well established. The two ladies would retire to their sleeping chamber when the crew arrived to turn out the great room. Nicole had learned to slip into the fine dresses herself, submitting when necessary to Emily's help with out-of-reach buttons. But tonight the weather had grown chill, with a strengthening wind straight out of the north. So Nicole selected the heavier dress of midnight blue, which she could do up unaided. The dress had a high collar and long sleeves and small froths of lace that tickled her chin and wrists. The buttons that ran up the front were the only adornment. Yet nothing else was required, because the buttons were matched pearls as big as her fingernail—thirty-six of them—spaced less than an inch apart and marching from below her waist all the way to her chin, with another six down each forearm.

As usual, Emily inspected her. She nodded her approval, then asked, "Shall we take a turn on deck?"

Always before, Nicole had declined, preferring to remain seated on her bed, dreading the moment ahead when she would walk through the doorway and be met by the assembly of ship's officers. They were a grand lot at these dinners, for the captain had begun his career in the Royal Navy and held a strong liking for spit and polish. The officers stood stiff and proud in their best uniforms, bowing and murmuring their greetings. Nicole was typically famished by evening, yet found it hard to eat anything, because their eyes never seemed to leave her. She felt she was always being watched. Always. A ship's closeness had never bothered her during the journey north from Louisiana with her uncle Guy and his family. Only now, when she was dressed like a doll on display and every motion she made seemed wrong, was she conscious of others' eyes on her.

Tonight, however, Nicole gathered her courage and said, "Yes, all right."

Emily's eyes widened with surprise. "My husband spoke with you?"

"H-he did."

"He is a good man, despite what you may think of his manner. The sea is a harsh place to ply a trade, and a master must hold the respect of his men. But he is a good man nonetheless, and you can trust his word." She offered Nicole the lamb's-wool mantle with a smile. "You are doing the right thing, my dear."

Nicole followed her through the great room, where the two crewmen stopped their polishing of the silver platter long enough to bow to her, pulling their forelocks. The two women continued down the hallway and up the stairs and into the gentle light of the setting sun. The sea was tossed by the brisk, biting wind. The ship gave a mighty lurch just as Nicole reached the quarterdeck's top step, and because of the tall-heeled shoes she wore, she risked tumbling back down the stairs.

Fortunately the captain was close by to offer her a hand. "Steady as she goes, Miss Harrow."

"Thank you, sir."

"Think nothing of it, ma'am." He bowed slightly, first to her, then to his wife. "A fine night, by the looks of things. We'll be making record time—that is, if the weather holds." The captain peered beyond the two women, and a frown suddenly creased his face. "Avast there! You there at the mizzen, tighten out that luff! Your business is out to sea, man, not what goes about the quarterdeck! Hold steady to the course, steersman, or I'll have your hide!"

Nicole joined Emily by the windward rail and thrilled at the wind's soft buffeting.

Young Andy Potter moved up alongside, doffed his hat, and said, "Evening, ma'am. The captain said I might dine with the officers tonight." He pointed out across the wind-tossed ocean. "The watchman just spotted a whale off the stern. Keep a careful eye, if you will please, for you might just . . . yes, there she blows!"

Without warning, a great black hump

appeared a mere stone's throw from where they stood. The water rolled white and foamy off the broad back. Then there was an enormous puff of breath and a geyser of white water shot high as their heads, which was immediately followed by a sucking hiss sound when the whale inhaled. The tail large as the ship's rudder flapped once, then the whale rolled down with the sea closing swiftly in around it. Soon no sign remained that the beast had ever appeared.

Nicole released the breath she had not realized she'd been holding. The air was biting, and the salty tang sparkled deep with each breath she took. "I love the sea."

"Aye, there are grand moments to the life on board a ship." The captain's second officer stepped up to her other side. Gordon Goodwind was a tall, rakish man with copper-colored hair and a long saber scar down one cheek. He doffed his hat and gave a stiff bow. "Captain's compliments, Miss Harrow. He has granted me the privilege of seeing you into dinner."

Nicole had always found the man frightening. She was intimidated by the combination of his dashing looks and officer's poise. But tonight she offered her hand as she saw Emily do to Andy Potter, and said, "Thank you, Lieutenant."

As they proceeded down the passage-way to the great room the young officer continued, "Of course, there are the harsher faces to the world afloat. And they temper one's affection for the sea, if you catch my meaning."

The captain directed each man to his position, the lieutenant holding Nicole's chair as Potter did for Emily. Only after the women were seated did the men then take their places.

"That's as may be," the captain said, "but with the wind steady out of the north quarter, we may well make landfall before we run out of fresh provisions." To Nicole he explained, "A diet of hardtack and salt pork might nourish the body, but it does little for the spirit. But when the sea shows a mean face, we have little choice but to batten the hatches and wait her out."

It was at this point that Nicole ordinarily dropped her head and held to a tight silence throughout the ordeal of dinner. But she caught both the captain and his wife studying her, waiting, clearly offering her a chance. So she took as great a breath as she could and said, "I have known an Atlantic storm."

"Ah?" The captain's eyes sparked. "And when was that?"

"Last summer, off the Virginia coast. I was traveling up with my father's brother and his family. That is, my French father." Then she stopped, ashamed of her accent and clumsy words.

Before she could lower her head, the lieutenant beside her said, "Pray do go on, Miss Harrow."

Nicole risked a sideways glance, finding no derision there, only a keen gaze fastened intently on her. She cleared her throat quietly and said, "We were becalmed for almost a week. It was very hot and very still. Day after day we sat and cooked."

"Well do I know those times," the captain replied. "The diabolical waiting, searching the horizon, praying for wind."

"Just so," Nicole agreed. "But none came. The sun beat upon the sea like an anvil on a great steel mirror. I have lived most of my life in the Louisiana bayous, but never have I known a heat such as this. Then at midday on the eighth day of our waiting, there came a single sudden breath. And all the ship's crew raced to the side and searched. No one spoke, not for the longest time." Nicole then realized all eyes were upon her. She blushed to the roots of her hair. "I beg your pardon, I am carrying on too long."

"Quite the contrary, Miss Harrow!" The captain's words were echoed by all those at the table.

Nicole saw Emily giving her an approving smile.

The captain continued, "Cook tells me the crew landed six fine halibut this very afternoon. We should be dining upon a stew fine as you'll have anywhere on earth." He waved at the waiting crewman, who turned and left the chamber. "Pray continue, Miss Harrow, if you will."

"They searched and they searched," Nicole said, suddenly caught up in the memory. "Then, for no reason that I could see, the entire ship exploded into action, racing up the masts and across the booms, the captain and all his officers shouting orders and running with the men. Everyone moved so fast, I did not know where to look next. Then I happened to glance out over the rail and I could not believe my eyes. Out of nowhere a great black mass of clouds had appeared and was moving toward us rapidly. It looked like nature was sending an invading army, all aimed at us."

"Well said, Miss Harrow. Most well said. There is nothing like one's first glimpse of a nor'easter. Nothing at all. What did you do?"

"We were bundled down into the central hold, where we crouched for a day and a night and most of the next day. The waves crashed and tossed us about like peas in a great wooden pod. The children were terrified, and sick, of course, and the lanterns were doused. They shut the hatches, so there was no light and very little air. Then it was over. It passed like it came, there one moment and gone the next. I shall never forget the beauty of walking back up on deck, seeing sunlight again, and breathing calm, clean air. Never, as long as I live."

"Was there much damage, Miss Harrow?" someone down the table asked.

"We lost one mast, chopped down like a felled tree. Ropes were scattered everywhere. The men exhausted. And we were leaking badly. The ship put in at Boston for repairs."

"You made it, though, and that's the important thing. You survived." Lieutenant Goodwind's brow furrowed in thought. "But why, may I ask, were you placed in the central hold and not in the aft cabins where you belonged?"

"Because we did *not* belong there, sir," Nicole replied simply.

"I beg your pardon, Miss Harrow, but—"

"No, no, it's time we gave the young lady a respite. That tale and all the rest shall await us another day." The captain paused until the servants' settling of their steaming plates blocked his actions from notice; then he rewarded Nicole with an approving nod.

Chapter Nine

Cyril started to rise and protested, "Anne, you really must let me get up."

"I won't do anything of the sort." She was able to force him back with the gentlest of pressure. "You're still not well. You must rest, and that's that."

His face looked more flushed now, lying as it was on the stark white pillow. "But my patients—"

"Must wait," she interrupted. "The doctor is ill." Anne feigned a calmness she did not feel. With one hand supporting the small of her back, she straightened and walked to the window. She swept back the drapes, revealing a second curtain of falling flakes. "Look at the weather, my husband."

"Snow in late May. Whoever heard of such a spring?" Several strands of hair lay plastered to his forehead with perspiration. "Warm and bright one day, freezing the next. No wonder so many remain sick."

"Momma has gone to see Dr. Camberly and tell him he must carry on."

"I've been down a whole week now," Cyril said. "I cannot let the old fellow continue to cover for me."

But it had not been a week. Today was in fact the tenth day Cyril had been in bed. He had lost three days to delirium. But there was nothing to be gained by sharing this with him. Nor the panic that threatened to choke off Anne's breath as she had stood by helplessly and watched her husband thrash and cry and pour forth his feverish sweat. At least this had passed. Never had she prayed so hard. Never. "You must rest, Cyril. Now, no more arguments."

To her great relief, he subsided. Then the familiar tenderness flickered faintly from his gaze. "You are such a dear good wife," he whispered.

Walking back over to his bedside, Anne took up a towel and dabbed the beads of sweat from his face and neck. "My beloved, would you take another cup of peppermint tea?"

"Never have I grown so tired of anything as I am of peppermint tea. I taste it in my dreams."

"I must return to the kitchen. I am

preparing another poultice." Anne needed both hands to straighten herself. She gave her patient another love-filled look, then left the bedroom.

Midway down the hall, she was halted by the baby kicking. The baby had taken on such a strong kick, Anne was certain she carried a boy. She stood there, her hand cradling the tautly stretched belly, and wondered how it was possible for her to manage both this weight and the worry over her husband.

Finally the baby eased, and she continued on to the kitchen. The room reeked of fumes from the poultice. She opened the pot that simmered on the iron rail above the fire. Anne shielded her face the best she could, hoping the fumes would not affect the child. Using the wooden ladle, she plucked out the cheesecloth sack. She held it over the pot for a while, allowing the excess water to drip back in. A few drops fell on the fire, sending up puffs of foul-smelling smoke.

When her arms grew tired, she turned and laid the sack into a waiting bowl. Then she grabbed a large piece of cotton bunting—cloth she had originally purchased for making diapers—and stretched it across the kitchen table, folding it twice. Picking up the bowl and the ladle now, she walked to the basin for waste water, tilted the bowl, and used the ladle to press out the remaining water. Then she walked back to the table, pulled out the cheesecloth sack, and settled it on the bunting. After wrapping it up, she lifted the bundle and walked swiftly back to the bedroom.

As soon as she opened the door, Cyril groaned a wordless protest.

"None of that, now. Peel back your bed linen." Anne waited as he pushed down the blanket and sheet. "Now open your nightshirt."

He obeyed, but with a grimace. Cyril hated the poultices almost as much as he hated lying sick in bed. "I have decided this is my punishment for ordering my patients to use them."

"It helps and you know it," Anne said as she settled the steaming bundle on Cyril's chest. The poultice was made according to Cyril's own recipe and contained fresh mustard leaves, two entire peppermint plants, twice-boiled tea leaves, and a dollop of camphor. "You always say there's nothing better for drawing out the contagion."

As she started to move away Cyril captured her wrist. His grip was feeble, his hand moist with sweat. "I have never appreciated you enough."

"Oh, stop that." But something in his countenance and the desperate way in which he spoke the words left her heart feeling pierced straight through. "You're talking—"

"Or loved you as well as you deserve." His hand dropped away. His eyes began to close. "You are the embodiment of everything I ever dreamed for myself."

"Oh, Cyril." She had to stop and swallow a sudden desire to weep, for the words did not bring the joy she might have expected. Not at all. "My dear darling husband."

Sleep and illness drew his eyelids closed, yet the words continued as a soft murmuring. "The clearest vision I have ever known of God's love has been the moment you awaken, looking into your eyes."

"Shah, my love." She stroked his brow and felt her fingers scalded by his unnatural heat. "You must rest now."

Although the bent-over position pained her mightily, Anne remained there till she was certain he was asleep. Finally his rasping breath eased, and she used both hands to push herself erect.

As Anne left the bedroom, she heard the

front door open. She walked into the parlor, where Catherine stood unbuttoning her snow-dappled coat. "This weather is positively atrocious!"

"Even so, Cyril wanted to go see to his patients."

"Perhaps that is a sign he's improving." When Anne did not say anything, her mother demanded, "How is he?"

"I . . ." Suddenly it seemed as though the parlor no longer held any air. She worked her lungs again, then said, "I fear his fever is returning."

"Oh, Anne, no."

"It happens, you know." She tried to be the doctor's assistant, speaking an honest summary. But the words caught in her throat, until it was a struggle to make any sound at all. "He has been so weakened by this, I cannot help but fear he may be struck by another bad night."

Catherine moved up beside her daughter. "Have you eaten?"

"I am not hungry."

"Yet eat you must. There's a child growing within you who must have nourishment."

She allowed her mother to guide her back toward the kitchen. Thankfully the poultice's fumes had lessened somewhat. "I hope the baby does not grow too much more. I feel tight as a drum already. I honestly don't see how I can carry this child another month."

"Just sit yourself down and rest. You do far too much as it is. I'll warm you up a nice bowl of stew and then prepare some good fresh bread for baking with the evening meal. That should do you and your husband both a world of good."

Anne blinked away the morning's second wash of tears. "I don't know what I'd do without you here, Momma."

"That's what mothers are for, haven't you heard?" Catherine's voice was overenthusiastic, as though seeking to dispel the surrounding gloom with the force of her words. "Now as soon as I've fixed your stew, I am going to go upstairs and write your father. It has been three days since my last letter, and I am certain he must be wondering what on Earth has happened to us."

Chapter Ten

The Portsmouth docks held the largest collection of men and ships Nicole had ever seen. With the midday light strong as the westerly wind, she was forced to shade her eyes with her hand as she came up the stairs from the captain's great room. She had stood at the railing and watched the ship's furious activity as it had maneuvered down the long channel, finally answering the port's signal gun with cannon fire and flags of its own. Then at Emily's suggestion she had gone down to change into the dress of midnight blue. Though it would make for a warmer overland journey, Emily felt the somber air would make a more fitting first impression. "After all, my dear," she had reminded Nicole, "it is not just your uncle who will be greeting you. There will be the servants and the coachmen and any friends or relatives who might be gathered."

"Charles has no other living relatives in England," Nicole said, but her mind had become preoccupied by the word *servants*. How ever was she going to cope?

Emily noticed the sudden rush of anxiety and patted her hand. "Rest assured, my dear, you will do fine."

"How can you be so certain?"

"Because I have watched the effect you have had upon the men gathered here. If you can charm the likes of my husband and his officers, I have no doubt that you will make your uncle very proud indeed."

The words had eased Nicole through the final stages of packing and dressing. But now, as she came up from the belowdecks and found herself facing the bustling harbor, she quailed. "It's positively enormous."

"Aye, some say the busiest port in all the world," Captain Madden said proudly. "Home to His Majesty's fleet, not to mention half the London-bound trade. Tea from India, spice from the Orient, silks from China, gold from the colonies. Trade is the backbone of our nation, you mark my words."

Nicole forced herself to turn and offer the captain her very best smile. "I cannot thank you enough, sir."

The ship's master plucked the hat from his head. "Your servant, Miss Harrow."

"I mean this sincerely. You and your dear wife have taught me well and graced me with friendship besides."

The captain's chest expanded, and his vast sideburns seemed to bristle further. "The pleasure has been all mine."

"Ahoy there!" A voice drifted up from over the side. "I say, do you carry a passenger by the name of Miss Nicole Harrow?"

The captain walked to the rail. "Who wants to know?"

"Gaylord Days is the name, sir. Privy to Lord Charles, earl of Sutton."

"Then the answer is yes." He turned to the bosun and ordered, "Rig the rope ladder and the bosun's chair."

"Aye, sir."

Then the captain bent back over the rail. "Mr. Days, how did you know? We made a record crossing. There's no chance of the mail packet having beaten us over."

"You're the fifth ship I've come out to meet, sir." The rope ladder was tossed over as the vessel was moored, and then a solid man who appeared to be in his fifties made hard work of clambering aboard. He paused at the top to adjust his periwig and straighten the lapels of his long coat with its shining gold buttons. Then he gave a deep bow. He wore dark breeches tucked into knee-high white stockings, a frilled shirt, and square-toed shoes with bright gold buckles. "Your servant, sir."

"The fifth ship, you say?"

"Aye. I've been lodged here in Portsmouth for six days now, with orders to meet every ship that arrives from the northern colonies. Lord Charles is all afire to have . . ." His eye then caught sight of Nicole standing well away from the discussion, not hiding, but certainly not pushing her way forward. The stocky man could not help but gape. "Y-you are Miss Nicole Harrow?"

"Yes." Even to her own ear, her voice sounded quieter than the gulls' constant crying. Lost and small and afraid. "I am."

"I am ever so glad to make your acquaintance, ma'am." He bowed, then resumed his staring. "You'll forgive me, but Lord Charles said nothing of my being sent to meet, well, a lady such as yourself. Dark-haired, tall, and fetching was all the description he cared to give me."

Captain Madden seemed to find the servant's surprise most amusing. "Her beauty is nothing compared to her charm, I assure you."

"Thank you, Captain," Nicole said.

"With your permission, Miss Harrow, my officers have requested to pay their respects and see you off." The captain gestured them forward. Behind the row of officers, dressed in their very best uniforms, stood many of the ship's crew, who had also turned out en masse to bid her farewell. For

Nicole's dinnertime stories had filtered down through the ranks, and not a one of the men had remained untouched by the young lady's tales.

Nicole made her way along the line of brightly uniformed gentlemen, thanking each in turn.

Next to last was the handsome Gordon Goodwind, who removed his hat and bowed so sharply his saber's tip rattled against his boot. "You have brought us good fortune, Miss Harrow, and graced us with a memorable voyage."

"You are too kind. All of you." She searched for something to make her good-bye more personal. "Mrs. Madden informs me that you are to be brevetted a captain. Did I say that correctly?"

"Aye, ma'am." The lieutenant's gaze was as straight and pointed as his sword. "This grand lady of a vessel is to be mine."

"I have no doubt you will make Captain Madden very proud."

"I thank you for the words and the confidence, my lady." Goodwind colored slightly as he bowed a second time. "I shall be visiting relatives in London between journeys. Perhaps you would be so good as to permit me to call—"

"That will do, Mr. Goodwind," the captain broke in.

Nicole did her best to soften the captain's chop. "I would be honored, if I am there." She then stepped over to Andy Potter, whose face turned so brilliant red it looked as if he might explode. "I shall always remember your welcome, Mr. Potter."

"Oh, thank you, miss," he stammered. "I . . . I count it a great blessing the day you boarded our ship."

"As do we all," the tall lieutenant said.

Nicole turned to Emily, hugged her close, and whispered, "I cannot do this."

"You can and you will." The lady's face was wreathed in smiles. "What is more, my dear, you will *shine*."

"Will you come to see me? That is, if it's not too far?"

"Actually, we live in London when my husband is not abroad. If you're sure you would like to see us, we would be honored, wouldn't we, James?"

"Delighted. We would be delighted."

"But I thought Uncle Charles lived in the country."

Emily smiled even more broadly. "Oh, the things you will see," she said and patted Nicole's arm. "The wonders still to be discovered."

Nicole had no choice then but to turn back to where the manservant waited. "I am ready, sir."

"Very good, ma'am." He had a discerning eye and so took a moment to study the way the entire ship seemed poised and waiting to honor Nicole's departure. "I can see Lord Charles was not mistaken in his choice, Miss Harrow."

"Far from it," the captain declared.

Gaylord Days made equal hard going in his descending from the vessel, taking another moment at the bottom to readjust his wig and coat. He received the chests and settled them himself, then waited as Nicole was helped into the bosun's chair and eased gently over the side.

As she began her descent the captain commanded sharply, "Present arms!"

The officers doffed their hats and stood at attention as Nicole disappeared over the rail. Gaylord Days met her with, "They do you great honor, Miss Harrow. I've not seen such a display other than when there's an admiral or royalty about. Not ever in all my born days."

She was seated alongside Gaylord amidships, as fore and aft the six men leaned heavily into the oars. Gradually they pulled away from the ship, drawing hard across the inner harbor's protected waters. Nicole kept her eyes focused on the vessel, watching as everything she knew and had gotten comfort from moved farther and farther away. She whispered to herself, "Where am I going?"

"Harrow Hall, Miss Harrow," Gaylord replied, for his ears were as keen as his eyesight. "Lord Charles has delayed his move to London until you have time to settle yourself."

She straightened and tried to clear herself from the tides of uncertainty. "How far is it from here?"

"A good day's journey by carriage. There's a coaching inn midway, where we can overnight in comfort and safety."

"Carriage?"

"Aye, miss. You can see it waiting us there upon the quayside."

Nicole gasped at the sight of the gleaming coach. It was tall, shining with gold leaf, and drawn by six of the finest dark steeds she had ever seen. Three men stood awaiting their arrival, all in longcoats and powdered wigs. Above the carriage door was embossed an elaborate royal seal.

She turned back around and stared at the ships and the harbor, but saw nothing. She then murmured to herself, "Carriage."

Chapter Eleven

Charles paced impatiently back and forth across the forecourt. Never had he felt so anxious. He pulled the gilded pocket watch from his waistcoat, glanced at it, and let out an indignant snort. How was it possible for time to crawl so?

That morning, a young man had arrived from the coaching inn between Harrow Hall and Portsmouth Harbor, shouting with the excitement of bringing good news. The servant, Gaylord Days, had ordered him the previous night to leave at first light. But the boy had ridden the first hour by moonlight, so elated was he by the prospect of earning a reward of silver farthings. Would Lord Charles recompense him for the news that the carriage would be arriving that very day? Indeed, Charles had sent the weary but immensely pleased innkeeper's son off on his return journey with a handful of silver jingling in his pocket.

"*Here* you are, sir!" Maisy Days rushed down the front stairs. She was a broad woman, with a cheery red face that looked for reasons to smile. But she was not smiling now. She carried herself with a rolling gait across the forecourt, stopping only when she was close enough for Charles to see the indignant flush to her cheeks. "Here it is just gone two o'clock in the afternoon, and my good cooked lunch has gone stone-cold, sir. Stone-cold!"

"I am not hungry," Charles said.

"That's your head talking and not your middle," she retorted. "I've been with you nigh on forty years and I know you well as anyone on this here earth. And within the hour you'll be hot as a boiled rooster, stomping about and giving everybody the sharp end of your tongue. Now is that the impression you want the young lady to have of this place?"

"No, no, I suppose you're right."

"'Course I am." She shooed him back across the cobblestone concourse. "Give me no end of trouble, you do. If Will were to try your tricks, he'd soon hear from me, if I may say so, sir!"

Charles crossed the outer hall from which he could see the two downstairs maids frantically completing their cleaning. Will was also at work, standing on a ladder and polishing the top panes of the open front windows. From his perch he looked down and grinned conspiratorially. All the staff wore smiles that afternoon, all except Maisy Days and himself.

Charles asked the indignant woman, "Do you think Nicole will like the old place?"

"What a question. I wish you could hear yourself, I do. Walking about like a man what's lost his way, squinting into corners and not seeing a thing."

"There's a great deal riding on this, you know."

"And not a thing that'll come from your going on so." She pointed him into the smaller dining chamber. "Sit yourself down there, while I go warm up your soup. Again."

"I'll just have a bite standing in the kitchen."

"No, sir, if I may be so bold. A meal I have prepared will be eaten sitting down." She handed him a linen napkin and waited until he had assumed his position at the head of the table before turning back to the kitchen, muttering as she went, "Greeting the young mistress what's come all this way, wearing a waistcoat dripped with his lunch. Not in my house, sir. Not in a thousand years." Her words were punctuated by the kitchen door shutting firmly behind her.

Charles pulled a wad of folded pages from his coat pocket, notes he had written three mornings before. There was so much he wanted to say to Nicole—words of welcome and explanation—he had decided to jot them down rather than risk forgetting something vital. Yet now as he looked them over, they seemed so formal, so very wrong for the occasion.

Maisy returned, bearing a steaming bowl and a plate of freshly baked bread. "Here you are now, a goodly portion of stew. It'll warm you right up."

He refolded the pages and stuffed them back into his pocket. "I wish I knew what to say to the lass."

"None of that, now. She's not coming for the night, you know. She made the promise you wanted, did not you tell me that?"

"Two years, that's what she said." Charles took a spoonful of stew but tasted nothing.

"Well, then." Maisy crossed her arms, clearly intending to stand there and make sure he ate. "What's important is how she finds things over time. It'll all be new at first, but she'll grow to like the place."

Charles looked up at the woman he had known all his adult life. "You think so? Truly?"

"She's coming all this way, is she not?" But she saw the desperate appeal in his face and so softened. "I will tell His Honor something I've not said, no, not ever. You came back from your journey to the colonies a changed man. And if that young woman has an ounce of sense to her name, she is going to see this as well."

"I think," Charles said, "she already knows."

"If she's half the woman you've described to me, I am not the least bit surprised. Such things as this are what's important. Not the old place and all these here trappings. I've heard you say that often enough. Give her time, I say, and she'll see this as well."

Charles felt the first faint easing of tension since his greeting the young rider that morning. "You are a dear woman, Maisy Days."

She turned fierce once more. "I am annoyed at the hole you've made in my day, is what I am. Here with a guest arriving and me with a kitchen to run. Now you sit there and finish what's been set before you." She then patted his shoulder before whirling around and walking back to the kitchen.

But once Charles was alone again, all the worries and tensions returned. He forced himself to eat, yet he might as well have been spooning dust into his mouth.

"Sir! Oh, sir!" Young Will Days clattered down the ladder and raced across the hall. "I hear horses!"

Charles overturned his chair in his haste to rise. He rushed to the front door and then stood motionless, as all around him gathered the excited household staff.

"Quiet, everyone!" But all he could hear was the hammering of his own heart. So he pushed open the door and walked to the edge of the front terrace. He strained and then caught the drift of a faint drumming of hooves. "That must be them!"

Maisy's voice rang out, ordering the staff to come together for the formal greeting. Paying particular attention to the younger people, she went down the line and made sure the livery was spotless, the maids' caps were in place, their aprons tied properly.

Charles walked a few paces away from them, frightened. What if Nicole despised the old place? What if she despised England? What if he had made a terrible mistake in bringing her here?

As if in response to his questions, the answer formed. Ask and it shall be granted. So Charles bowed his head. *Father, I am afraid. I don't even know what to pray for.*

Thy will be done. I can ask for nothing more. Thy will be done.

He stood there, head still bowed, willing for more or better words to come. And in the quiet there pealed forth a sound, one that silenced even Maisy. Charles raised his head and listened. There it was again.

The warm summer breeze carried the unmistakable sound of a woman laughing.

Charles found himself hurrying in disbelief down the lane that led toward the front gates. He watched as the carriage slowed and then turned through the gates. As the horses started down the treelined avenue, he heard it again. A laughter so clear and carefree it caused him to shiver.

Then he saw her, seated beside the driver, sharing the reins with him.

"That's it, my lady," he heard the driver call. "Draw back even, the two lines in together. Call to them, now."

"Whoa! Slow down, there!" The laugh was clearer now, close enough for Charles to see the beaming face and the young woman's excitement. "Oh, oh, they're doing what I say!"

"Pull harder, now. That's it." The horses came finally to a halt next to where Charles was standing. The two front steeds, the most spirited of his team, pawed at the earth and whinnied. Clearly they had felt a new hand at the stead and enjoyed it.

The driver then sobered as he turned all his attention toward Charles. "Your pardon, my lord, but she asked and asked—"

"It's fine, truly," Charles said. And it was.

Nicole seemed reluctant to release the reins. "I am sorry, Lord Charles, but never in my life have I known such a thing as this."

"She's a natural, your honor," the young driver offered. "The horses mind her better than they do me."

"That's not true," Nicole cried. "I could do this only because he sat beside me and helped hold the reins."

"I did naught but show her the way," the driver countered.

Gaylord Days pulled open the door to the carriage proper as the two footmen dropped from their rear stations. He glanced up at the young woman, then gave Charles a deep bow. "I hope I was not wrong in giving the lass her head, your lordship."

"Not at all." Charles could not help staring at Nicole, nor could he prevent his smile.

Gaylord moved in closer still and

murmured for Charles's ear alone, "A most remarkable young lady, my lord. Charming and spirited besides."

Charles reached up both arms and smiled his pleasure. "Welcome, my dear. Welcome to Harrow Hall."

Nicole looked down from the carriage's high perch, so overwhelmed by all that had just passed she could not recall the fear she had known that morning. Upon waking, her mind had quaked over the thought of seeing her uncle and everything she did not know. Now, however, her heart overflowed with the joy she had found in watching the world pass with such smooth power. "I hope I haven't done anything improper, Lord Charles."

"Call me Uncle or Charles, I beg you. And not in the slightest. Come, let me help you down."

Nicole accepted his hand. "It was such a beautiful day, I couldn't bear the thought of not sitting up top and watching the sunlight through the clouds."

"I quite understand. Put your foot on the metal step there, that's it."

"It seemed the most natural thing in the world to ask to hold the reins." She stepped lightly onto the ground, gave him a carefree smile, then reached over and patted the nearest horse's shoulder. "These are the grandest and most beautiful animals on all the earth."

Nicole then glanced up to where Jim sat grinning down at her. "And you are a wonderful teacher. Thank you."

He tipped his hat. "A pleasure, my lady."

She stepped back from the carriage and tried to pat her hair back into place. "I must look a mess."

"On the contrary," Charles said with quiet conviction. "You look divine." He offered her his arm. "Would you like a cup of tea now?"

"Oh, I am very thirsty." Nicole took his arm and walked with him around the carriage, where she stopped in her tracks.

"Now, now, none of that."

All the day's joy drained away. Before her stood the most magnificent building she had ever seen. It loomed higher than the trees. In fact, it seemed high as the sky from where she was standing. All the fears she had known returned with a jolt. "Do you live here?"

"*We* live here," he corrected softly. "This is Harrow Hall."

"All of this?" Her voice squeaked in her ears.

To her surprise, Charles did not lead her toward the waiting staff. Instead, he turned her around and started back down the tree-lined lane.

"Let me share with you a confidence," he said. "Before you arrived, I was absolutely terrified."

"You? Why?"

"Because I had so much riding on this moment. The future of my family's name. All the hopes I have invested in a future beyond my own life. Trivial matters when faced with the things of eternity, I admit. But important to me just the same. And now you were coming, traveling across the wide blue sea, and what would you find? How would you feel?" He halted and faced her square on. "I even wrote a speech of welcome. It's here in my pocket, and there it shall remain."

Nicole bit her lip, as much from his tone as the words he expressed. "I confess to being terrified as well."

"Of course you are. It is only natural. But the nicest moment of this entire time of waiting, my dear, was hearing your laughter ring ahead of your arrival. More than anything else, I want you to be happy here." He reached forward and touched her arm. "This old place has been empty of laughter for far too long."

She raised one hand to cover his own. "Dear Uncle Charles. Thank you."

"For what?"

"For reminding me of why I came."

He relaxed a trifle. "Shall we go now and see your new home?"

Nicole felt once more a twinge of apprehension, but tried to keep it from her face. "Very well, yes. Let's."

Chapter Twelve

Nicole took her time going up the stairs, for the servants lined the broad stone steps, one to each side. Charles seemed pleased that she would want to meet them. He introduced each by name. But there was so much to take in, especially as each stride took her closer toward the palace.

One person stood out immediately in her mind, an ample, smiling woman, whose cheeks were pushed out as if they held a pair of ripe plums. "This is Maisy Days," Charles said. "She and her husband,

Gaylord, run the house for me. And run it well."

Maisy did her best to curtsy. "An honor to meet you, my lady."

"Thank you, ma'am. I fear I have given your husband a great fright on the way here. He did not seem to think much of my climbing up on top the carriage."

"Nonsense, my lady. A woman of spirit is just what this old house needs." She reached behind her and pushed forward a sturdy-looking boy. "Might I introduce our youngest boy, my lady. William Days is his name, though round these parts he mostly answers to Will. He's ten years old now."

Nicole watched as the boy bowed, his face flaming. "What a charming young man. May I call you Will, also?"

"If it pleases you, my lady," the boy mumbled, clearly embarrassed by the attention. But his mother brightened so that her cheeks glowed apple red.

Will's words gave Nicole the courage to turn to Charles and say then and there, in front of them all, "If you will permit me, Uncle Charles, I find my title jarring. Especially here among people who live with us."

Charles blinked in evident surprise but said merely, "Would you prefer they use your proper name?"

"Yes, please."

"Very well, it's settled then." He offered his elbow again. "Shall we continue?"

Nicole started toward the front door, her eyes arrested by the towering edifice before her. The door had been set at the center of eight enormous pillars, not separate from the building but made to be half-emerging from the magnificent façade. Nicole saw that the windows to the first two floors were taller than she was; then she stumbled on the steps.

"Now, now," Charles chided quietly. "None of that."

"But it's so *big*."

"Aye, far too big for one lonely old man." He reached over with his free hand and patted hers, where it rested on his elbow. "Remember, my dear, all this pales compared to the gift you've given me of your presence today."

They then stepped across the threshold. The front hall was a marble-encased cube, fifteen feet to a side and fifteen feet high. The ceiling was the shape of a cupola from which hung a great brass chandelier. Charles paid it all no mind as he led her into what was the largest chamber Nicole had ever entered. So large, in fact, that the walls flanking the dual curved staircase contained full-sized portraits of men on dancing steeds.

Nicole pointed at the paintings and asked, "Are they family?"

"They were. A long time ago."

She found comfort in the fact that she would not have to greet them. They both held a stern look, and one waved a saber over his head. Nicole knew she would feel uneasy using that particular staircase and walking beneath the raised English sword for a very long time.

"Now then," Charles said, "a bit of history. The house was originally built during the time of Charles the First, but my grandfather rebuilt it in the style you see today. It's called Georgian. We are now ruled by the third of the Hanoverian kings, George the Third. Although thankfully much of his power has been passed on to our Parliament."

Nicole tried to pay attention, but she felt overwhelmed by all the wealth surrounding her. "What is this room called?"

"This?" Charles waved a dismissive hand. "The first inner hall."

Nicole looked at him. "There is a *second* hall?"

He inspected her a moment, then said,

"I suppose the history lesson can wait for another time, yes?"

"All right."

"And perhaps we should go ahead and get the worst over without delay."

"The worst?"

In reply, Charles turned and said, "Gaylord."

"Yes, m'lord."

"We shall see to the formal halls first."

"Very good, m'lord."

As the butler scurried up the stairs in front of them, Charles continued, "Downstairs in front are what you might call our family rooms—the breakfast room, Chippendale room, music room, dining hall, smaller dining chamber, reading room, winter garden. In the back are the servants' quarters, kitchen, and pantry. To the north side we have what remains of the original structure, now fashioned into three bed-chambers, sitting rooms, dressing rooms, and a guest apartment. Upstairs—"

Charles cut off his explanation and grasped the stair railing. He let go of Nicole with his other hand and then gripped his chest—hard.

"Uncle, is there something the matter?"

"No, nothing."

"But you've gone all pale. And you are perspiring."

"It's nothing, really." But the words came in quick, short gasps. "The excitement. At times I . . ."

She was about to call for Gaylord, when as swiftly as it had come, the spell passed. Charles's color returned, his breathing eased. He relaxed his holds on the banister and his chest. Managing a smile, he said, "There. All better now."

"Should I call for help?"

"Not at all, my dear. And please don't mention this to anyone. I get these spells only from time to time. They come and they go."

Reluctantly Nicole permitted him to continue leading her up the stairs. "Have you spoken to a doctor?"

"There's nothing anyone can do for me. And it's all a trifling affair. I have simply been far too excited for my own good. But you are here now, and all is well. Truly." And he did look fine as he rested there on the landing, near where Gaylord stood proudly beside a pair of ornate double-doors. "This is known as a seven-bay house, with three rooms to either side of the front entrance. Upstairs we have the formal rooms, used mostly for visitors. Of course, you may take one as your own and do with it whatever you like."

Nicole could scarcely believe her ears. "But not as my bedroom?"

"No, your sleeping quarters will be in the old house."

"You mean I can have *another* room all to myself?"

Her question caused Charles to exchange a quick glance with Gaylord. "I think the best thing for us to do is simply proceed through the entire affair."

"Whatever you say, Uncle."

"All right then. Remember now, these are merely trappings. What's important is the gift you have made to me this day."

But his words and the assurance they carried vanished like smoke in the breeze while they strolled from one large room to another. Charles took her in a right-hand circle, naming each chamber as they leisurely made their way around the manor.

The first drawing room opened up to the garden drawing room, and this gave way to the first formal salon. From there they proceeded into the mirrored salon—the only room where the walls were not covered with oil paintings. Instead, each wall held a single beveled mirror within a heavy gilded frame. Nicole found herself staring back at her reflection a hundred times over, and every face appeared frightened. She was glad to leave the salon behind and enter the portico drawing room.

Soon they walked into the long gallery, where Nicole finally had to stop. "It's all too much," she whispered.

"It *is* rather grand," Charles admitted, giving her time for a longer look.

Walls of amber damask rose forty feet to a gilded domed ceiling, where skylights of stained glass diffused a rainbow of afternoon shades. Dozens of pillars were crowned with gold-leaf cherubs holding aloft silver ribbons that crisscrossed the dome. The floor consisted of a mosaic of marble and fine woods. And the gallery's furniture was carved and covered with gold leaf to match its surroundings.

"The long gallery here is used for our larger parties," Charles said. "I had hoped to give a reception in your honor, my dear. Once you have had a chance to settle in and become comfortable. But everyone is away just now. It's the season, you know."

Nicole nodded, not understanding, but unable at the time to speak. The room went on and on, and was ringed by a balcony deep enough to contain tables and chairs. Nicole felt her head beginning to spin. She couldn't take it all in, so she sought something to fix her attention on. Her eyes landed on a painting, one so beautiful she cried aloud, "Oh, look."

Charles followed her gaze and then guided her forward till they stood directly before it. Yet it was to the butler that he spoke. "Have you ever seen the like, Gaylord?"

"Quite remarkable, m'lord."

In a tone more tender than she had ever heard him use, Charles said, "This was my mother's favorite painting. It hung in her bedroom all her life. The one which will now become your bedchamber, if you like."

"This is the most beautiful thing I have ever seen," Nicole breathed.

"It was painted by a Flemish man named Rubens nearly two centuries ago. It is called 'Christ Praying in Gethsemane.'" As Nicole continued to stare intently at the painting, he went on, "I think we should move it back to your bedchamber. Will you please see to that, Gaylord?"

"Immediately, m'lord."

Nicole spun around. "You are giving this to me?"

Charles gave her a soft smile. "My dear, *all* of this is yours. Whatever you like, you may claim as your own."

The implications of this simple statement left her utterly without words as they walked on into the yellow drawing room, the striped drawing room, and the Etruscan drawing room with its embroidered silk benches that encircled the chamber. Only after they had entered the formal dining hall, which included a thirty-foot long table and centerpiece of Portuguese silver, did she react at all—and then with a shudder.

"What's the matter, my dear?" Charles asked with a concerned look on his face.

"Nothing, it's just . . ." She pointed at the walls. "All the paintings in here are of war."

"Ah. Yes. Of course. This was my grandfather's choice, and my father left them here out of respect for his memory. I should have thought of this, given your heritage." He then turned around and said, "Gaylord."

"Yes, m'lord."

"Every painting to do with soldiery, officers, battles, and war."

"Soldiery. Yes, m'lord."

"Remove them to the back garden and burn the lot."

"Immediately, m'lord."

"No!" Nicole cried out. "You cannot!"

149

"If they offend you, my dear, then I must."

"No, it's just . . ." But when she looked again at the scenes of battle and mayhem, she couldn't completely hide another shudder. "Please, don't destroy them."

"Very well. We shall instead collect the paintings and store them in a room you shall not need to enter. Which of the rooms did you care for the least?"

Nicole hesitated, then admitted, "The one with the striped benches."

"Gaylord?"

"Every military painting to the Etruscan drawing room. We shall begin on this at once, m'lord."

"No need to hurry. We shall not be using this room for a few days yet."

Struggling to make sense of the jumble in her head, Nicole blurted, "You have so many paintings."

"Indeed we do. Several of my ancestors were great collectors." Charles took her arm, and together they entered a pair of small antechambers, both fitted out with writing desks. "There are pictures and portraits by Ribera, Raphael, Van Dyck, Rubens, Steen, Titian, Correggio, Brueghel." Charles stopped when he realized she was no longer listening. "What is it, my dear?"

"No one," Nicole said slowly, "can possibly own this many books."

"Ah. You like my library, do you? I am so very pleased. I spend as much time here as I can."

The chamber was as tall as the long gallery but included two balconies rather than one. Two of the walls were covered by glass-fronted cases, and every case was crammed with books. The third wall had shelves as well, but these were built to rise up and frame a huge marble fireplace. The fourth wall was given over to a beautiful leather-topped desk flanked by tall windows. The furniture was simple compared to the rooms they had just left behind: a great Persian carpet spread over the polished wooden floor, leather settees, and tables piled with books and documents. Books everywhere. "May I come back here?" she asked.

"Nothing would give me more pleasure. We shall claim this chamber as our own, shall we? The place where we meet in the evening and speak of our day."

Above her confusion and all the opulence, Nicole heard her uncle's desperate plea for her to be happy here. She patted his arm and said, "You are such a good, dear man."

Charles seemed to deflate, releasing the tension he had been holding since her arrival. And long before. Suddenly she was looking into the face of the man she had come to know in Halifax. "You must be tired from your journey," Charles said. "Come, let me show you to your private chambers, and you can have a rest before dinner."

Nicole started to say she had no intention of resting, but her mind was caught when Charles had said *private chambers*.

Down the staircase they went, through a trio of rooms somewhat less regal than those upstairs, yet only by degree. Then through a doorway with an odd point at the top and up another flight of side stairs, narrower than the front hall and much older. The steps creaked a gentle welcome beneath her feet. The railing was made of dark wood and appeared scarred from centuries of use.

Charles tapped on another of the tall peaked doors, set now in frames carved from stone. "My chambers are through here," he said. He then led her down a hall decorated with tapestries to another doorway. "And here is where you may reside."

He pushed open the door and waited for her to enter. Though it was very hard,

Nicole forced herself to move forward.

Before her stretched an array of four rooms. The front room held a writing desk, settees, and bookcases, with ancient-looking windows shaped like the doorway. The walls were comprised of carved wood, oiled so that they shined a rich welcome in the afternoon light. And on the left and right sides of the entrance were fireplaces, so tall she could have stepped inside them. Nicole gasped when she looked into the next chamber and saw the vast canopied bed. To one side there was a narrow doorway, open to the afternoon breeze, which revealed a balcony and stone railing smothered by blooming lilacs.

"Your dressing chamber and washroom are through there," Charles said, pointing. "I shall leave you now and give you a chance to settle in. Welcome, my dear, to Harrow Hall."

Chapter Thirteen

Anne's and Catherine's prayers and their unrelenting care could not keep Cyril's fever from returning. And five days after Anne's fearful admission, both women were now exhausted from the work and the strain.

Anne emerged from the house in time to greet the symphony of twilight. She eased her back with one hand and clung to a porch post with the other. As she squinted at the globe dipping behind the western hills, she felt resentment over the day's closing beauty. How could the heavens be so gloriously lit? How could the air hold such a warm promise of summer?

Then the door opened, and Catherine came out to stand beside her. "Is he resting?"

"Finally." But what got Anne's attention was not her mother's question. Rather it was the odor that had escaped through the door with her. She knew the smell. She had faced it many times in the homes of Cyril's patients. He had once told her he could often tell the degree of illness long before he examined his patient, simply by being exposed to the home's odor. She did not have his gift or training. Nevertheless, she had studied hard and learned much, and she knew what she smelled.

Her eyes were then drawn toward the raucous shouts coming from the lane beyond their front garden. Their planting had been over a week late. Finally that morning, three of Cyril's former patients had stopped by to dig the small furrows and plant some vegetables. The neat rows of tilled earth gave off a fragrant promise Anne found easier to ignore. Instead she focused on the three men sauntering by on the other side of the white picket fence.

The governor had ordered that two fields beyond their home be turned into garrisons for soldiers on their way west. One of the fields was now home to a hodgepodge of adventurers, mostly German mercenaries who had come to fight alongside the British. Late at night when Anne lay in bed, she could hear their carousing.

The three men brandished sabers, wore high muddy boots, and carried themselves with a jaunty air. One of them spoke in a language she did not understand. Anne felt no fear, no anger over their leering and rough talking. Having nothing to say, nor the will to hide what she was feeling, she simply stared back at them. And something in her gaze was enough to silence them. They turned away from whatever they found in her and her mother's face, continuing on without another word.

Not long after the soldiers had passed, Anne heard a horse trotting. She did not turn, though, thinking it was one of the motley officers responsible for the garrison. Then she heard her mother gasp.

Catherine flung herself down the path, struggled with the gate, then raced toward the horseman. The figure was caught in the glare of the setting sun, so that at first Anne could only see that both the rider and horse were near exhaustion. For the horse's head drooped almost to the ground, and the rider's shoulders were bowed, with the head leaning slightly to one side.

Then she suddenly realized this was her father.

Anne started down the stairs, but it seemed that suddenly balance was impossible to maintain. It occurred to her that this was not just the result of fatigue or her being with child. She found herself needing to grip the railing with both hands, to pause on each step, breathe, and then gather herself for the next step. She watched as Catherine reached up and embraced the exhausted Andrew. She heard the quiet weeping, the first tears Catherine had shed since her coming.

Anne then heard her father say, "I left just as soon as I received your letter. I've ridden straight through. How is he?"

She managed finally to get to the bottom stair and take the first step along the path.

She noticed how her mother did not respond with words but with weeping, stronger than before. Her father then slid from the horse without releasing Catherine. Rubbing her face back and forth on Andrew's shoulder, her mother clung to him with a look of desperation, her body shaking from the irregular sobs.

Anne's feet could no longer hold to the path, nor her eyes see to find her way. The stench from the house, their little cottage, wafted out and wrapped its cruel tentacles around her. She felt the moist earth beneath her feet, and it seemed to her that she stood at the edge of a grave. She knew her father had turned toward her, yet how she knew this she could not have said. It appeared as though the odor now blinded her to all but the sudden realization. She had been at Cyril's side when other pastors had come. Other ministers, some strangers and some friends, called to the bedside with urgent haste. There to help, to offer the final solace. There to pray.

She did not so much faint as give up. All the strength she had been holding, all the will she had left—all was suddenly gone. It felt to Anne that the ground had risen up and caught her. The last thing she remembered was the scent of soft, sweet earth.

Chapter Fourteen

Gradually Anne began to return from the land of unconsciousness. But her eyes resisted focusing, and her mind struggled to sort out what was going on around her. Ghostlike images drifted in and out of the mist, murmuring words she couldn't comprehend, touching her with hands she did not feel. She wanted to scream in her confusion and protest, but only a groan escaped her lips. It brought immediate response from the ethereal figures hovering over her. A hand reached out to stroke her brow. Then she felt it and understood its meaning.

A voice spoke, her mother's. She fought to make sense of the sounds, trying hard to focus her eyes on the face that wavered before her. She licked dried lips and finally found a voice to express her confusion. "What happened?" The words were weak and breathy, and she did not recognize them as her own.

The hand again. Stroking her forehead, brushing back the hair that had somehow escaped from her carefully pinned topknot, now wisping uncontrollably about her face.

"We're here. Your father and I are here," the voice above her said.

That I know, but why? Anne wanted to respond. *What has happened?* She felt the urge to scream. Why was she in this peculiar state? She had to know. The questions pounded through her benumbed brain.

"The doctor has left. You—"

But Anne interrupted. "Doctor? Why was a doctor here?"

"You have a son," her mother murmured, trying to bring some lightness to the strange announcement.

"A son?" Anne fought to raise herself from her prostrate position.

Catherine's hand forced her back against the pillows. "Just relax. You are still very weak. You must conserve your strength."

"A son?" Anne still puzzled. "How? When. . . ?"

"A short time ago."

"Is he. . . ?"

"He's fine."

"But he's early. He was not to arrive . . ."

"I know." Anne relaxed against the pressure of the hand on her shoulder. She did not have the strength to push herself up anyway. Her eyes searched frantically around the room for clues as to the bizarre happenings. If she could only think clearly.

"Please," she implored her mother, searching for some sense of her world. "Start at the beginning."

She saw Catherine blink back tears. This was not the way a new grandmother usually delivered the news that a baby had arrived safely. Anne felt terror grip her soul.

"You fainted," Catherine began.

Anne struggled to remember. Yes, she had fainted. Just after her father had arrived. Her father. Was he here? She strained through the fog of uncertainty. Perhaps it was he by the foot of her bed.

"I fainted," she agreed with a barely perceptible nod of her head. Somewhere in her dim memory came the remembrance of pain. Pain. It was all so strange. "But why?"

"Cyril has been . . . ill."

Cyril. Of course. It was Cyril. It all rushed in on her now. Cyril was ill. Desperately ill. She must go to him. She must. She pushed against her mother's hand, exerting all the strength she had left in the attempt to raise herself up.

"You must remain calm," Catherine said, but her words blurred with tears.

Then her father moved up beside her. "You went into early labor—because of the strain and anxiety," he said. Even his voice sounded different to Anne. "The baby's small but quite strong. He's a little fighter. And he's going to be fine."

"Cyril?" mumbled Anne, shaking her head in hope of clearing the confusion. Was this all some horrid nightmare? Would she soon awaken to have her world restored again?

Andrew took her unresponsive hand and rubbed it between his two strong hands. It was some time before he found his voice. "Cyril's prayer was answered," he said softly. "He was able to tell his son that he loved him."

Anne puzzled. What a strange thing to say. So strange it cleared some of the fog from her brain. "What are you saying?"

Again a long pause. "My dear . . . I would give my life not to have to say this to you, but . . . your beloved Cyril has left us and gone to glory."

"What. . . ?"

"Cyril passed away, my dear. Not long after he held his newborn son in his arms. His last prayer was for you—and your baby boy."

"You're mad," Anne screamed as she heaved herself to a sitting position, despite the hands that tried to hold her. Never had she spoken to her father in such a way, nor to anyone, but she was beside herself with fear. "I want to see Cyril," she demanded. "I want to see my baby."

"Hush, my dear, hush." Catherine sought to comfort her. "You will only bring harm to yourself. You must think of your child. I'll bring him to you. It's true that his father is gone, but the baby is right here with you. You must think about him now. That is what Cyril would want."

As Andrew held Anne tightly, trying to still her trembling while the sobs shook her body, Catherine turned and left the bedside. Soon she returned and placed a small, frail bundle in Anne's arms. Her son. With all the strength she could muster, Anne gathered him close to her heart. It was true. She had a son. But her mind couldn't escape the accompanying fact: that it must also be true Cyril had lost his battle with the ugly disease that consumed his body.

Tears of grief streamed down her cheeks as she mourned for the man she had lost. How would she ever live without him? How could she bear to spend her days and nights alone? What would happen to the child in her arms? Baby John, whom they had looked forward to welcoming to their home. The little one who was to bring them such joy and make their family complete.

Oh, dear God, her heart cried out silently, *please, please help me.*

Chapter Fiveteen

Three weeks after her arrival in England, Nicole and Charles set out for London. As with everything else to do with life in Harrow Hall, their departure was an enormous affair. Gaylord and Maisy had left the day before. One of the maids shared the wagon's front bench, young Will perched himself high on a heap of belongings, and a footman went along as driver and guard. Charles had explained he wouldn't have subjected her to a journey so soon after her arrival, but the London season was drawing to a close. And it would be more fitting if they attended at least one event.

Nicole did not mind at all. Little seemed to touch her very deeply these days. The contrast between England and everything she had known previously was so extreme, it had left her without a profound reaction to anything. Her days had been occupied with a flurry of activity as she learned her way around the manor. Yet nothing seemed to reach beneath the surface. Charles doted on her as did the household staff, everyone seeking to anticipate her wishes. But she had none. It was proving hard enough to accept the idea she had been brought there so that she might become heir to Charles's estate. So that everything she saw—the house and gardens and furniture and paintings and opulent fittings—would become hers someday.

The staff gathered to see them off, a duty made pleasant by their genuine smiles. Then, just as Nicole was settling into the coach, one of the gardeners came rushing down the long, treelined front lane waving the familiar leather packet over his head. "Just arrived, sir! Just arrived!"

"Well done, Harry. This is a good sign for the journey ahead, wouldn't you say, my dear?" Charles accepted the post through the window, then called out, "Let's be off, Jim!"

"Right you are, m'lord!" The young driver cracked his whip, and the horses wheeled about and headed off with a clatter of metal shoes on cobblestones.

"Is there any word from home?" Nicole asked.

Charles had to work at masking his wince over the word *home*. But Nicole caught sight of it and immediately understood how hard he tried to be happy for her as he hefted the thick envelope from among the others. "I say, this *is* a gift towards a good journey!"

"Finally!" Nicole's hands shook as she took the envelope and broke open the wax seal. She unfolded the letter, and then a second page fell out. "Look, I also got a letter from Mama Robichaud!" she cried.

Charles sat in silence and let her read, then reread the two letters. Nicole devoured the pages, one in English and the other in French. The first one was all Catherine, brisk and bright in spite of the heartache she felt over Nicole being so far away. Catherine closed with a further note that caused Nicole to raise her head. "Anne does not write. Apparently she's busy tending Cyril, who has come down with the chest ailment."

Charles showed not the least worry. "He's a strong young man and a wise doctor. He should have no difficulty in throwing this off, particularly so late in the season."

"Yes, you must be right."

"What do your relations in Louisiana have to say?"

Nicole found it helped to translate the

letter. Otherwise there was the threat of losing herself in the soft French words, the sweet memories of fragrant green waters and of a home far removed. "They say all the family are fine, and the spring harvest was the most bountiful anyone can remember. But there are signs of trouble on all sides."

Charles's expression hardened. "The war?"

"Yes, it seems to be coming ever closer. The English occupy the fort at Baton Rouge and have warned the Spanish in New Orleans not to become involved." She could not hold the tremor from her voice. "My family and Vermilionville are directly in the middle."

"I should not worry." This was not Charles the kindly uncle who spoke now but rather a man of power and knowledge. "No doubt they hold Baton Rouge to keep the Spanish well apart from this conflict. They shall now go after the main strongholds farther to the north and not scatter their forces by trying to occupy the smaller villages. Especially when the locals are deemed non-combatants." He stared out the window, seeing strategy and harsh images. "What utter nonsense this whole affair is, what balderdash, what tragedy."

"You are against the war?"

"More than that, my dear. More than that. I am against the *principle* of this war." He drummed his fingers on the windowsill, his face as serious as Nicole had ever seen. "These are not foreigners within some land our army has chosen to occupy. The largest contingent of American colonists is British! Do you know what it means for them to rebel against the nation that many of them still consider their homeland?"

She found it difficult to see much further than her own aching heart and the longing she had for places and people across the sea. But the conviction with which Charles spoke helped her to set her homesickness aside. At least for now. "They must be very angry."

"They are *wounded*. We, our British government, have done such a horrid job of ruling, they see no other course than to cast us aside." He waved his hand out the open window, not at the green English countryside but at more distant lands. "We cannot hope to conquer a people stretched over such a vast continent. Either we rule them in peace and harmony, or we grant them what they wish. Anything else is utter futility."

The carriage rocked and drummed its

way onward, until Charles refocused on the moment and inquired, "Might I ask what else they say?"

"Mama writes with news of the family. My brother has a new baby, a boy. Both mother and child are well." Nicole swallowed hard against the sadness she felt in her mother's words . . . Louise's yearning to see her darling daughter, the void in her kitchen and her home and her heart. "My father is not a man who writes much. He says merely that if I am in Canada, I am to go. And if I am in England, then I am to stay."

"A wise man." Charles examined her face and saw beyond the brisk tone Nicole had adopted. "I do so hope you enjoy your time in London, my dear."

Nicole took a hard breath, then pushed out the air and the sorrow both. It would do no good to regret her decision or yearn for what was not possible. The only answer was to throw herself fully into life in England and try to make a success of it. "I intend to do just that."

"That's the spirit," Charles replied as he pointed ahead. "If you look out your window, you will have your first sight of one of my villages."

"*Your* villages?" Nicole turned and sat

beside him. "We are still on your land?"

Charles coughed discreetly. "A bit of explanation is in order. The title of earl was Saxon in origin and granted to someone who ruled a province or county in the king's name. Our own earldom has been handed down now for more than two hundred years. My land continues quite a ways yet, so far in fact that we shall overnight at an inn that's still within my holding." He patted her hand fondly. "In the last century, my forefather did a great service for the king and was granted yet more land in Wales and the second title of viscount. This is considered a lesser honor than earl, so with the king's permission, it was deeded to the appointed heir. Thus you, my dear, will be referred to as viscountess, that is, once the rites of passage are completed."

Nicole was saved from having to respond by the carriage slowing and clattering into the village proper. The houses were ancient mortar and wood, with roofs of deep thatch or slate tiles. Nicole was astounded by the sight of people emerging from the doors and windows. "What are they doing?"

"Oh, I suppose they wish to greet me. It's a formal thing, you know."

But it did not seem formal at all. Many

children and some of the adults trotted alongside the coach, calling out their greetings and their respect to his lordship. Ladies stuck out of upstairs windows and waved kerchiefs. There were numerous smiles and shouts of God's blessings on his honor. Charles called to many by name, smiling back at them and waving to all.

One young man clambered aboard the side and clung to the windowsill. From behind, the footman yelled, "Here, you! Get off!"

"It's all right," Charles said, patting the man's arm. "You're looking well, Tom. How's the wife?"

"She's splendid, your lordship. We cannot thank you enough."

"All recovered from the birth, is she?"

"Aye, and a fine bonny lass we have!" He then beamed at Nicole and said, "You're seated next to the grandest man in all of England, m'lady!"

"None of that," Charles said mildly. "Now, be sure and give your darling lady my best wishes."

"I will. We've named the lass after you, m'lord. Charlotte Tiles, she is, and may she bear the name proudly!" The man dropped off and ran alongside for a while, waving his hat as the village border was cleared and the horses gained speed.

"What was that about?" Nicole asked.

Charles seemed embarrassed by the effusive man now disappearing behind the coach. He looked out the window while they sped along the higher road, then finally said, "Since my return, I have tried to administer my holdings as God's servant. I make a mess of things more often than not, but I do try."

"And the young man?"

"My father employed an overseer who ruled by fear. To my great shame, I let the man stay on. He died when I was in America, no great loss to anyone. I have decided to release all my tenants from debt and have begun to build public barns in which to store winter grains. Some of the younger men have been willing to learn new methods of farming. In return, I have rewarded them with greater holdings."

It was the perfect thing to hear at that moment, for the words included not only a new insight into her uncle's character but a challenge for herself. "I shall try to make myself worthy to carry on after you, Uncle."

He turned to Nicole, gratitude shining from his face. "I could ask for nothing more." Then a thought struck him. "I say, would you like to give Jim a hand with the horses?"

She clapped her hands in delight. "Oh, could I? I was afraid to ask."

"Never be afraid, my dear." He used his walking stick to rap on the roof. "I say there, Jim! Pull over, will you. The lady wishes to have another go."

Chapter Sixteen

The Canadian summer turned out to be as bright and constant as the spring had been cold and harsh. The entire world was alive, the fields so fruitful and the forests so full of game every family in Georgetown was busy salting meat and storing produce for the upcoming winter. The children grew red and round as little piglets and raced around the village from dawn to dusk.

Yet there were two dark clouds on the horizon. One was the news. From everywhere came word of battles fought and more still to come. The British won here and lost there. Catherine felt helpless, as if she were caught in the vortex of a maelstrom, and there was nothing she could do but watch and listen as all around her the world was being threatened by forces out of control. On market days, people grumbled over the high prices charged for anything not homegrown. Everyone prayed that the war would remain far beyond the horizon.

The other cloud was the great worry over Anne. She remained cloaked in a darkness all her own. The baby John had been a delight to all. The boy's great-grandfather took on a new life. If allowed, Grandfather Price would spend all day clucking and cooing over the baby. John was a fine, strapping infant, big and lusty and growing fast. He was happy almost all the time, but if he wanted something, then he let all the world know with his howling. There was no concern over understanding John. He was all of a mood, as the saying went. Every fiber of his being was caught up by whatever the moment held. A smiling face above his crib was enough to bring robust kicks with his little arms and legs. He could fasten his hand around a person's finger and hold on for ages. And his toothless smile was enough to brighten the darkest night and the most sorrowful heart—except for his mother's.

Anne had become a wraith. She drifted in and out of rooms, barely disrupting the air with her passage. She would set her hand to whatever task was given her, but her mind remained locked in grief. Often in the middle of some activity she was involved in, such as when feeding little John, tears would spill from her eyes. She did not sob aloud, except at night, when her cries for Cyril kept Catherine and Andrew awake for hours. During the day she seemed only half there, and if left alone, she would just sit and stare into space for hours. Even the baby did not seem to help, for when his coos and cries brought a smile to Anne's face, this would soon be followed by more silent tears. And Catherine had to order her to stop helping in the kitchen because of the possibility of injuring herself with a knife during one of her absentminded moments.

Twice Catherine had spoken with her daughter about the ongoing malaise. The second time had been three days earlier, and when Anne responded with silence, Catherine's tone had grown harsh. "For the baby's sake, if not your own, you have to pull yourself out of this! Yes, it is tragic that you have lost your husband. But look at the baby! You would scoff at a blessed gift like this?"

For once, her daughter had focused on her fully. Her voice sounded soft and dry as the scraping of autumn leaves. "I scoff at nothing."

"You do! Your every action suggests you don't care that at least the good Lord saw fit to leave you this small portion of your man!"

Anne's face turned toward the crib by the fire, lit to ward off the cool breeze coming from the bay. "He's not a small portion, Momma. I look at him and see Cyril." Tears began cascading down her cheeks. But she did not seem to notice their presence, and as more tears came, she neither wiped them away nor attempted to clear her eyes. "His smile is Cyril's. His little hands, the set of his eyes, his feet, his . . ."

"Anne." When she remained fixated on the crib, Catherine reached over and shook her arm. "Anne! Look at me!"

Her daughter turned, revealing the ravaged features of a woman who appeared twice her age. The tears continued, and again no notice was given. "I have not lost just a husband. I have had the heart torn from my body. Why am I even alive?"

"How can you say such a thing?" Catherine said, struggling now against her own welling up of tears. "For your baby! For John."

"Yes? I am a good mother? I shall be a good guardian and teacher? He shall look at me and find someone who can offer him hope and joy?"

"Anne, you must heal. You *must*."

She turned her face back toward the crib, where a tiny hand was waving along with the cooing sound of contentment. But Anne seemed to see none of this. "I never understood the word *cripple* until now. What it means to lose a limb and know it is lost and gone forever." The empty look enveloped her features. "How does one fashion a crutch for a crippled heart? How can you mold a limb for a desolate spirit?"

Catherine washed the flour from her hands and then dried them on her apron. Grandfather Price had convinced Anne to take the baby out to the cliffside tree stump with him. Andrew was off seeing to some parishioner's needs. The house was full of light and the sound of birds singing. Knowing dinner was not for another two hours, Catherine decided she couldn't put off writing the letter to Nicole any longer. Andrew was taking her into Halifax the next day to do some urgent shopping and collect some things from Anne's house. They had not been back since the funeral. So there was business to take care of and items to gather and bring home before any soldiers thought of looting their empty dwelling. Hopefully they would locate a ship headed for England to carry the letter to Nicole. Hard as it was to write such tragic news, Nicole had to know.

There were, though, many happy things to report, such as Catherine's work in the Acadian school. At Andrew's urging, she had accepted the invitation to teach the younger children. She helped them learn the official language of the province and in so doing put a friendly face to the English. Catherine had found such joy and fulfillment in the work that she could hardly contain herself. Her pupils had become a vital part of her days now. It seemed to Catherine her heart had been longing for a chance to offer other young ones her love. The Acadian village recognized her worth and her gifts and, with no urging from her, had come to call her *Tante* or Auntie. The simple act had enriched her and also helped to ease the burden of Anne's deep grief that had weighed so heavily on her.

But she wouldn't begin her letter with the good. No, there was nothing to be gained in putting off the bad. Catherine lit a tallow candle and then carried it over to the small writing desk in the corner. She lifted the lid and pulled out some paper and a quill and inkwell. She did not hesitate, for this was not the time for seeking the exact or proper word. Anyway, there was no such thing with such a letter. She must simply write and tell all.

Chapter Seventeen

Charles and Nicole overnighted at the coaching inn and then continued their journey the following morning. Before they reached the outskirts of London, Charles stopped the carriage so Nicole could climb back inside to enter the city in ladylike fashion. Her enthusiasm over having driven the horses the previous afternoon and much of this morning soon evaporated. The outskirts of London were foul, the occupants miserably poor. Few faces turned as the carriage passed, and those who did stared in mute indignation. After a while the squalor gave way to respectable abodes and well-tended lanes, yet the poverty that lay behind them had somehow branded itself into Nicole's mind and heart.

Charles understood all too well. "I wish

there were some way you could have avoided seeing that."

"Is there nothing that can be done?"

"There is much," he countered. "A lifetime's work and more. I am struggling with a number of issues and hope to do more in time. My only regret . . . well, perhaps it would be best not to discuss such things so early on."

"No, please tell me, Uncle."

"It's only since my return from the colonies that I've come to see the abject state of many British subjects. Before, I am ashamed to say, I saw little and cared far less." His face creased with regret. "All the wasted years, all the meaningless quibbling over status and convention, all this shall I be forced to lay before the throne one day."

"At least you're trying now," she consoled.

"And doing far too little." He gave her a weak smile. "Perhaps in time you shall manage even more."

The London residence looked small, but only in comparison to Harrow Hall. The whitewashed townhouse fronted a broad intersection where Charles Street met Princes Gate. And beyond the leafy green of a tree-lined park rose the peaks and towers of Buckingham. A long line of carriages and open drays clattered past the townhouse's front garden.

Gaylord and Maisy were there to greet them and escort Nicole into the home. The front hall opened into a high-ceilinged formal parlor. Eight recessed columns guarded either side, ascending to carved rosettes that adorned the domed ceiling. The rosette design was repeated in the floor in marble and mother-of-pearl.

"The house has a strange intensity about it, at least for me," Charles told her, stepping up alongside. "I was actually born here, not in Sutton. Born here, christened here, and wed here twice. And I hope to be laid to rest in the back garden."

Nicole was led upstairs to her chambers and left to freshen up after the long journey. Later when she returned downstairs, she found her uncle standing in the front hallway, holding a letter box overflowing with papers and ribboned documents. With him stood an older gentleman, who was busy pointing to the top document and speaking in a low tone.

Charles looked up at her approach and smiled. "Ah, there you are, my dear. May I have the pleasure of presenting Lord Percy Fulton. Percy is the London solicitor who handles most of my affairs. He's also an elder deacon at Westminster Abbey. I have the honor of naming Percy among my closest friends."

Percy was a short man built to appear shorter because of his portliness, harboring most of his weight in his bulging middle and in his jowls. Yet his lower half was spindly. To Nicole's eye, he looked like a pear perched on two matchsticks. He was bald except for two fluffy white bushes sprouting wildly from above each ear, making him the most ludicrously unbecoming man she'd ever met.

Still, Nicole had caught the significance of Charles's words quite clearly and so gave what she hoped was a suitably deep curtsy. "An honor to meet you, sir."

"And likewise, my young beauty, and let us pretend to an affection that I do hope will not be long in coming." He spoke with a voice so low and sonorous, he would have put a bayou bullfrog to shame. Percy kept his eyes fastened way above her head as if aiming his words toward the hall's distant corner. "Long have I awaited this moment, for your uncle has done little more than speak of you during this past long winter."

Charles ushered them into the front parlor but did not join them. "If you will forgive me, there are a few pressing matters I must see to."

"Certainly, my dear boy. Be gone, and allow me to press my case in an atmosphere of suitable intimacy." Lord Percy lowered his head to search his waistcoat pockets for his snuffbox. The action left his chin disappearing in the folds of his sagging jowls. He took a pinch and applied the snuff to each nostril, then let out an enormous sneeze. "I do beg your pardon. A horrid vice, but my only one, I assure you."

Nicole found her lips quivering from the sudden impulse to laugh. She couldn't decide which was sillier, the man's appearance or his words. "Would you care to sit down?"

"A kindness I might never hope to repay." He walked over to a pair of high-backed chairs that were set before the large central window. Then he sat down, but his legs proved too short to reach the floor. Only the tips of his buckled shoes grazed the carpet. Percy Fulton must have noticed the way she studied him, because he said, "Alas, there is naught I can do about this earthly vessel. Yet I am not without charms, or means, for that manner. But you strike me as one who pays little attention to the crasser elements of societal courtship."

Nicole settled slowly into her chair, for

it granted her a moment to realize the man was actually paying suit to her. She stared at the strange dwarfish man, with his protruding red waistcoat being held up by his bent legs and his chin lost in the jowls that drooped onto his cravat. "I beg your pardon?"

"It is I who must apologize—for the quality of the man you see before you. But the spirit within this chest of mine is of spun gold, I assure you. Gossamer wings of heaven don't touch it. No, nor diamonds."

Nicole hid her smile behind her hand. "Your pardon, sir, but I scarcely know what to think of this."

"Think of heaven, my young fairy queen. For that is what I propose to offer you. Heaven on Earth." He punctuated his proposal with another double pinch of snuff and an even greater sneeze than before. "Your pardon, ma'am."

Nicole did her best to keep her laughter at bay, her voice trembling slightly from the effort. "You are making fun of me, sir."

"Not at all. Not in the slightest. I am speaking the poetry of lyrical invitation. Make me the happiest man on earth by accepting my humble offer."

She dropped her hand and gazed

openmouthed at him. "You are asking me to marry you?"

"Indeed so. And nothing could make me happier." Then the gold snuffbox was flipped open yet again, and the powder applied to both nostrils. The sneeze that followed nearly lifted Percy off his seat. "Your pardon."

Nicole found it impossible to contain herself any longer. She rocked back in her seat, a giggle finally escaping.

"I take it my suit has been rejected?"

She clutched her side with one hand, covered her face with the other, and nodded.

"Alas, alas. Though my heart is torn asunder in my chest, I shall endeavor to survive and continue along this mortal coil." Another pinch of snuff and a sneeze. Percy whipped an unusually big handkerchief from his rear pocket and wiped his eyes. "Of course, I shall have the distinct pleasure of naming myself as the first suitor to have been refused. There will be a few meager crumbs of comfort in that, I suppose."

The prospect was enough to stifle her laughter. "You think there shall be many, sir?"

He examined her with gray eyes that seemed too bright and clear for his frame.

"Surely you jest, Miss Nicole. May I call you that?"

She realized then what he was about. The strange words and the even stranger proposal had been intended to breach the impossible distance between them. Percy only wanted to make her laugh. More than that, he wanted to make her feel comfortable with him. Nicole settled back in her seat, liking him already. "Please do," she replied.

"Of course, Charles has told me a bit of your background, but seeing you seated here, showing such beauty and poise, it now escapes me." There was none of the bumbling jester now. "A lady of your evident charm, soon to become one of the wealthiest heiresses in the land. I should think you will soon find yourself under siege."

"What horror," she murmured.

"Yes, I can well imagine it might seem so from your perspective. That is, unless you prepare yourself."

"And how, pray tell, might I do that?"

His eyes grew keen again. "Arm yourself with friends. Trust your defense to people who have your best interests in mind. Allow them to advise and to buffer you."

Nicole hesitated. "I am not sure what you mean."

"Such a lady as you, full of dance and spirit as you are, must find this whole matter of polite English society rather dusty and dull."

She then wondered if she could truly trust the man. Yet Charles held Percy in high esteem, and she had come to trust her uncle implicitly. Nicole also felt the overwhelming need to confide in someone, so she softly said, "These weeks since my arrival, I have felt very hemmed in."

"You poor thing. Of course you do. Coming from a place where you had both clan and work to surround you, it must be quite stifling."

"Work," she repeated. "I had no idea how much that word meant to me. I feel so useless here."

"You are to be your uncle's heir," Percy reminded her.

"Yes, but what am I to *do*?"

"There's much to be done, as you will see for yourself. Much good to be done. Great wealth will be placed in your care. And with wealth comes power. I know you shall wield both well." He seemed ready to launch into a vision of what the future might hold for her, then checked himself. "But that does not help you now, does it?"

"No," she said morosely. "I feel

186

confined by things I don't understand. I must abide by rules that make it difficult to be who I am. I cannot cook or care for my home. I must give orders to others, then stand by and watch as though I were without hands and legs of my own." Nicole felt her throat tighten. "And I am told I should never leave the house without an escort!"

"London is not your home village, Miss Nicole, where all are either friends or relatives or both."

"I don't care for the reason! I only know that I am trapped, and it matters not that the cage is lined with gold and fine paintings."

"Of course you don't." He reached over to pat her hand. "And I am your answer."

"I beg your pardon?"

"Your morning glory has arrived." A brilliant smile spread across his chubby features. "Charles has begged me to help find you a suitable escort. My response was simple. I have all but retired from the active life, and my young associates are far more skilled than I could ever hope to be. It's only your dear uncle who insists upon my personally handling his affairs. My church activities and my work for Charles hardly require two days a week. I have been widowed for ten years. Therefore, I am here to propose that I become your escort."

"I understand now," Nicole said, "what Uncle Charles sees in you, sir."

"Call me Percy, I beg you." He almost toppled from the chair as he reached and patted her hand again. "For those kind words I shall consider myself ever in your debt."

Then Charles reentered the room. Seeing the two of them seated there, he smiled, clapped his hands, and said, "Ah. You're becoming friends. What joy. Come, there's just time enough for a walk about the garden before we dine."

Chapter Eighteen

Nicole stepped hesitantly from the carriage. "You're certain this is the correct address?"

"Lincoln's Inn Fields. Yes, ma'am." Jim pointed ahead with the hand that held the whip. "Number thirty-nine is just up there."

Looking out through the open door, Nicole asked, "What if she does not want to see me?"

"That is the beauty of polite society." Percy rested his cane between his knees and smiled encouragingly. "You shall never be forced to suffer the indignity of rejection. Simply leave your card with the maidservant who answers the door."

"I don't see—"

"The lady of the house will then have the opportunity to return the favor if she wishes. Then you can meet and have tea or perhaps stroll through Mayfair together. Otherwise she writes you a nice little note, listing a motley collection of excuses. I have acquaintances who have politely avoided seeing one another for a dozen years and more."

There was nothing left for her to do but walk away from the carriage's safety. This area of London was unknown to her, but Percy had assured her that it was most respectable. The houses were built snugly against one another, all facing across the lane toward a tree-shaded field that stretched out in gray silence. The day was cool and clad in a mist too fine to be called rain. The weather was like much of England as far as Nicole was concerned—irritatingly genteel.

She had discovered two distinct worlds existing within England. One was a universe of bejeweled gowns and balls, music recitals, and Sabbath services at Westminster Abbey. The other consisted of a flagrant poverty, which left her sickened and horrified. Of course, it was possible to avoid the worst sections of town by simply drawing the carriage curtains. And the way Nicole had heard others speak at the receptions and banquets and tea dances, this second world might as well not have existed at all. But she couldn't blind herself and had no desire to do so. A glimpse down an alley was enough to fill her dreams with images of people living in smoke and squalor and starving children wearing rags. It was then that she felt the most trapped and frightened.

Nicole climbed the front stairs and pulled the brass handle beside the door. Somewhere inside the house, she heard a bell tinkle. Reaching inside the small beaded purse that hung from her wrist, she took out her card. The fact that she had such cards at all still bewildered her. Yet it was one of the first things she had done with her uncle after arriving in London. They went straight to Kedrick's of Bond Street and ordered stationery and cards of bonded vellum, the Harrow crest stamped in silver. She fingered the script beneath the crest, which said in heavily engraved lettering, *Miss Nicole Harrow*. No address, no information of any kind. Charles had assured her that nothing further was required.

The door opened, and a young woman in starched apron and cap stood before her. She ran an eye over Nicole's day dress and little hat, then gave a quick curtsy. "Good morning, ma'am."

Nicole was about to drop into a curtsy of her own but then halted. Instead, she repeated the words that Percy had instructed her to say. "Please, if you would be so kind as to inform Mrs. Madden that Miss Nicole Harrow wishes to call upon her and—" She stopped midsentence, because the woman was no longer paying any attention but was gaping at something behind Nicole. Nicole turned around and saw nothing but her carriage and the footman standing by the open door. Percy remained seated inside, fiddling with the head of his cane. "Is something wrong?" Nicole asked.

"Oh, no, m'lady . . ." Then the maid dropped into another curtsy, deeper this time. "Excuse me, please."

But Nicole's fragile poise was shaken. "If you would just give Mrs. Madden this card." She shoved her card into the maid's hand and started back down the stairs.

Before she had reached the carriage, a voice behind her cried out, "Nicole!"

She spun around to see the captain's

wife lifting her skirts and racing down the stairs. "Oh, my goodness, I can hardly believe my eyes!" She grasped both of Nicole's hands. "What a delight it is to see you, my dear."

Nicole felt such relief at the greeting, she said, "When you did not contact me, I thought it was because you did not want to see me again."

"Oh, my dear sweet young thing, nothing could be further from the truth. Now you must come inside and have a cup of tea," Emily demanded as she gave Nicole's hands a tug.

Nicole extracted one of her hands and then motioned toward the open carriage door. "May I introduce Lord Percy, my uncle's solicitor and friend."

"A grand good morning to you, my lady."

"You must come in as well, your lordship."

"I am quite comfortable here, thank you."

"Nonsense, I wouldn't think of such a thing. Climb down this very instant!" Emily cast an astonished glance around the carriage, murmuring to herself, "My neighbors will be positively agog." Then she pulled Nicole back up the stairs and into the house. Percy clambered down from the carriage and followed obediently behind.

Soon they were settled in plush chairs by the front bay window, overlooking the lane and the park. The polished oak flooring reflected the morning's soft light and the fire's glow. The walls were adorned with paintings of harbors and majestic seagoing vessels. Sitting on the corner table was a large globe. And two cabinets were stacked high with charts and scrolled documents carrying royal blue ribbons.

While the maid served them tea, Emily explained, "Once we arrived and settled in, it occurred to me that you might not wish to have me call."

"But why?"

"Because life ashore is different." Both her tone and look seemed good-hearted. "It might appear inappropriate for a shipowner's wife to call upon the heiress of an earl." Emily reached over and lightly patted Nicole's knee. "But never mind all that. You are here, and now you must tell me how you've been."

"I honestly don't know." The chance to open up to another woman left the words feeling caught in her throat. "I am not unhappy. Yet I cannot help my feeling trapped . . . and so very confused."

"And lost from time to time, I would imagine."

"Utterly." The relief at being understood left her weak. "I have been here two months now, and still I don't understand what is expected of me."

"My dear, that's not a surprise. England is so—"

"Different. I know. Everyone tells me I must give it time. But how much time? And why must I feel so closed in? There's much I would like to do, so many people are in need. But all I hear is, 'Give it time.'"

Emily did not offer such a platitude. Instead, she sipped her tea and studied Nicole over the rim of her cup. "And have you met many suitors?"

"Of all ages, shapes, and sizes."

When Percy coughed discreetly, Emily turned to him and said, "You must forgive us, m'lord, for ignoring you so."

"Not at all, Mrs. Madden. It is my honor to call Miss Nicole a friend, and she has so longed for the chance to confide in another woman."

"Of course she has." Emily shifted her attention back to Nicole and quietly urged, "You were saying that there have been many interested men, my dear."

The floodgates opened, and Nicole

blurted out a jumble of disjointed thoughts. She told of parties with sweeping lines of debutantes and eligible bachelors, of suitors who fawned about her, of grandes dames who seemed not to see her at all. She spoke of meeting people who boasted connections to the Harrow family that went back generations, of people who appeared to know more about who she now was than she did herself. At first, Nicole had been impressed by the wealth and others' attitude toward her as Charles's niece. But as London society swept her up and carried her forward on a wave of chiffon and taffeta and polite empty chatter, she found most potential suitors to be boring, bald, and pompous.

Emily listened with a steady watchful silence, her eyes as calm as her demeanor. When Nicole finally quieted, she asked, "And what does your uncle think of all this?"

"He seems pleased," Nicole said with a trace of doubt in her voice.

Lord Percy cleared his throat and broke in, "If I may say, Mrs. Madden, Lord Charles is delighted. He has thrown this poor young lady in at the deep end of the sea, and she has not only managed to survive, but to do herself and her uncle quite proud."

"Uncle Charles wishes I would spend more money," Nicole said rather glumly.

"That is because Miss Nicole has but two gowns and six dresses," Percy explained.

"That won't do," Emily agreed.

"Why, with the prices the seamstresses are asking," Nicole protested, "I could feed my village in Louisiana for a year!"

"But you're not in Louisiana," Emily said. "My dear, would you accept a bit of advice?"

"Of course." Nicole leaned forward in her seat. "I would be happy to receive it."

"Perhaps you should wait till you have heard what I have to say before you speak of being happy." Emily set down her cup and folded her hands in her lap. "In fact, I would suggest to you that this is not concerning your happiness at all." She paused to give Nicole an opportunity to object. When Nicole did not utter a word, Emily straightened in her chair and then said with calm intensity, "I would suggest to you that the issue at hand is not one of happiness, but rather of *duty*. The idea that life must orient itself to make you happy is the attitude of the young and privileged. But anyone with open eyes can see that life is full of difficulty and tough decisions."

"What you say," Nicole said slowly, "makes perfect sense."

"With every gift, there comes an equal responsibility," Emily went on. "Your uncle has offered you a great gift, that of wealth and position. Yet with this gift comes the duty to use these wisely."

"But how?" Nicole asked. "This life leaves me so confined! My days are filled with frivolous things that help no one."

"You must learn to walk before you can fly," Emily replied. "Direct your efforts toward learning the lessons at hand. Slowly you will find ways to use your new gift in helping others."

Percy cleared his throat again. "Your pardon, Mrs. Madden, but I promised to deliver Miss Nicole to her uncle in a half hour's time."

Nicole stood and asked, "Might I please come again?"

"Nothing would give me greater pleasure." Emily offered her hand. "My dear Nicole, these few minutes have revealed two remarkable features about you. First, despite what you may think, you're making great strides toward settling in England with dignity. And second, you remain genuinely unconcerned with your own beauty and wealth. You have no idea how rare that is, my dear. I am certain your uncle is most delighted with you."

"I wish I could be so certain," Nicole said.

Emily smiled. "You will do him proud. You will accept the duties of your new station and, in time, will find fulfillment. On board ship, you spoke with my husband about your faith in God. I suggest you remember that God does not promise us a path strewn with flowers in their full bloom. He simply says He will be with us always, through everything that life brings."

"Is my hair all right like this?"

"You look an absolute stunner, if you don't mind my saying, Miss Nicole." Maisy took a step back. "Turn around now, dear, and let me see you." The new gown was striped taffeta silk of emerald green, with a series of silk flowers cascading down the back. "Now, you be sure and gather up that train when you're sitting, else them flowers will look all mashed flat."

"Thank you for helping me, Maisy."

"Oh, it's a pleasure. I was only half-sorry to hear that the maid had come down with the grippe. I do so love this! It's like watching a lovely little doll take shape."

And that's just how I feel, Nicole thought as she looked at herself in the full-length mirror. *Like a porcelain doll made up for others to stare at.* "But what about my hair?"

"Don't you be worrying about that. Them little crowns are all the rage, I hear."

It was not a crown at all but an arrangement of tall green stalks set in an Oriental design, which shook with the slightest motion.

Nicole stood up straight, gathered up her bustle in her right hand, and practiced her curtsy. The evening's event at the Portuguese embassy would be the first truly formal outing of her life. Charles had done his best to introduce her gradually to the pomp and ceremony of London society, taking her only to places where friends and allies would shelter her and forgive her mistakes. But tonight was different. The London season was drawing to a close, and the Portuguese ambassador's party was the last opportunity for a formal appearance. She knew how important this was to her uncle and so wanted to do everything just right.

"Duty," she whispered to herself and then watched her reflection carefully as she folded downward, extending one white-gloved arm out in a sweeping gesture. She rose back up and asked, "How was that?"

"Graceful as a swan," Maisy said, her hands clasped over her apron. "My, but you will please his honor."

"I hope so." Then she repeated the word to herself. *Duty.* The more she thought of Emily's advice, the more convinced she was of its wisdom. She had been acting frivolously. There was a need for her to learn the lessons of polite society, of how to fit in and behave properly. Then and only then could she begin to take on responsibility and put her privilege and wealth to use. This was not just to bring her happiness. It was to do the best she could with what she'd been given, to do good and thereby fulfill what she knew was her assigned task. *Duty.*

But as Nicole descended the stairs, she felt more than her corset constricting her. It seemed as though every breath was a struggle against the restraining elements of a world she did not understand.

She couldn't help but glance at the side table as she entered the front parlor. On a silver platter were piled the day's deliveries. Another six engraved invitations had arrived that day, along with three cards from those stopping by to pay their formal respects to his lordship and the new heiress.

Nicole repressed a shudder at the thought of more teas and exhibitions and dinners and chatter. "I am ready, Uncle."

"You look splendid, my dear!" Charles beamed proudly as he surveyed her standing there. "I must say, the dressmaker has outdone herself."

"Thank you again for the gown."

"Now, now, there's no need to thank me." Charles was a strange one to place such emphasis on her buying new clothes, for he was dressed in the same dark longcoat, breeches, and gold-embroidered waistcoat he always wore for such events. "I only wish I could induce you to spend more at the dressmakers. But never mind that. My dear, I have a surprise for you."

As soon as his hand reached inside his jacket, Nicole exclaimed, "A letter!"

"It just arrived while you were dressing. I thought it best to wait till you came down."

Nicole used the silver letter knife to break the seal. She scanned the first few lines, then cried, "It cannot be!"

"What is it?" Charles was instantly at her side. "You've gone pale as a ghost. Here, you must sit down." He guided her onto a nearby settee. "Now tell me what it is!"

"It's Cyril. He's . . . he's dead. The grippe took him."

"That's impossible!" Charles sank down beside her. "Such a strong young man—he couldn't have succumbed."

"But he did." Nicole finished reading the letter. "Anne is devastated."

"Of course she is, the poor sweet girl. How they loved one another. Such happiness as they shared, those two . . ." Charles shook his head. "And the baby?"

"He's fine. Mother Catherine says he's the light of their days. They named him John, after my grandfather."

"Catherine's father, of course. A fine man."

Then the date of Cyril's funeral finally registered. "He's been dead almost three months!" The letter dropped to her lap. Never in all her time here had she felt so far removed from the world she knew or from the family she loved. *Three months.*

Nicole looked up and saw the wary concern on Charles's face. She was coming to know her uncle and so realized immediately what he was thinking. Charles expected her to say she wanted to return home, which indeed had entered her mind. And he dreaded having to remind Nicole of her promise to give him two years.

"I wish I knew what to do," she murmured.

Charles drew a deep breath as he massaged his chest, a motion that had become a familiar habit. Then a new light dawned on his features. "Might I suggest you write and invite Anne to come to England?"

"What did you say?"

"Certainly. A change at this point might do her a world of good. Grant her an opportunity to see the tragedy and her future from a different perspective."

"Oh, Uncle, that's a wonderful idea!" The thought of seeing her sister and friend again filled her with an almost desperate longing. "But do you think she would come?"

"We shall never know unless you write and ask." He then reached for the bell. When Gaylord appeared, Charles said, "I must prepare a note of regret that I wish for you to take to the Portuguese ambassador. We have just received some tragic news, so shall not be attending this evening's event."

"Yes, m'lord." Gaylord bowed in Nicole's direction. "I couldn't help but hear, Miss Nicole. Might I say how very sorry I am to hear of your family's loss."

"Thank you, Gaylord." Nicole was tempted to agree with Charles's decision and to use the terrible news for postponing her entry into formal society. She couldn't have asked for a more perfect excuse. But something in her rebelled. She straightened her shoulders and rose to her feet. "That won't be necessary, Uncle Charles."

"My dear, I couldn't possibly ask you—"

"You have said yourself how important this evening is. My eyes are not smudged, are they?"

"They are perfect." Charles stood alongside her, his face a picture of pride and gratitude. "My dear, I know nothing to say except that you do me proud."

Chapter Nineteen

On the trip back to Georgetown from the new French settlement, Catherine found herself sitting next to an Acadian farmer and marveling at how good life had been to her. At an age when many women began thinking about settling back and taking one's ease, she was filled with a fresh sense of purpose and joy.

And the season matched her mood— vibrant and humming with the powerful south wind. It was the warmest autumn she could remember, where the sun turned fleeting showers into golden curtains. Rainbows appeared nearly every afternoon, sweeping bands of color that often spanned the entire sky.

They crested the final rise before Georgetown, and then the farmer halted the horses, granting the weary animals a breather. The wagon creaked under the weight of the summer's final produce and the first jugs of fresh cider. A taciturn man, the farmer had spoken but a few sentences during the whole journey. But Catherine did not mind at all. After two long days of dealing with seventeen children, a little quiet was a welcome change.

The wind was strong enough to buffet their wagon and have her holding tight to her bonnet's strings. Yet it was such a warm and cloudless afternoon, she could sit and watch the world below in comfort. Between them and the steeple of Andrew's church, everything seemed to toss and shiver with a hundred shades of fall colors. The wind stripped the trees and sent their leaves swirling in such impatient haste, she could see little else. At the hill's summit, all around was sunlight and blue sky and whistling wind. Below them rushed an autumn tide of russet and gold.

The farmer clicked to the horses and snapped the reins. Slowly they descended the bumpy road that gradually led them into the maelstrom below. Catherine shielded her eyes against the debris. Once they were within the shelter of the towering trees, she looked up in wonder. Now the sun flickered and danced through the waving branches and flying leaves as if throwing off sparks from a heavenly fire.

As they approached Georgetown, Catherine pulled from her shoulder bag the list she'd been working on and checked it once more. Everything seemed to be in order. She handed it to the farmer and said in French, "You will please buy these things and take them to the new family?"

"It will be as you ask, madame."

Then she gave him a leather pouch. "This should take care of the cost, but if not, then I will pay you the rest when we meet next week."

Charles had continued to send them money, and Andrew no longer objected. This was good for many reasons. Andrew's joints persisted in bothering him, which resulted in his having to quit leatherworking. Also, the parish had been growing quite rapidly along with the demands on Andrew's time. But the chief reason they were so thankful for the extra money was that it had meant they could assist the newcomers with their making a fresh start.

Colonists loyal to the Crown were pouring into the Canadian provinces at a prodigious rate. Each week boatloads arrived, crammed to the gunnels with more Loyalists fleeing the growing conflict farther south. Some brought wealth or tools of their trade, others little more than tales of fighting and woe. Catherine and Andrew had little time for the tales, for their own allegiances were divided, and the news became increasingly distressing. But these were people in need, and their hearts went out to them. It was important to offer support to families struggling to prepare their homes before the winter set in.

Catherine went on. "I've included money to pay those helping to build the Parkers' cabin."

The silver coins jingled as the farmer stowed the pouch in his vest pocket. He squinted down the road, then after a while, said, "Does not do any good, you having us stay quiet over where the money comes from. Sooner or later word gets out."

"Regardless, that's how we want things to remain." She and Andrew were in agreement that they wanted to keep their giving as anonymous as possible. It did not stop people from finding out and thanking them, but it did mute a lot of the fuss.

They also used Charles's money to help make peace among neighbors as they paid French settlers to construct cabins for new English-speaking immigrants. The French were newcomers themselves, in dire need of cash, particularly as market prices climbed continually upward. It meant most new-comers were far too grateful for the aid to complain about their neighbors.

"It will be as you say," the farmer said. He then pulled the wagon to a stop at the turn near her house and waited for her to step down. Reaching behind the seat, he lifted out an earthenware jug and handed it to her. "Thought you and the reverend might like a taste of the new season."

"Why, thank you. Andrew does love his cider."

Without another word, the farmer clicked to his horses, tipped his hat to Catherine, and continued on to market. She turned and walked swiftly up the lane, eager now to be home.

The stay overnight with the Acadians had been hard at first, but it made good sense. The twelve-mile journey was over hills and included a very rough road. Going back and forth each morning and evening had proven to be exhausting, so one of the farmers had converted an old shed into a cabin just for Catherine. Then the local farm community had fitted it with a make-shift floor, a table, some earthenware, and utensils. This was their way of saying thank-you to the Englishwoman who would not accept anything else for her work.

Catherine had found it a trial to be away from her family, yet also felt blessed. It was the first time in her life she'd ever spent a night alone. The sounds seemed stranger, and the silences rang with remarkable power. The nights alone had given her time to reflect. Praying and reading the Scriptures took on new meaning, and it felt to her that God spoke in a different way during these times by herself.

Catherine pushed open the gate and sensed the familiar joy of homecoming as she hurried toward the front door. Grandfather Price must have been busy in the front garden again, for the last of the root vegetables were pulled free. The kitchen windowsill was piled high with carrots and turnips. A large basket of dirty potatoes sat by the front door.

She swung open the door, and before she could speak, Anne came rushing forward to announce, "I am not going and that's that."

"Very well, dear. Let me get off my cloak and bonnet." Catherine took her time with the actions, as she wanted to consider this change in Anne. Her daughter was filled with renewed vitality, pacing the floor, wringing her hands. The difference was shocking. Anne had shown little energy since Cyril's death. Yet now she walked back and forth like a caged animal, her black skirt rustling angrily about her ankles.

"How is little John?" Catherine asked.

"The baby's fine." Anne obviously did not wish to speak about the baby. "A letter has come from England."

"Oh, I am so glad. How is Nicole?"

"She's fine. At least, I think . . ." Anne said with a dismissive shrug. "She does not really say."

"Why not?"

But Anne remained quiet.

So Catherine walked over and seated herself by the cold fireplace. "Come sit down, my dear."

"I could not possibly."

"Sit." Catherine disliked having to use a hard tone with her adult daughter, but Anne's moods had been coming with such force that sometimes it was the only way to break through so that Anne heard her at all. "I cannot concentrate on what you have to say with you pacing like that. Please, sit."

"Oh . . ." Anne dropped onto the bench opposite her mother. "I cannot understand what came over them, making such a ridiculous suggestion."

In a flash, Catherine knew what the letter said. Still, she needed to hear it for herself. "Please, tell me what they suggested."

"Nicole and Charles want me to bring baby John over for a visit. To England. Whyever would I want to go to England?"

Catherine studied her daughter. Anne had always been slight in build, both as a child and now. But since Cyril's death, Anne had become even more fragile looking. How she managed to feed the child was a wonder to everyone. Sadness clung to her. As a result, her complexion had turned sallow, and her skin stretched over the bones, making her look as fragile as a tiny bird. Her dark eyes were huge in her head, her expression pinched—now devoid of the happiness that had once reigned there.

"Who in their right mind would propose such a thing to me?" Anne continued. "Especially now, at this time in my life."

Catherine's attention turned inward.

This was another manifestation of her time spent alone, the newfound ability to withdraw from outside tumult. It was a Godsend, this disconnected space, because it meant being spared from the worst of Anne's suffering. Otherwise it might have been too easy to drown in her daughter's grief.

"I have a baby to raise. I have a husband to mourn. I have . . . I have things to do here. To think I would simply pick up and travel thousands of miles across the sea. . . . Why, it's all madness!"

Catherine turned and looked out the open window. The windswept clouds of dust and leaves flew past their little cottage, portents of the many changes striking the world beyond their village. She wondered at how she could feel so calm. Perhaps she was just numb to it all, but she did not think so.

"I cannot imagine what came over them, to even suggest such a thing!"

Catherine looked at her daughter and asked, "Where's Grandfather?"

"I don't . . ." Anne seemed to run headlong into Catherine's simple question. "He took the baby on a walk. Is that all you have to say?"

"I think I had better start dinner." She rose from her seat and moved toward the kitchen. Suddenly she felt very tired, and the simple motions of a lifetime became a burden.

Anne stepped over next to her mother, staring at her in disbelief. "But don't you have anything to say about the letter . . . about their request?"

"I haven't yet heard everything they said." She started scrubbing the carrots and cutting them into thin slices. A stew would be nice. Andrew likes a piping hot stew. "And it seems you have enough words for the both of us."

"I have. . . ?" Anne steadied herself by placing a hand on the counter. In a calm voice, she asked, "Do you *want* me to go?"

"Want? No. Of course not." Catherine resumed paring the vegetables with a slow, deliberate motion. "I want you to stay here with us always. I want to watch little John grow up and become a man. I want . . . I want many things."

"Good," Anne said, only slightly less confused. "Because I am *not* going, you know. I am not going anywhere."

Catherine had to set down the knife. Her vision had suddenly blurred, and she was afraid she might cut herself. She turned toward the window and watched the wind whip the trees opposite their little house.

With a mother's wisdom, she knew. Yes, there was no question. She knew.

Chapter Twenty

Another letter came, this one from Nicole. Anne had been laboring over how to word her answer, but thus far had only succeeded in supplying sheets of writing paper to the fire. Now as she broke the seal on the new envelope, her fingers trembled. She hoped Nicole had changed her mind about the outlandish proposal. Anne had planned to respond firmly, which should settle the issue once and for all. Go to sea with a young child? Quite out of the question.

But Nicole's second letter was not a bold petition at all. On the contrary, and it shocked her with its strangeness. The letter spoke of longing and loneliness. Nicole said she wished she were home to help console her sister in her time of sorrow, adding that she'd board a ship and return home right away were it not for her promise to their uncle.

As Anne read on, she kept waiting for the expected request to be reiterated. Instead, Nicole told of the busy social season she had been thrust into. Yes, thrust. For although Nicole's time was taken up with lavish parties and dinners, she seemed to take no pleasure in them. This brought a frown to Anne's forehead. Was Nicole really as lonely, as empty, as her letter sounded? *I miss you all so,* the letter concluded. *I would give anything to see you again. Even for a day. An hour.*

How many times over the past months had Anne's heart expressed a similar cry? Oh, if only she could see him again, hold him for a single moment. Anne suddenly felt a new understanding for Nicole in her loneliness.

Another guilt niggled at the back of Anne's mind. Twice Cyril's mother had written from Wales, expressing her sorrow and deep desire to hold her grandson in her arms. With the background that Anne herself had suffered, she understood all too well the importance of family. Her dear husband's mother deserved to meet Cyril's son. And baby John deserved to have more than just knowledge of his kin. He needed relationships. Especially since there was little chance he'd ever meet his grandparents on his mother's side. The arduous trip from Louisiana to Nova Scotia would likely never be repeated. It would soon be impossible for Uncle Charles to hire a ship, and Anne had no intention of traveling alone to Louisiana—especially now with war about to break out.

She felt torn between her paralyzing grief and the needs of others whom she loved. Bedraggled and confused and without the capacity to make a sound decision, she took it all to prayer. Anne laid aside her indecision and left the matter with her Lord. But later she struggled with taking back the load on her own frail shoulders and reasoning her way through the dilemma. What should I do? What would Cyril want me to do? What was right for John? "Lord, I need some kind of sign," she whispered in her anguish. "Show me what you would have me do. If I am to go, I must go soon. I fear that before long there will be no more ships sailing because of the war."

Furthermore, it did not seem the right time of the year to be setting sail for England. Already fall was flowing into winter. By the time arrangements were made and passage booked, they would be past Christmas and into the coldest months. The thought of a storm at sea in the dead of winter made her afraid. It was hard enough to face an ocean crossing during the mild months, but in wintertime? That seemed like a foolhardy venture indeed.

But if God wished her to go, would He not then take care of the dangers?

It had been some months since Anne had been to her home in Halifax, but she felt it was now time to return, if only to take care of things and settle her finances. She could not bear the thought of living on in the beloved little house without Cyril. His memory would be everywhere, calling to her with the chime of the clock he used to set faithfully every Sunday morning . . . creeping up behind her and looking into the supper pots when she was preparing a meal . . . tugging at her sleeve when she stepped toward the cold outside, to remind her to put on her shawl. No, Anne did not think she could live in the house ever again.

But she needed to go back. She hated the idea of asking her folks to accompany her, yet knew she could not make the trip alone.

Andrew and Catherine did not appear surprised when she voiced her request. "Of course," her father had said for the both of them. "I shall make the arrangements straightaway." Then things happened far more quickly than Anne had wished. She needed time to prepare herself, to pray. To steel herself against pleasant yet haunting memories that were sure to greet her the minute she stepped in the door. But this had to be done while they rattled over the rutted frozen road, winding their way along the familiar trail.

Thankfully the baby slept well. And when he was awake, he seemed preoccupied with the adventure, noticing every branch that hung close to the road, every bird that winged over their heads.

Andrew smiled. "That boy does not miss a thing," he said with a grandfather's pride.

Anne passed the child to Catherine. Her arms ached from holding him, but even so she hated to give him up. The closer they got to Halifax, the more pronounced her grief. This would not be an easy time. Not for any of them. Anne bowed her head in prayer once again. She would need all the help heaven could give to make it through the next few days.

The following morning she called on Cyril's banker. Andrew drove the rig, while Catherine stayed home with baby John. Surprisingly, Anne, who had felt in a daze, was able to take charge of her own business matters. Cyril's medical practice was to be sold to another doctor. The new doctor was also a Loyalist, one of the many who had migrated to Halifax to escape the impending war.

Anne tried to ignore all the talk of trouble that surrounded her. Talk of fear and of fleeing. Anger and hate and rebellion. Talk she was afraid would eventually lead to a large-scale conflict, where homes would be lost, families displaced, and men killed. She shivered at the thought and longed for a lasting peace, for a world where the life of her boy would not be threatened. For although the grievance was between the new colonies and England, the Loyalists were now crowding Canada's shores with ships used to escape the war. So might not the war then follow them and Nova Scotia become haplessly embroiled again?

"Please, I beg your indulgence," Anne said to hush the words of terror, "but I must get back to my infant son. You do understand?"

The men nodded, and the torrent of words ceased to flow. The papers were pushed forward and dealt with in quick fashion, then the new doctor left. After the banker resolved a few more minor issues, Anne was free to hurry home. She breathed a deep sigh as though washing her soul of confusion and fear.

Anne knew now she would not be staying in Halifax. She'd allow her home to be sold. With all the Loyalists milling about, whom the city now harbored, it would no longer be safe for her and little John. Surely it would be the first place the armies would strike should the war spread beyond the shores of the American colonies. Therefore, she'd move inland, to one of the villages hidden among the forests. There her family should be safe. With this thought, Anne felt the constriction gradually ease around her heart.

The following day Anne forced herself to return to Cyril's office and collect his personal items. She hated the prospect of walking into the rooms where she and Cyril had served together. But Cyril's papers needed to be gathered. And she could serve neighbors who had no access to a doctor once she had Cyril's medical aids at hand.

Anne was surprised at the sameness as she stepped through the door. As always, the room was teeming with those seeking medical attention. Anne let her eyes travel over the chairs lined against the wall. Thankfully, she did not recognize any of their former patients. For one awful moment, she imagined herself back in time. Anne found herself having to resist the ridiculous urge to hang up her coat on the hook behind the door and take her position behind the small table that serviced the patients coming in. Another woman—much older and seasoned by life than she—now occupied the chair that had once been hers.

"Is Dr. Warren in?" she asked in a shaky voice.

"Yes, miss. But you'll need to wait your turn just like everyone else," the gray head said gruffly, never lifting.

"Oh no . . ." Anne said, taken aback by the woman's retort. "Please, I am not here to see him as a patient. I am Mrs. Mann. Mrs. Cyril Mann."

The woman looked up. Her ashen face showed a glowering expression.

"The previous doctor's wife," Anne stumbled, then added, "widow, that is."

The woman rose from her chair, pushing it back noisily. "Come along," she said, her words and manner conveying what she thought of the interruption. "He said you would be stopping by. He's with a patient.

Guess you would know that."

"Yes. Of course."

Anne followed the woman, though she could have led the way with her eyes closed. They went into the side room where all the supplies were kept.

"I expect the doctor will want you to make a list of everything you'll be taking," said the woman bluntly. "There were things included in the purchase price. He'll be wanting those left behind."

"Of course," Anne replied, taken aback that her honesty was questioned.

The woman left after supplying Anne with paper and quill to record what she would be taking. Anne flung aside her coat and hurried with her task. She could not escape the confines of the little building a minute too soon. Her eyes blurred with tears as she worked. There really was not much to be claimed; most of the supplies were sold along with the practice. She retrieved Cyril's black medical bag, stroking it lovingly as she set it among the other things she'd gathered in a small crate.

Taking one last look around to be sure she had not missed anything, Anne wiped her eyes and heaved a deep sigh. God had helped her through another difficult chore. She had taken one more step in her break with the past. She reached for her coat and then picked up the crate and the list she had written out. She would hand it herself to the sour woman who now ran the office.

Anne braced herself as she wiped at her face again, using a small cotton hankie, then left the room.

She had taken only a few steps when a voice stopped her short. "Aw, now. 'Tis Mrs. Mann herself."

An elderly woman hoisted herself with some difficulty from her chair and crossed over to Anne with a ragged gait. Anne recognized the woman at once. But before she could say anything, the woman had reached out and caught hold of her hand. "So sorry we did lose the good doctor."

Anne felt herself reel under the unexpected expression of sympathy. She could only nod. But she managed to give the woman's hand a slight squeeze.

"He was a gem of a man, to be sure. Always giving hisself no matter the hour of night or day."

"Thank you, Mrs. McKenzie," Anne said finally. She made an effort to withdraw her hand. She knew if she did not leave soon, she'd be breaking down in front of a room full of staring strangers. Mrs.

McKenzie had attracted the attention of everyone.

"And you yourself. What are ya to do now?"

"I . . . I am with my folks," Anne stammered.

"Aw, but we be needin' ya here," the woman continued. "I know it's too soon for ya to be back yet, but in the future—"

"No," cut in Anne. "I am sorry, but I won't be back."

"You're givin' up helpin' the sick? But you're so natural at it." The woman's hands tightened on Anne's. She leaned in closer to Anne's face.

"Well . . . I am not sure. I have my baby . . . our baby, that is, to care for now. Perhaps sometime in the future." While Anne struggled to explain, she became conscious of a man who had gotten up from his chair and walked over to them.

"You're a trained healer?" he asked bluntly.

Anne turned to him. "No. I merely served as my husband's aide."

"She's more than that," Mrs. McKenzie contradicted. "Far more. Everyone who came knew the wonder in this lady's touch. She could soothe the most fretful bairn, she could."

"God be praised," he said, so quietly Anne barely caught the words.

"I beg your pardon. I don't understand. . . ."

"Cox is my name. Paul Cox. I desperately need someone to tend my wife, Matilda." He turned and waved a hand at a pale woman propped in a chair in the corner. "She is very ill. But she longs to go back to England. She's sure she'll get better if only she can reach home safely. But I am no good with that sort of thing, you see. A ship's captain will take her aboard only if she has someone to care for her. Please, ma'am. I should pay you well."

Anne felt the world spinning around her feet. "But I . . . I have a child."

"I shall pay your child's fare, as well."

"But I had not thought . . ."

"Then would you think on it? We're desperate, you see. And soon. I fear we don't have much time, due to the war that's coming."

Anne swallowed hard and shook her head as she tried to collect her thoughts. The whole thing was preposterous, unthinkable.

"Would you be so kind as to give me your name and where you can be reached?" the man continued. "I should like to talk with you further. Here's my card if you wish to check my references. Please, I pray you, give this serious consideration. Of course, I shall also arrange for your return voyage. Just as soon as you wish to make the journey back. But perhaps it would be wise if you spent the winter in England. I can arrange for that, too."

"No," Anne said, shaking her head. "That would not be necessary. I have kin there."

"Splendid!" For the first time, he gave her a smile. Anne watched as years dropped away from his eyes. He was not nearly as old as she had first suspected. It was his worry that had pressed his features into looking prematurely aged.

"I haven't given my consent yet," she corrected him, then immediately regretted being the cause of the darkness that fell over his face again.

"But you *will* think on it?" he urged.

"I will do better than that," she said. "I shall pray about it."

The tension relaxed in his face a bit, and his eyes took on a new light. "Then perhaps my prayers have been answered," he said with confidence. Then he took a step back and doffed his hat.

Visibly shaken, Anne bid good-day to

Mrs. McKenzie and took her leave. Was she to be the answer to someone's prayers? Was this the sign she had asked God for? She did not know, but she dared not dismiss it as mere coincidence.

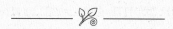

Over the next several days, Anne met with Mr. and Mrs. Cox, and a sympathy for them grew within her heart. She saw their distress and felt a strong desire to help them. Still, was it right to pack up little John and travel all the way to England? Finally she went to her parents and asked, "What do you think I should do?"

They discussed it for a while, looking at it from different angles, at the good but also the potential risk and heartache.

"Certainly, if you feel that it is God's calling, then you can do naught else but to obey," Andrew concluded.

Anne nodded solemnly. "But how can I know, for sure, the will of God in this?"

"Which decision would bring you peace?" he answered. "There is where you most likely shall find the right answer."

"But I feel torn both ways."

"And I, too. But in my heart I feel that,

at this time, perhaps England is a safer place for you and John than here."

"You think war is truly coming, then?"

Andrew hesitated before responding, and when he did, his voice sounded low and somber. "I fear that is so."

From this point on, Anne no longer wavered. Word was sent to the Coxes that she was willing to accompany them to England. Gradually a sense of peace permeated her heart and mind. She had prayed. She would now trust God that she'd found His answer.

Chapter Twenty-one

It was not till February that passage was booked for Anne and the Coxes. But December and the Christmas season had found Anne beginning to look forward to life beyond her present sorrow. Though she did not offer much cheer to the holy days, there was a relaxing of tension and a hint of the former warmth in their home. January was given over to packing and preparations, which became so frenzied that any lingering doubts had to be set aside.

Soon it was time for their departure. This entailed a frigid journey into Halifax, prayers at the quayside, and rejoining the

Coxes—all a tide of action that plucked Anne from the known and flung her into the storm-tossed Atlantic winter.

In some ways, the voyage turned out to be easier than Anne had expected. Yet in others, it proved quite perilous. The wind and waves and freezing rain bothered her far less than it did some of the hardier passengers. Anne found the adverse weather almost comforting, as if she were bringing some of her beloved homeland with her. For the weather remained almost constant the whole way to England.

The day they had sailed from Halifax was blustery and cold, punctuated by a wind-lashed rain that held out day after day. Many of the passengers were frightened by the howling wind. But not Anne. She took comfort from the stoical sailors, who seemed to find nothing distressing in the weather that pounded their ship. In fact, she heard one of the officers say how the weather was with them. For as long as it blew hard from the north, there was little chance of being struck by an unpredictable storm of greater and more dangerous power. "The wind is with us and holding steady," she heard repeatedly from the sailors on board. With each passing day, England grew ever closer.

Anne never suffered from seasickness, though many others weren't so fortunate and had become desperately ill. Mrs. Cox was among the afflicted. It was left to Anne most days to see to the children's needs. There were two other young mothers on board, both of whom were laid out by the ship's lurching. But Anne was glad to help with their babies, and she welcomed the work.

By the end of the second week at sea, she no longer found it hard to make her way across the pitching deck. There was a certain timing to the ship's motions, one she had learned by watching the sailors. The ship would ride steady over the longer combers, then give warning to a swooping rush by first raising its head high. Then followed a crashing impact that seemed to almost burst the ship's seams and brought shrieks of fear from many of the women.

The constant damp was also a great nuisance. Anne was bothered by how mold had found a way to attach itself to nearly all her garments. Yet Anne had spent a lifetime wrapped in layers against the wet cold of the Nova Scotia winters, so she knew how to adapt to such hostile surroundings and endure.

Baby John seemed to love everything

about the voyage. He cooed and laughed. His only fretting came from the rash that most of the children had picked up from wearing wet underclothes. But not even his rash dispelled his happy nature for very long. And at night the ship's incessant rocking sent him into a deep and settled slumber.

Another dinnertime was signaled by the sailor's piping and the subsequent drumming of wooden-clogged feet. Anne waited till the commotion died down, made sure the recently fed John was resting comfortably, then climbed the narrow, steep stairway up to the main deck.

Snow whipped about her in fitful blasts, and the wind lashed her face with stinging cold. Two men in woolen caps stood at the wheel, almost lost within the folds of their greatcoats. Icicles clung to the wooden rails and from many of the windward lines. The sea roared and crashed. Darkness crouched beneath a low gray sky.

Anne returned belowdecks and followed the long passageway that connected the passenger hold to the ship's kitchen. The chef beamed his welcome, a great smile made comical by the hole where his two front teeth used to be. "How's the missus this grand evening, then?"

"No one in their right mind could refer to such a freezing dismal day as *grand*," Anne replied. "I am fine, though."

"And that strapping young boy, is he well?"

"Fed, content, and sleeping," Anne said proudly.

The chef and his two assistants exchanged grins. "Born sailor, that one. You mark my words."

"I will not!" Anne shot back. "No son of mine will ever go to sea."

They seemed to find her comment witty and so responded with boisterous laughter. "How many are you feeding this day?" the chef asked.

"I haven't checked. Let me have a trayful, and I shall return for more later if I need to."

"The doctor and captain are glad enough to have you on board, ma'am." The chef began ladling out steaming bowls of soup made from dried peas and salt pork. One of his assistants piled hardtack on the side of her tray. "Saves them a ton of worry and woe, it does."

Anne smiled at him and said, "I just do what I can."

"Mind you don't make yourself ill. The way you carry on, you work harder than those what're earning the king's shilling."

Anne hefted the tray and started back, carefully timing her motions to the roll of the ship. Typically the passengers were expected to eat after the sailors had been fed, but the cook did not mind her coming and getting food for those too sick to move. She entered the passenger hold and, as always after being on deck, found the air to be very stagnant and smelly. No wonder, since the weather had halted all but the most basic of washing. From the bunks and hammocks lining the room, several pallid faces watched her with mixtures of hunger and misery.

She set the tray down on the center table and took the first bowl over to Mrs. Cox, who greeted her with a subdued moan. "Go away, I beg you."

"I will not. Please, you must eat."

"It smells vile."

Anne did not respond, but she was secretly amazed the woman could smell the soup at all. She sat on the dank mattress next to where Mrs. Cox was lying and said, "Must I feed you myself?"

The woman groaned as she labored to sit up. She took a few tentative bites, her expression giving clear indication her stomach was rebelling against the food. "That's all."

"No, four bites more. For the baby."

This was enough to persuade Mrs. Cox not only to swallow four more spoonfuls but to hold it all down. She forced the last one down and then collapsed. "No more."

Anne set down the bowl. "Would you now take a turn on deck with me? The fresh air will do you a world of good."

"Perhaps tomorrow," Mrs. Cox said weakly. Her gaze was pinched and squinty, both from her recent illness and now the strain of the voyage. "Thank you. You are so good to us. So very kind and good."

"An angel in mourning," said a voice from a neighboring bunk. All the passengers knew of Anne's losing Cyril. There were few secrets among them.

Anne rose from the bunk and occupied herself with giving aid to the others who were ill, also helping to wash and change one of the babies. After checking on John, she joined some of the passengers for prayer and the evening meal.

Soon after, the candles were extinguished and they all settled in to endure another turbulent night at sea. Anne lay alongside her small son and reflected at how the nights had become her enemy.

It was during these times, when she was no longer busy caring for others, that she saw the work for what it was. She was fleeing as hard as she could from her grief and Cyril's absence. She shut her eyes, willing herself to give in to sleep. Her final thought was how perhaps this was why she did not much mind the storm outside, as it seemed only to reflect what she felt within herself.

Chapter Twenty-two

Nicole sat by the window in Harrow Hall's morning room, thinking that if she were asked to rename March, she would call it the Month of Change. The February winds had carried on till almost the middle of March, storms born in the wilds farther north that had swept in with armies of snow and blistering cold. Just the day before, the clouds had advanced across the sky, the windows shivered from the great blasts of wind, and the manor's chimneys blew like cold brick trumpets. Then that evening all went quiet and still. And with the night descended a bone-chilling frost.

Now in the morning, the world remained imprisoned by the cold. The front lawn was transformed into glistening pinpricks of silver and green. When Nicole had entered the morning room, she lit the fireplace, taking pleasure in the simple chore. Then she made tea and enjoyed it along with her breakfast of dark bread and honey, the Good Book laid open before her.

Nicole was an early riser and had grown to relish her quiet time in the hours before the house and the world awoke. Soon after their return from London, Charles had apologetically told Nicole that he'd no longer be joining her for morning prayer, as he found the extra sleep to be a great strengthener. They had taken to studying and praying together in the evenings instead, nestled as they were on the library's leather settees. Nicole liked it this way, however, for she'd come to depend on beginning her days alone, in the stillness of the empty chamber. The staff were given strict instructions not to enter the front rooms before Charles had descended the back staircase. Nicole had even managed to get Maisy to understand that she wanted to prepare her own breakfast, that she liked having time to herself in the kitchen.

A new sound crept into the morning room, gradually pulling away from the noise of the crackling fire. Nicole set her finger on the page to mark her place and turned toward the front of the house. Yes, she was certain now. There were horses trotting down the front lane.

She got up from her chair and searched the frosty dawn outside the window, but all she could see was the gently drifting mist, some white-encrusted bushes, and the reflections of her candle and the fire. Then there came the jingle of a harness, the stomp of a hoof, and the snort of a horse as the driver called for the steeds to halt.

Nicole was entering the front chambers when she heard a faint keening sound, so oddly frightening that she felt herself become exhilarated. It sounded like a baby crying. Her entire body clenched up tight.

As she raced across the inner hall the bell sounded. Nicole made it to the front door and then flung it open. She stared uncomprehendingly at the shadowy figure that stood before her, shivering and exhaling tiny white plumes. The frail bundle on their doorstep looked like a beggar wrapped in layers of cloaks and blankets. It was a woman, Nicole determined. It had to be. The shape was far too dainty and narrow to be a man. Besides, the bundled figure held a mewling baby.

"Yes? What can I do for you?" Nicole asked politely.

"You can take little John, sister." The

words were mumbled by a mouth turned rigid by the cold. "My arms have gone all numb."

"Anne!" The morning light was enough to reveal cheeks so hollowed, her sister looked the victim of famine. Exhaustion had reworked her features, and tragedy her eyes. Nicole scooped up the baby with one arm and embraced her sister with the other. Even with the layers of padding, Anne felt light and fragile as a little waif. "Oh, Anne! I cannot believe you're really here."

"Begging your pardon, ma'am." The driver was so wrapped up, only his eyes and bright red nose protruded from his wool scarf. "But the lady said you would be paying me."

"Of course!" Nicole handed the man his earnings and invited him inside to warm up. She then guided Anne into the morning room and to the fireplace. To her great relief, she saw a figure in a voluminous dressing gown appear through the back doorway, no doubt drawn by the ringing bell. "Maisy! Come help me, please!"

"What is it? What's going on?" Maisy rushed forward, her eyes widening at the sight of the crying child. "The poor little bairn—he looks half-froze."

"Go prepare something hot. Soup

would be good. Make some of your spiced tea, too. And wake Charles." Nicole then helped her sister get settled into the chair by the fire. "Why did you not tell us you were coming?"

"I did." The words had escaped through half-frozen lips. "I wrote you a letter, but perhaps the ship did not make it. The storms were terrible. Is that tea?"

"Yes, but it's gone cold by now." Nicole held out the baby to Maisy. "Take him for a moment, will you?"

Maisy received the baby and said, "Gaylord told me his lordship did not retire until late last night."

"Never mind that." Nicole pulled another seat up close to the fire. "You look to be freezing, sir. Come, sit here and warm yourself," she said to the driver.

"Thank you kindly, ma'am, but I can take my comfort by the kitchen fire."

Nicole turned to Maisy. "Now take the child and lay him down in my chambers and then see to the tea and soup. Raise the household while you're at it," Nicole ordered. Then she pointed to the chair and used her most commanding voice. "And you, sir, set yourself down!"

"As you say, m'lady," he said, then did as he was told.

"But his lordship . . ." Maisy protested.

"It's all right. Just go tell my uncle that Anne is here."

"Anne, the lady of your tales?" Wide-eyed, Maisy drew in for a closer look. "The second changeling? The sister of no blood kin?"

"The very same." Nicole gently unwrapped Anne's layers, rubbing thoroughly her frigid limbs. "Have someone stoke all the fires and prepare a hot bath. I shall be right in to see to the baby."

Three weeks after Anne's arrival, Nicole sat in the morning room and observed another dawn. Spring had finally arrived, heralded by the first crocuses pushing up through the earth. She reflected on how her world seemed transformed by Anne and the baby's presence. Nicole had difficulty imagining the time before their arrival. Anne had brought neither happiness nor cheer into the manor. Instead, Anne had come burdened with a funereal sadness. Yet her appearance had transformed everything, for Anne had brought with her the one thing Nicole had lacked most—a sense of *purpose*.

Only this morning, Nicole's thoughts were far removed from Anne and the baby. Her second cup of tea had long since grown cold, and her breakfast remained unfinished. She loved these quiet moments before the day's activities began. Normally she would delve into the Good Book and draw near to the Divine. But today her attention shifted back and forth between the passage in front of her and the previous day's events. She had attended a party given at one of the adjoining estates. Simply because Anne had arrived did not mean that Nicole's social duties had ended. Yet now there was something to give her relief from what she had felt was far too empty a life. Now there were others who needed her. So it was that Nicole could depart for such functions with a sense of fulfillment that had been utterly lacking since her arrival.

Yesterday's reception had started off as most such events did, a swirl of carriages and fancily dressed people and lighthearted chatter. Then one man in particular had stood out from the crowd—Lord Reginald Harwick. He was one of the members of the House of Lords along with Charles, and a landowner of several large estates. He was in fact quite handsome in a craggy, forceful kind of way. There was something of the pirate about Lord Harwick, a sense of power that pervaded everything around him. But his domineering air had left Nicole wondering if he heard her at all. He had sought to win her with his charm, together with the blinding attributes of his wealth and might. There was a definite magnetism to the man. Certainly she had found more substance to him than she'd seen in many of the other would-be suitors, with their foppish manners and snobbish talk.

So Nicole was pleased to accept his invitation for a quiet walk out on the terrace. There he had addressed her with the blunt manner of one accustomed to wielding power over others. "I've seen you before, you know. And we have been introduced," he said.

"I am sorry, sir, but I do not recall."

"Oh, I would not expect you to remember. I was one of a hundred men all bowing and scraping about you like courtiers before the queen of France." He wore an ensemble of black on black. The only hint of color on his person was a flashing cravat, which looked woven from threads of real gold. He adjusted it now as he eyed her and continued, "The only reason I accepted this fellow's invitation was because of my desire to see you again. I made certain you and your uncle had agreed to come."

"You do me great honor, sir."

"I speak the truth, m'lady. I care naught for hunting, nor the trappings of country life. My estates are for creating wealth and making employment for those who depend upon me for their livelihoods."

"It's nice to know that you are concerned with the welfare of others, sir. I do not find enough of this."

His eyes were gray and sharp in the torchlight. They searched her hard. "I have heard you follow the ways of your Lord Charles when it comes to such matters."

"Yet you are a man of fairness and just causes?"

"Like every loyal subject, I must uphold the Crown and the Church." He paused, then added more softly, "When it suits me."

The night seemed suddenly chillier. "Perhaps we should rejoin the others, Lord Harwick."

He turned with her, moving up close enough for her to catch a whiff of some strange scent. Nicole was immediately reminded of the fragrance of the Orient—mysteries and spices of which she was not aware. She knew she should move away but found herself drawn to the man and his haughty force.

"I hold no small amount of power in court, Miss Nicole," Lord Harwick said. "May I call you that? No small power, I assure you. There are always barriers to the transference of title and inheritance, especially when the bonds are tenuous between one generation and the next. A discreet word spoken within the royal chambers can make a remarkable difference." He hesitated, his hand spread firmly against the closed door that led back to the ballroom. "I make it a point to be a good ally to my friends. A worthy and potent supporter."

Nicole reached forward and pulled the door open herself, feeling less like a lady being courted than a city under siege. "It has been a pleasure making your acquaintance, Lord Harwick."

Nicole sat and pondered the words of the Bible in her lap together with the peculiar circumstances in which she had found herself. An unexpected peace settled over her, a peace that added to the beauty of the sunrise and made her senses come alive. She breathed the soft odor of woodsmoke and burning embers from the fireplace.

From beyond the windows came the sound of birdsong. She spied a squirrel racing from one tree to another. Then from beyond the stone wall that bordered the garden, she heard the metallic chuckle of a pheasant calling his mate.

A voice from behind her said, "May I join you?"

"Anne, of course. Good morning!" Nicole set her Book on the table, then stood and stretched. "How are you feeling today?"

The question seemed to throw her off balance. Anne froze there in the doorway, so Nicole walked over, took her arm, and directed her to the chair opposite her own. The settee was high-backed and stuffed with horsehair, making it as padded as a bed. Anne nestled in deep, allowing Nicole to tuck a blanket over her lap. "Do you always rise this early?" Anne asked.

"It's my quiet time. I come here and study the Word and remind myself why I am here." She hovered by Anne's chair. "Can I get you anything? Some tea, perhaps?"

"In a little while."

"Does John need tending?"

"He woke an hour ago. I fed and changed him, and he's gone back to sleep.

He won't awaken again for a few hours. Just sit with me for a time, please." She waited till Nicole had reseated herself to say, "I feel all I've done since coming here is sleep and eat and take care of John. Then sleep some more."

"You've been through a hard journey."

"It was not the voyage." Anne's gaze was empty. "I haven't rested since the funeral. Not really."

"I am so sorry about Cyril," Nicole said, as she had so often before. "He was such a good, dear man."

"Yes. Yes, he was. I've been upstairs thinking about him. Lying there for hours, thinking." The words seemed to agitate her. Anne's gaze scattered about the room, clearly wishing to speak of something other than her grief over Cyril. She spotted the Bible opened on the table. "What have you been reading?"

"The Psalms. But not reading—not this morning, anyway. Just looking up verses I partly remember and seeing how they fit with what I've been thinking lately."

"And what is that, pray tell?"

Nicole thought for a moment. "Perhaps we should wait until you're better."

"Why? Or is it that you don't want to tell me?"

"No, not at all. It's just . . ." Nicole felt divided. She had been waiting for the chance to speak with Anne, but the woman seated opposite her was still so frail. "What I've been studying is hard to talk about without also telling you *why* it's so important to me."

Anne squinted as the sun cleared the horizon. She sank back further so the chair's border shielded her eyes. "You have changed," she said quietly.

"Yes, I suppose I have."

"I have the feeling I could tell you anything right now, and it would not surprise you."

Nicole heard a request beneath her words, a testing. "All right. Try me," she said, matching Anne's soft tone.

Without getting up, Anne shifted her chair so that her face was more in the shadows that were being thrown off by the chair and the steadily rising sun. "I was awake because I dreamed of Cyril. I've never done that before. Before arriving here I often thought of him in my sleep, and those simple notions were always enough to wrench me so I should wake up crying. Many such nights I wept until my heart felt torn from my body."

Anne stopped there, watching Nicole

closely. There was a measuring quality to her look. Nicole responded by folding her hands in her lap and saying nothing. No words could express the sorrow she felt, and certainly Anne was not confiding in her to receive some meaningless platitude. So Nicole sat and waited.

The response must have pleased Anne, for the hollow eyes drifted away from Nicole and over toward the fire. "Last night was different. I haven't cried since leaving Halifax. The grief is with me always, but more tears now seem useless. Cyril has been gone from me for many months. The tears may come again, but the agony over his passing is over. I don't know how or why this is so clear to me, but I am certain just the same."

They sat in silence for a while, Nicole content to remain there through the whole day if necessary. Soon enough the house would begin to stir, but she had learned to speak with force if the need arose. A single word to Maisy and they would be left undisturbed. And Charles never emerged from his chambers this early. So there was no need to hurry. The silence around them seemed to carry great weight, as though there was a rightness to the waiting.

Anne became aware that her musings

had drawn her far away. "Where was I?"

"You said last night was different."

"Oh yes. Very different, indeed. In my dream I saw Cyril standing on a shore. At first I thought he was back in Nova Scotia, and the dream meant I had made a terrible mistake in coming here. But as soon as I thought this, I realized it was incorrect. Cyril was not in Nova Scotia, because the shore on which he stood was someplace I had never been." Her voice took on the uneven cadence of one half sleeping. "He looked so calm. And so strong, untouched by the illness that ended his life. He stood there and he watched me. I felt his love and wanted desperately to go to him. Yet as I looked at him, I was on a ship moving farther and farther from the shore, out into the open sea. There was nothing I could do about it. I just stared as he grew smaller and smaller, then finally disappeared on the horizon. All I was left with was his love."

The fire gave a faint hiss, and one of the logs cracked and sent sparks flying upward. Nicole rose and used the tongs to push the embers together. When she had returned to her seat, Anne asked, "So what do you think of my dream?"

"That it was not Cyril's love you felt. Not *just* his love, in any case."

The words seemed to heighten the intensity in Anne's expression. She gazed at Nicole for a long moment and then pressed down on the arms of her chair. After rising to her feet, she said, "First I shall have the tea you offered and perhaps some breakfast. Then I want to hear what you were reluctant to tell me."

But after breakfast, Anne went upstairs and quickly returned. "The baby's still sleeping. Might we take a walk around the garden?"

She followed Nicole out, while marveling at the day's gentle warmth. Where Halifax would still be lying brown and fallow, the English fields were a rich silvery green, and the flowers planted closest to the house revealed their first blooms. In the three weeks since her arrival, winter had been banished.

The house sat on a promontory, which at the back sloped gently down to a vast array of carefully tended fields. Somewhere far below there ran a broad stream, for down to her left Anne could see the sun glinting off the liquid ribbon. The cultivated and well-tended air eased Anne greatly and gave her the ability to speak words that before she could not possibly have said or even thought.

"Last night after the dream woke me up, I lay there thinking about my life since Cyril's death. I have gone through seasons of my own now, dark as a winter night. And I've tried my best to run from what I have known all along. I fled into deep despair, drawn back only by my little John. On the voyage over, I worked myself to the point of exhaustion. Since getting here, though, I've done little but sleep."

As she spoke Anne was keenly aware of her sister walking beside her. Nicole still possessed the same striking beauty, with her long dark auburn tresses and glowing green eyes. Yet for all her strength and energy, there was a new quietness about her. In ways Anne could not explain, she knew her sister had experienced a profound change. She had grown, deepened, and become a woman in her own right.

Anne took a deep breath and continued, "But I've awakened now. I've slept long enough and have fled as far as I can from the fact. Last night it came to me, and the knowledge is all around me. Cyril is gone and he's not coming back. I must pick up

251

the shattered pieces of my life and go forward."

Anne could have supposed any number of reactions from Nicole. The stronger woman, she would have thought, would most likely want to sweep her up in a sisterly embrace, willing her own strength into Anne's more frail form. But Nicole neither spoke nor made any movement toward her, except to look deep into Anne's face and share the silence of confession.

And this enabled Anne to walk on calmly, though her heart remained heavy. Somehow Nicole's example of strength helped her to finish speaking her thoughts, sharing her burdens. "My problem now is to determine *where* I belong. In other words, what's the meaning of my life now?"

"You have John," Nicole reminded her.

"I have many things. But I cannot see my life or the road ahead. My whole reason for living was wrapped up in Cyril, so that now there seems to be no sense to anything, save in loving my son."

"Come, let us take a seat over here on the bench." Nicole led her to a carved stone seat surrounded by a neatly groomed hedge. "This has become one of my favorite places. The seat faces south and catches the sun all day long, and the bushes are tall enough to shield us from almost any wind. We're visible only from the library windows at one end of the house and from Charles's private chambers at the other." She offered a small smile. "You would be amazed at how much this tiny patch of privacy has come to mean."

Once they were comfortable, Nicole went on, "You asked what I was reading in the Bible this morning. I've been trying to learn some lessons on my own. You'll meet the local parson this coming Sabbath if you feel up to joining us for church. He's a good man, but his homilies don't challenge me. So I spend my early mornings feeding my soul with God's Word. I confess I know so little that it's like the fumbling motions of a blind person."

Again there was the sense of hearing someone Anne knew intimately, yet did not know at all. Nicole's speech had become more precise in her months here, her accent much softer. But there were other signs, too, such as the erect way she held herself and the new depths to her countenance and voice. "Tell me what you've been studying," Anne said.

"It all began last summer, when I had an occasion to speak with a woman I met on the voyage over here. Since then I have spent a good deal of time thinking about the meaning of *duty*."

Nicole waited, uncertain whether she should proceed. But Anne remained quiet, so she said, "At some level, I think I've always assumed that when I found my place in the world, then I should be happy. Yet in all my searching of the Scriptures, I haven't found a single instance where God promises this. In fact, nowhere is such a thing even requested by His servants."

Anne slid farther from Nicole, partly because she wanted to see Nicole more clearly. But also Anne suspected that these words were meant for her. Perhaps this was why she'd been awakened by the dream or even why she came to England at all. So that she could sit here in the sunlight, on this kind spring morning, and listen to these words.

"It has made me realize that all my life," Nicole said, "I've measured how well I was suited to a place by how happy it made me. Only now, as I learn my way through English society, have I come to see that, although happiness is a fine thing, it comes and it goes. So long as I base my happiness upon what I have or how life suits me, it will always remain fleeting. For as soon as something changes, as soon as a cold wind blows through my life, as soon as life takes an unpleasant turn, my happiness would be gone. But is this what I want to base my life upon? No. But to just say this, that I don't want my life centered on what comes and then quickly passes, is far easier than making this actually the way I live or the way I manage my days."

The strain of shaping these thoughts left Nicole's features pinched. She gave Anne's shoulder a light pat and said, "I am sorry. I haven't spoken of such things before. It all probably made no sense to you."

"No," Anne said, so softly she barely heard herself. "No, you're making perfect sense. Please continue. I want to hear this, truly."

Nicole turned back toward the sunlight and the day dawning before them. "My studies have shown me that I need to find my happiness in God, and in Him alone. By placing my life in His hands and seeking to live as He wants me to, I now have a peace that's greater than whatever struggle I might face. My frustrations and my difficulties, all these will pass. But He remains always. And it's in His eternal promises that I must abide."

"I . . . I don't understand." Anne had to disregard her own internal musings to take into account what lay behind Nicole's words. "You're not happy here? But you have—"

"Everything," Nicole said quietly. "Yes, I've been granted many gifts." She kept her eyes level, pointed toward what only she could see. "And with each gift there comes a responsibility."

"But why—" Anne halted, then sat listening intently. She heard it again, the sound of a baby's cry. Instantly she was on her feet. "I must go see to John."

"Of course." Nicole settled back, her face impassive.

But as Anne turned away a thought came to her. She looked at Nicole and asked, "Would you mind terribly if I joined you in these morning studies?"

Nicole displayed the day's first smile. "There is nothing that would give me greater joy."

Chapter Twenty-three

Even the smallest of things in Charles's life were somehow transformed since his return from America. When growing up, his family had never eaten breakfast together. His father had considered children to be fit for society only after they'd been brushed, dressed, and fed by the nanny. He realized now that his own nature had mirrored traits he never much cared for in his father, such as keeping a cold distance from others. This was one of many things Charles struggled to overcome now. But the habit of having his breakfast alone remained with him still. Yet this had now become his time to reflect, to study the Word, and often to confess.

These days he found himself spending a great deal of time on his knees, searching for ways to make restitution for his earlier life. Though Charles was very grateful for his remaining days, his remorse had become a wearisome burden nonetheless. It was only with Nicole's coming to England that he had begun to feel a loosening of the grip that regret had on him. In Nicole he sensed someone who might become his future and carry on his purposes. This was not in the sense of living for him, but rather in helping to accomplish some of the things he was destined to leave undone.

Often Charles had to show restraint, for he was not a very patient man. And the strides Nicole had taken during her time with him were nothing short of remarkable. He realized how little progress she felt she was making, yet he knew better. Nicole was a woman now transformed. Charles was fairly certain she'd be coming into her own this summer, ready to move beyond the realm of polite society and share with him the greater scope—toward doing good and instituting positive change.

There were many duties he wished to discuss with her, challenges that, for the moment, he struggled with on his own. Currently in the House of Lords, Charles was fighting the issue of land enclosure, which threatened to force hundreds of thousands of families from their homes.

Then there was the war with the American colonies. Charles was one of the few Tories who advocated peace. It had cost him many friends and left him isolated. But he felt he was right—quite certain, in fact. These thoughts conjured up an idea of what to expect when they traveled up to London. As the day of their departure approached, the thought of what he might face caused Charles to wince from the pain in his chest.

He heard voices from the back garden now. Moving to the open window, he looked for anything to chase away any further thoughts regarding the course he had set for himself.

He caught sight of the two girls seated together. Once more he wondered at the difference in Nicole that Anne's arrival had caused. Nicole had never been a particularly jubilant person, no surprise given her background. She had brought with her a discontented heart. Charles knew this, but never discussed it with her because he felt there was little he could do. Either Nicole would stay on and become his heiress, or she would sail back to Nova Scotia.

The possibility of her leaving sent another lancing pain through his chest. The pain hit more often now, so much so that he had learned to shrug it off as best he could. It would come, shoot through his ribs and twist his body in torment, and then be gone. But he knew time was running out for him, and that the issue of his successor had to be settled soon.

Watching the two of them as they talked helped to calm him. At first, Charles had been concerned about Anne's visit to England, for she had brought with her a shadow of gloom. However, the change in Nicole could not have been greater. She had truly come into her own. She had cast aside her hesitant nature and rushed to care for Anne and her child, directing the staff to prepare the guest apartment so that Anne might feel comfortable. Charles realized that her caring for the bereaved woman had provided Nicole something she'd been lacking. For the first time since entering his manor, Nicole felt needed.

Then a sudden thought yielded a smile to Charles's face, and he turned away from the window. He pulled on his housecoat and hurried for the stairs. After tapping on the door to the guest apartment, he called to the nanny, "Is his lordship awake yet?"

"Just listen to the little lad, I ask you." The gray-haired nanny was Maisy's sister, a woman of gentle disposition and mother to six of her own. "Kicking and cooing like he was the happiest boy on earth."

"Leave us a moment, will you, please." Charles stepped across the room to where the crib stood by the recently stoked fire. As soon as Charles's face came into view, John gave him a beaming two-toothed grin and then increased his kicking motion. "Who's my big boy, then? Who's my jolly lad?"

The child waved his arms and gurgled with delight, for Charles was his favorite toy in all the world. Charles wore great shining buttons and took him on swooping rides around the nursery. John screamed with delight as Charles hefted him out of the crib. "Where would you like to go today, my lad? Ah, you want at my buttons, do you?" He held the child up close, so the tiny fists could close over his housecoat buttons in an effort to pull the spangles loose. When this did not work, John promptly fitted one of the buttons into his mouth and gummed it vigorously.

Charles laughed as he watched the boy slobber all over his front. He was astonished by the effect this infant had on his days and life. His greatest joys were found in the simplest acts now. He could spend hours upon hours with little John and never tire of his presence.

"Good morning, Uncle Charles."

He spun around, embarrassed at being caught in such a silly position. "Your pardon, Miss Anne. I . . . did not wish to intrude."

"How could you say such a thing? This is your home."

"But these are your private chambers." He pried the child loose from his housecoat. "Let go there now, John. That's a good lad." Reluctantly he offered the baby to his mother. "Never have I met a more adorable child."

"He finds great delight in you, as well." Anne smiled as the child bounced hard in Charles's arms, excited now by the prospect of being held by his mother. For an instant, the shadows lifted, and a trace of the woman's former beauty returned. She brought her face in close to the boy's and cooed, "You are such a happy boy this morning, aren't you? Yes, such a big happy boy."

Charles started for the door, then paused and said, "We're having a few friends over for a dinner tonight. Two families from outlying areas and the squire to the land north of mine. I know them all quite well. It would be a great honor if you joined us."

Anne kept her face fastened on the baby's. "Thank you for the invitation, Uncle. But I think not."

"Of course. I certainly understand." Charles hesitated a moment before deciding there was no harm in adding, "But perhaps it might help you if you were to come out occasionally and meet new people. Not to mention the aid and comfort you would offer Nicole."

Chapter Twenty-four

There was not any sharp transition, nothing Anne could point to that indicated where exactly she had made the turn. Instead, there was a gradual shifting of her world, so delicate it would have been easy to overlook completely. But Anne had no intention of permitting the change to go unnoticed. She asked Charles for one of his smaller leather-bound ledgers and used the fresh cream pages to begin recording her thoughts. She said it was to chronicle John's growth, for indeed the baby seemed to be growing and changing daily. But in truth it was to mark her own revelations, soft and almost unbidden, yet coming to her just the same.

These revelations were especially evident in the mornings while she studied and prayed with Nicole. Sometimes John was there with them, adding his own little morning noises to their words. But usually Anne would feed him and either put him back down for a time or leave him with the nanny. The longer she studied with Nicole, the more she treasured their moments together.

April had turned into May, and so they

decided to make the trip up to London. The social season actually began in late March, but Charles did not operate strictly according to others' calendars. Furthermore, the war had been creating serious rifts within English nobility and the London scene. Charles had offended many of his former cronies by defending the colonists' right to determine their own course. The result was that the social invitations dwindled both at Harrow Hall and in London. Neither Charles nor Nicole seemed to mind, however, and to Anne's eyes, their days remained filled with an endless stream of visitors and activity.

Anne took to joining them for the formal dinners at home, and twice she accompanied them for evenings out when she knew the hosts and was assured there would be no dancing. She even grew accustomed to wearing her widow's weave of black dress, gloves, hat, and half veil. The dark clothes afforded her some distance from everyone and the means to keeping herself slightly apart from the activities so as to fit gradually back into things. Eventually her sadness eased, and the terrible moments when it seemed she'd drown in her sorrow were now becoming memories. Her smile came more readily, too, especially when around young John.

The baby had but one bad week, when both the croup and teething had struck him at the same time. This occurred toward the end of their stay in London. In the blink of an eye, John went from an angel to a little red-faced screamer and remained so for eight long days and nights. Strangely enough, it was Charles who never seemed to lack the patience and fortitude to rise from his bed at all hours, lift the bawling child out of his cradle, and then pace the floor with him. The London townhouse was smaller, and noise carried to all the sleeping rooms. So Anne would often get up to the sound of John's fretting only to find Charles already taking care of things. He'd be standing there for an hour and more, his nightshirt tucked into his breeches, dipping his finger in the peppermint oil and letting the baby gnaw on it. Only after the baby had drifted back to sleep would Charles return him to his cradle. Then he'd stand and rock the cradle till he was sure John was content.

It was on such a night, when all the house lay slumbering, that Anne threw on her quilted robe and joined him in the nursery. As she watched him lower the child gently into the cradle, then run one finger down the baby's sleeping face, she whispered, "It's a pity you never had children of your own."

Charles's speedy reply suggested he must have thought of this often. "Perhaps it was because I was not ready to be a father until now."

Anne observed him in the light of the single candle. His weathered features looked gaunter now than when she'd last seen him in Nova Scotia. She saw in his face traces of Andrew's kind strength. The two shared the same steady glow in the eyes. Then a wave of homesickness rose up inside and threatened to overwhelm her. Anne swallowed hard, shifted her thoughts, and asked, "What does the word *duty* mean to you, Uncle?"

His smile also resembled Andrew's. "Strange that you would pose such a question in the night's wee hours."

"You're right. I should ask another time."

"No, no, it matters not. I am not sleepy, but I confess I am curious. Why duty, and why now?"

"It's something Nicole and I have been discussing during our morning times, when we study and pray."

"Ah. I think I understand." He

pondered a moment as he rocked John's cradle. "Duty is what I am obligated to do. I have a duty to my country, to my fellow man, and to my God. These are the givens of my life. I am called to walk uprightly and to love my neighbor as myself. And I am called to love God and serve Him with all that I am and all that I have. These are not invitations, to alter or ignore at my whim. These are *duties*. These are the constants upon which I must base my actions."

"I see," Anne said quietly, "that you have thoroughly considered this, as well."

"Many times, and especially now."

She noticed the hardening of his features and asked, "Are you speaking of the war?"

"I am British to the core," Charles replied. "This is the country of my king. Yet I have chosen to oppose England's stand on the colonies. I am against this war. But I take this stand from within my homeland. I do not alter my allegiance. This has made for certain . . . well, difficulties."

Anne reached out her hand. "You're a very good man, Uncle Charles."

He refocused on the night and the room. "I cannot tell you how pleased I am that you've come to stay with us for a time.

If you will excuse me for saying, it appears that you are healing."

She nodded, finally willing to admit it to herself. "I suppose I am."

"In that case, perhaps we should make plans to travel to Wales and present young John to his father's clan."

In her surprise, she bundled the robe up tight to her neck. "What?"

"I have holdings there I haven't seen in a long time. And it would make perfect sense to take the trip now during the summer. For travel will be more comfortable. Would you not agree?"

"But what about Nicole's time in the London social scene?"

"Nicole, yes." In an unconscious motion, Charles lifted one hand and kneaded his chest over the heart. "The constraints of this life have been very difficult for her. Surely you must see this as well as I."

"She seems determined to make a go of it," Anne said carefully.

"Yes, indeed so." The hand kneaded more vigorously now. "Indeed so."

"But you don't wish to press her," Anne continued, watching her uncle.

"It's her life and her decision. Yes." He caught sight of the way she observed his hand and so dropped it back to his side. "I doubt very much that she'd object to our early departure from the social engagements here." He turned to the candle's soft flickering, though his bleak gaze was directed far from the room's comfort. Then he said in a voice as glum as his features, "But there's one thing I must see to before we go."

Despite the interruption to her sleep, Anne was up and dressed and downstairs with the dawn. Maisy had taken to preparing a fire and setting two places at a little table near the front bow windows before retiring. A damp mist clung to the windowpanes and the morning.

Anne was busy striking a flint when Nicole shuffled downstairs and asked, "How's John?"

"Snoring like a little piglet," Anne replied, setting the kettle over the fire and joining Nicole at the table. "He kept Charles up half the night. Not that Charles complained."

"Uncle loves that little boy," Nicole agreed as she offered a small clay jar. "Honey?"

"Thank you. I spoke with Charles about what duty means."

"What did he say?"

Anne related their conversation and then added, "I wish I could say for certain where my own duty lies."

Nicole gave her an odd look. "Are you certain you're ready to hear such a thing?"

"What do you mean?"

With a careful, deliberate motion, Nicole set down her breakfast bread and knife. She seemed unsure of what to say, for her eyes moved across the table, finally settling on the two Bibles resting between their plates. "When the Scripture speaks of a servant's life, we hear of a time of preparation. Moses in the desert, David as a shepherd boy. The list goes on and on."

Then Anne set aside her own breakfast. "You're saying I have to endure such a time?"

Nicole hesitated. "I am not the one to speak to this, sister. I don't know enough to advise anyone."

"But if not you, then who?" Anne took hold of Nicole's hand. "Whom do I trust more? Whom do I have who knows me better?" When Nicole remained silent, Anne continued, "If I've learned anything since coming to England, it's how much I love you. We're sisters through miscast circumstances, and friends for life. For that's what you've given me—the gift of life. The only reason I am here at all is because you took my place upon the harsher road."

Nicole spoke then, her words coming slowly and directed down to her lap. "For the first time ever, I've found myself not just accepting the hardships of my childhood but being grateful for them. Because of those severe times, we have become sisters."

"And friends," Anne said, and then she raised a hand to clear her eyes. "*Best* friends."

Nicole lifted her face, revealing eyes soft and liquid. "I am sorry either of us had to endure such a road. But far better it was me than you."

Anne said nothing for a long time, just sharing the look and the moment. Finally she urged quietly, "Tell me what you were going to say."

"Perhaps this has been your time in the desert," Nicole said. "Your period of waiting. I know it seems silly to speak of all this luxury and wealth in such terms, but I have watched you. I see how little notice you take of our surroundings. And yet it all suits you perfectly. Your delicate nature has thrived here, and you have grown strong again. At the same time, you are enduring the desert within your own heart."

Anne was pressed back in her seat by the truth in Nicole's words. "You're saying I must leave here now?"

"Not at all." Nicole rose and went to the fire. She lifted the steaming kettle and brought it back to the table. As she filled the teapot, she continued, "The desert is within you. The question is, are you ready to leave *that* behind?"

Anne sat and watched her swirl the steaming water. Then she set the silver filter over the teacup and poured out the fragrant brew. "I think so. Yes, perhaps. Why does that frighten me?"

Nicole poured herself a cup and settled back into her chair. "Because you're moving into the unknown," she said.

Anne mulled this over as they ate. After a while, she asked, "What do I do now?"

Nicole winced. "I wish you would not ask me."

"Who else can advise me? Please, tell me what you think I should do."

"Perhaps," Nicole suggested, her tone very soft, "you should think of setting aside your widow's weave."

The words pushed Anne to her feet. "I . . . I must go see to John."

Nicole's features were sheathed with regret. "I shouldn't have spoken. I am so sorry."

"No, no . . . I must think. . . . Please excuse me."

Anne fled up the stairs and into her room. She leaned against the closed door, gasping with the force of her realization. Nicole was right, of course. It was time. Even so, the sudden insight left her breathless. Anne walked over to the crib and stared down at her sleeping infant. It was at times like this that Cyril seemed the closest, for his face was clearly imprinted on the baby's. "Forgive me, my love," she whispered.

The tears came easily, but the sorrow was not like it had been before. This was not the wracking agony of Cyril's death. She was merely taking a conscious step along a path she'd started down the day they laid her beloved husband to rest. It was time, she knew. There was a future beyond Cyril. She was being called to move on, to see where her new duty lay.

She went to the washbasin and rinsed her face. She then moved to the wardrobe and pushed aside the black dresses, all she'd worn since her arrival.

"Good morning, ma'am." The nanny's cheerful face appeared in the doorway. "Is his young lordship still asleep?"

"Hello, Nanny. Yes. He had another hard night."

"Poor little thing. I shall just collect my knitting and come sit with him, then."

When the door was closed once more, Anne found it hard to reach out and take hold of the dress at the back of the armoire. She forced herself to gather up the only dress she had brought that was anything but black. It looked strange to her now, something that belonged to another person and a happier time. She recalled the last time she had worn the frock, with Cyril at her side.

With a violent shake of her head, Anne pushed the thoughts away. Hurriedly she dressed herself. When she had finished, she bent over the crib, kissed her child, and murmured not so much to the sleeping face but more to the presence that reflected back at her from his tiny features, "Farewell, my love. You're always with me."

She hastened from the room, as she did not want to face Nanny's inquiring glance. Not yet. She made her way down the stairs only to find Nicole still seated where Anne had left her. Nicole's pinched expression turned to surprise when she saw Anne standing in the doorway.

Anne took a hard breath and said, "Shall we be off?"

Chapter Twenty-five

Every time the Wednesday supply cart rattled into Georgetown, Catherine rushed toward it in hopes that there would be some communication from her two daughters. Usually she returned home heavyhearted. Still no word had come.

And so Wednesdays always seemed longer and gloomier, leaving her wishing the carts did not come to the village at all. They were a painful reminder of the broken link between her and the ones she loved across the ocean.

It was midweek once again, and the long-awaited supply wagon still had not arrived. The late-afternoon sun had broken through the thin layer of clouds that hung close to the treetops. Birds flitted from limb to limb, playing in the feeble sun. Her father, who rarely strayed far from the fire on such a day, stretched now and rubbed at his troubling knee. He tipped his head to one side in an attitude of listening. "I believe I hear the dogs barking."

She put aside her needlework and

moved to the window. Again she marveled that her father's hearing had not diminished over the years. Indeed it did seem that something was astir. Catherine looked out to see the supply cart rumbling through the trail's thick dust, wending its way between the sturdy buildings. "The dray wagon has arrived!"

Catherine swung around and grabbed her shawl. Already the air held an evening's chill. *You're being foolish*, she scolded herself as she scurried to their front gate. *Just setting yourself up for another disappointment.*

The minister's wife had become a familiar sight to the driver, as she was always pressing through the throng of people gathered around his cart. The stocky man, with his pipe dangling between clenched teeth, removed his cloth cap and ran spread fingers through his unruly hair. The pipe bounced when he said, "I have a packet for you, missus."

It did not take him long to dig out the little bundle. Catherine gasped her words of thanks, clutched the packet to her chest, and hurried back home.

The packet contained letters from each of her daughters and a shorter one from Charles. Catherine laid aside the letter from her brother-in-law for Andrew to open when he returned and then broke the seals on the ones from her girls. She did not know which letter to read first, so she closed her eyes and picked one from her lap where she'd let them fall. It was Nicole's that she found in her hand. *Dear Father and Mother,* it began. *Greetings from England where summer now rests gently on the land.* Catherine smiled. Nicole's English had continued to improve.

The letter went on to tell of the daily happenings of their busy social life. Catherine wondered at the frantic pace of activity that, to her mind, seemed to accomplish nothing. Nicole did not speak of daily chores. What would it be like to live in a world filled with delights rather than duties? Catherine could not fathom such a thing. What satisfaction did her daughter have after laying her head on the pillow at night? No, the life of the wealthy was definitely not for her.

But as Catherine read on, the letter turned to other things. Nicole was busy learning, becoming more deeply involved with Charles and his service amongst the villages. This brought a smile to Catherine's face. Here was a worthy response to Catherine's silent query. Her daughter was discovering ways to help others. *Andrew will be so pleased*, mused Catherine.

The letter also told of Nicole's feelings regarding Anne's arrival: *I had not known just how lonely I was until I beheld Anne and her baby John at our doorstep. I have never been so glad to see anyone in my whole life. And yet I do grieve with her. She has lost so much. But Anne remains brave and does not mope about nor carry her grief as an adornment. Still, I see the pain in her eyes and it hurts me so.*

In spite of her sorrow, it has been such a joy to have them here. Johnny, I call him Johnny in spite of Anne's objection, is such a dear, sweet child. He entertains us all. Every day he seems to learn something new. He knows pat-a-cake and peek-a-boo and the gestures to "London Bridge." He knows a number of words now and tries many sounds we have yet to understand. He can become quite annoyed when we fail to grasp his meaning. We have to watch him carefully at all times. Uncle Charles is the one most likely to indulge him. He absolutely adores the child. The staff say that Johnny has brightened the entire house.

Catherine felt her chest tighten. She was missing so much. A tear slipped from the corner of her eye and traced a moist trail down her cheek.

We think of you always and speak of you

often, Nicole's letter concluded. *It would be so wonderful were you here with us. I am sure the warm, fresh countryside would do wonders for Father's health. We trust you are both keeping well. We pray for you daily and send our love and fondest regards. Your daughter, Nicole.*

Thoughtfully, Catherine folded the letter. She knew it would warm Andrew's heart just as it had her own. He would be home soon. She smiled as she thought of the wonderful surprise that awaited him.

Catherine picked up the second letter from the folds of her apron. *To my dearest parents,* Anne's letter began. *I cannot tell you how much we miss you. Every day John and I talk together about you. I tell him stories from over the years as I tuck him into bed each night. I am sure he understands because of the way his eyes light up. I don't want him to forget you, so I am doing everything in my power to speak memories into his little mind.*

He is such a dear little fellow. I know Cyril would take great delight in him. I see more of his father in him every day and I continually thank God for that gift. As you told me, Mother, John's presence is like having a bit of Cyril still with me.

Anne then wrote of how the English countryside intrigued her, as did the social climate. It was so different than what she'd known. *I am gradually becoming more involved in public life. Nicole shares with me all her adventures into society. I cannot help but lament some of the things I see and hear. There is such a vast distance between the titled and the common. A man does not seem to be of worth because of who he is or what he does, but rather by the name he bears. It seems so unjust. There is such foolishness, such pomp and arrogance as you would not believe.*

Returning to family matters, Anne said, *We shall hopefully travel soon to see Cyril's family. Some days I become so restless. I feel that John's grandmother is missing so much of his growing up. We have already celebrated his first birthday! Uncle Charles saw to it that it was a spectacular affair. I have never seen so many toys. I think John was just as entranced by the fancy boxes in which they came as the toys themselves. It made us all laugh, Uncle Charles especially. John puts him in such good humor.*

Again Catherine had to pause in her reading and clear her eyes. It was so difficult for her to be missing all of the happenings of the baby's life. And how she ached for Anne. The house felt so forlorn and empty without her familiar presence.

Anne gave her warmest greeting to her

Grandfather Price: *I wish he were here to walk with me along the hedgerows,* she wrote. *We could have such good chats as we strolled. I know he must have wonderful memories of his life as a boy growing up here in England.* The letter then drew to a close with further words of love and longing.

Catherine folded the pages tenderly, her thoughts many miles away. In all, it had been a cheery letter, despite Anne's disclosing that she'd spent some lonely days and even lonelier nights. At least the terrible wrenching sorrow seemed to be finally lessening. Perhaps time was indeed healing the deepest of Anne's wounds. Catherine prayed that it might be so and that God, in His mercy, would help the young woman find her way on life's path once again.

While wiping at her eyes, Catherine rose from the chair and handed the two letters to her father. "Andrew won't mind if you read them before he does." Then she proceeded to the kitchen to finish preparations for their simple evening meal.

Later that evening, as soon as she finished serving the family and cleaning the kitchen, Catherine took out a sheet of paper and began a letter of her own. She had decided she would reply while her daughters' words were still fresh in her mind and heart. Her letter would be one that would bring them joy and comfort, she thought as she raised the pen and dipped it in the inkwell. She would not write of the loneliness and pain that was in her heart. She would convey to them her love, not her sorrow. With this in mind, Catherine started her letter, writing each word on the page in carefully flowing script.

It turned out to be a folksy note. She shared the news of the villagers and made much of the ordinary things that formed her world. She wrote of weddings and new babies, of her work at the Acadian school and the acceptance they'd received within the new community. She dwelt on Andrew's ministry and the people who were showing interest in the truths of God. Of Grandfather Price's continued good health. Of sunny summer days and the promise of good crops in both the gardens and fields.

Nothing was written about the longing for her children or the pain caused by the absence of her grandchild. There were the usual admonitions concerning things spiritual, that they would follow the Lord's ways and seek His guidance for all life's decisions. She reminded them that they were prayed for morning and evening. Then came a great outpouring of words of love, and with a sigh, she signed, *Your loving mother and grandmother.* Catherine was folding the sheets that she'd filled—where she had carefully concealed her longings—when the tears gushed forth. She let them fall, as she needed to bring some release to her mother's heart.

Chapter Twenty-six

For Anne, the next few days held a breathless quality. There were several trips to the dressmakers on Bond Street. When Anne objected to Charles over the vast sums being spent, he expressed delight that finally Nicole was willing to have more clothes made.

While Nicole clearly took no pleasure in the activity, Anne felt guilty over the delight she found in the new clothes. The dressmakers had responded with excitement, as Anne's delicate frame and dainty features proved ideal for the current fashions.

Nicole took her everywhere. They began at Nicole's morning session with

Lord Percy, whom Anne had met on other occasions. Gradually Percy walked Nicole through Charles's affairs, which she clearly found hard going. Her sister, on the other hand, saw it all as very fascinating and several times was able to point out things that Nicole had simply overlooked.

Now that Anne had left her dresses of mourning behind, those she'd met before now greeted her like a newcomer. And perhaps this was the case, for certainly the world appeared different. The veil of sorrow had lifted, at least partly. It was not that she stopped missing Cyril, but that a new day had dawned. She often found herself praying silently for direction, asking the Lord to show her what was to come of her now, what service might she do, and whether it was time to return to Nova Scotia and start a new life there.

These feelings were strongest the morning a letter arrived from Catherine with an enclosure from Louise. As always, Catherine's letter began with the words, *My dear daughters.* The two sisters read and wept and clung together for support.

Charles, however, did not seem to take in the letters at all. In fact, he took little notice of Anne's gradual transformation. Ever since the late-night discussion with Anne, he had become increasingly self-contained. He was not normally a grim man, but his countenance had grown stern. He refused to be drawn out over what concerned him. Even the staff took to moving cautiously about the London residence.

That afternoon they attended a social gathering given by an Austrian princess at a women's club known as Almacks, located on King Street. Anne accepted a glass of orgeat from a passing waiter and gradually stepped away from the fray. Orgeat was considered the proper afternoon drink for a woman of high society and was made of crushed almonds, barley sugar, and orange-flavored water. Anne found it far too sweet, but if she held the glass, the hovering waiters would not continue to approach. She climbed the stairs leading from the main ballroom to an elaborate balcony shaped like a quarter moon. From there Anne was able to observe the homage paid to Nicole by the other debutantes. Most of them were younger, more frivolous, and far less attractive. Anne also noticed the stiff manner in which Nicole moved and spoke. It was quite evident just how burdensome her sister found the social events. Yet Nicole managed to carry herself well, responding with decorum. The men flocked to her, young and old alike. Nicole was kind and well spoken to all but touched deeply by none of them.

Anne moved toward a side table from where she could take in the whole sweeping affair of chiffon and clamor. Yet as she was seating herself, she heard a woman directly behind her ask, "Have you observed the Viscountess Harrow there?"

Anne shifted a fraction, just far enough to see the two dowagers looking down their noses at the swirling colors and people. She turned away as the other woman sniffed, "She's not titled yet. Lord Charles has shown the sense not to formally present the inheritance decree."

The first dowager had the rich, throaty tones of one to whom all had been given, and more. "You've heard the stories of her upbringing, I suppose."

"Simply scandalous," the other agreed.

Anne bit back on her sudden anger. That such ladies would speak with casual viciousness about her beloved sister left her almost choking with rage. But nothing would have been gained by speaking up, so she kept her back to them.

One of them demanded, "Who is that tall gentleman fawning about her now?"

"Surely you know Lord Harwick."

"Is that who it is? I thought he was on

the Continent somewhere."

"Vienna. Acting as the Crown's agent on some matter. Look at the way he bandies about with the strumpet."

"It would be shameful for a man half his age," the dowager said.

"It is such utter infamy, how the men fawn over the likes of that colonial upstart," the other snorted.

"You are here with your niece, I believe."

"Yes, Amelia is there in the yellow."

Anne spotted an anemic-looking twig flittering nervously across the ballroom. The color and cut of her dress only accented her awkwardness.

"How lovely," simpered the other lady behind Anne. "And my Leslie, see her in the lavender?"

The girl chose that moment to bray like a barnyard animal, causing one of the members of the string quartet playing in the far corner almost to drop his bow.

"A ravishing young thing," the other dowager offered. "Why those addle-headed gentlemen insist on making fools of themselves about that backwoods ruffian in silk is utterly beyond me."

Then the gentleman speaking with Nicole bowed and took a step back. Nicole turned and searched the gathering, clearly looking for Anne. Gratefully Anne used this as an excuse to rise from the chair.

Behind her one lady said, "But the young woman there is nothing near as bad as what Lord Charles himself is up to these days."

"You don't mean to say he's a nonconformist, then?"

"Worse. A Whig in all but name. I understand he's going to speak on the Revolutionaries' behalf."

"In public?" The woman's tone sounded horrified. "You cannot be serious!"

As Anne moved stiffly toward the ballroom floor, she heard the dowager respond, "Indeed I am. His poor father must be rolling in his grave."

Nicole watched as Lord Reginald Harwick cut his way through the crowd like a great ship parting the waves. He ignored the younger debutantes who fluttered their fans and sought to catch his eye. His gaze remained fixed on Nicole. He planted himself before her and gave her a rigidly formal bow. "An honor to see you again, Miss Nicole."

She curtsied with practiced grace. "Greetings to you, Lord Harwick."

He glanced around the gathering with distaste. "Once again I find myself attending a rather annoying event in order to seek you out. Did you receive my letters?"

As with the dozen or so other times they had met, Nicole found herself mysteriously drawn to the man's magnetic personality. Yet there also remained a foretaste of something more, and today it came out more clearly than ever before. "I did not."

"I feared as much. War has the spiteful habit of interrupting the natural flow of things." He nodded distractedly to an older woman and continued, "I've been on the Continent. Vienna, actually. Perhaps you know it."

Nicole found herself flashing back to another man, a handsome rogue of the bayous, a man she loved so that it tore her apart to leave him. Yet leave is what she had to do, for she knew there could be no future with someone who disregarded God's commands. Here again she felt attracted to a man of power, intrigued also by the challenge of taming him and molding him through her strong will. But this time she found the temptation far weaker than the warnings she sensed in her heart.

She realized the man was waiting for her reply. "I've never traveled anywhere other than here, sir."

"Ah yes. Of course." He paused, studying her face and form. "With your elegance and accent, I forget the fables of your mysterious upbringing."

"You are too kind, but they are not fables."

"I am many things, Miss Nicole. Blunt, impatient with many of the world's ways, too forceful for my own good. But certainly not overly kind. Kindness is a virtue I would hope to reap from an alliance with one fairer and more benevolent than myself."

Then Lord Harwick waited as if expecting some form of invitation. But Nicole had learned from her many contacts with other suitors that, on such occasions, silence was always the wiser recourse. So she snapped open her fan and waved it idly while looking up at him and saying nothing.

Her poise clearly rattled the older gentleman, and his expression tightened somewhat. "I've spent the previous months acting as the king's own emissary, Miss Nicole. He trusts me. That should speak for something."

Again she felt the battering of his power, but now she felt more certain of herself and of her direction. "Indeed it does, sir. Yet we are speaking of matters where the king holds no place."

"Does he not? Does he not indeed?" His face tensed further. "Do you perhaps remember what I said to you earlier, about how I am in a position to offer great aid to my allies?"

"I recall all our conversations, sir."

"It would do you much good to think on this matter, m'lady." He started to say something further but stopped himself with visible effort. He then bowed and said, "I have the honor of being invited to dine with you tonight. Perhaps we shall speak more on this matter then."

Anne decided not to speak with Nicole of what she had overheard. There was scarcely time to bathe the baby and herself and then get everything ready before the guests began arriving for dinner.

As usual, Lord Percy was the first to come. Normally he used such occasions to discuss business matters with Charles.

Tonight, however, he was there at the bottom of the stairs to greet Anne as she descended. "Madame, your presence lights up the room. And that dress—what a work of art you are tonight."

She gave him a genuine smile. Percy was an odd-looking character, his habit of taking snuff rather vile. But he had a heart of pure gold and he doted on Charles and Nicole. Anne lifted the hem of her new gown. The material was Chinese painted silk, the colors ivory and mint green, with a collar of Medellín lace. "The dressmaker called it a polonaise design."

"Upon you it looks positively ravishing." Percy bent over her hand. "Might I say, madame, it makes my heart glad to see you taking such a brave step."

Anne fluttered her fan. "Your eyes miss nothing, Lord Percy." And because the topic left her discomfited, she went on, "Might I ask where your own title comes from?"

"A trifle, madame. A chance encounter, an opportunity to do some royal a small service, which now escapes me." He dipped into his snuffbox, sneezed like a cannonade, then continued, "I am a landowner by chance and a Christian by choice. I am a lordship by sheer amazement. It's the clearest sign I have that God possesses a rich sense of humor."

He offered her his arm, which she accepted. As they walked toward the drawing room, Anne asked, "I don't suppose you could tell me what is troubling my uncle so."

Percy faltered momentarily, but then quickly composed himself and said, "Your eye is remarkably keen, madame. But some questions must be left for his honor to answer."

"Charles is lucky to have such a friend, Lord Percy."

"And Miss Nicole to have such a sister." Percy nodded in response to Gaylord bowing them into the drawing room. "Your presence has done her a powerful good."

"She will make a fine heir for Charles," Anne said, yet in her heart she could not help but wish that Nicole might find joy in the work.

Percy turned to her and said for her ears alone, "So would you, madame." Then he bowed and went to greet the other guests now trickling in.

The new dresses did not alter Anne's habit of standing to one side and observing the gathering. Before long, she sighted the familiar form of Lord Harwick as he closed in on Nicole. He said something to her, then grimaced at Nicole's calm response. Harwick spoke again, this time at length. Although Anne could not hear the words, she saw how Nicole noticeably tensed and then nodded acceptance.

Anne watched them walk together toward the balcony doors. They made a truly striking couple. Nicole wore a deep green gown of Lyons silk, and the color shimmered as she moved, like the shifting surface of the sea. But there was no joy to be found in either face.

There was another who scrutinized the couple, a young sea captain by the curious name of Gordon Goodwind. He had come as a late addition, a guest of guests, as the friend of Captain and Mrs. Madden, who spoke now with Charles. Captain Goodwind gazed at Nicole with undisguised ardor. He cut a dashing figure in his long black coat and frill-fronted shirt. He wore trousers in the newest fashion, long stovepipes that descended over the tops of his polished black boots. The only mark of color to his person was the blue ribbon with which he kept his long copper hair tied tautly back. On another man it may have looked effeminate, but with his hawkish features and the slash mark on his right cheek, the effect was quite stylish.

Yet Captain Goodwind made no gesture toward Nicole except to bow at their greeting. Then he went to hanging back and examining her every movement. Anne could well guess the reason for his reluctance to approach Nicole—a sea captain had little chance to cross the chasm that separated him from a viscountess. Besides, Lord Harwick kept a vigilant closeness to Nicole as they headed for the balcony.

Nicole walked with her head tilted high, her auburn hair cascading in well-managed curls. Lord Harwick maintained a possessive grip on her arm. The gentleman was perhaps fifteen years her senior, which in itself was not that great a difference. Yet he carried himself too stiffly, and his chin was set at too determined an angle. Anne noticed how others regarded the two, how several of the other young men stared at Nicole wistfully. It was a mystery to Anne how such a lovely young woman could remain not just unattached but isolated.

Anne stepped away from the laughing throng, and as the couple entered the narrow balcony, she moved alongside the open doors. She told herself she merely wished to ensure they were not disturbed, but there was something else. She desperately wanted to know what was happening between Nicole and this mysterious gentleman. Anne had never known a closeness like she felt toward Nicole. Their bond was one of friendship and sisterhood both. And yet there were new walls within Nicole, strange undercurrents that Anne did not yet understand. Even so, Anne was certain her sister was distressed, and if help was required, Anne wanted to be there for her.

Lord Harwick spoke with a deep baritone voice, rich in timbre and very masculine. "My dear Miss Nicole, I do wish you would grant me leave to pay suit."

Anne took a single step backward, closer to the balcony. She heard Nicole's utterly flat tone as she responded, "You would be disappointed, sir."

"Call me Reginald, I implore you." He then chuckled, but it sounded forced. "On the contrary, I am absolutely infatuated with you. I feel we would make for a perfect match."

"What makes you say that?"

"You must have seen the way people watched us tonight. Everyone here would most certainly agree we outshine the entire gathering. Not to mention the few moments we have shared together suggest a harmony that could only turn to deeper sentiments, if you would only allow—"

"Might I ask how you feel about the war with the American colonies?"

"What I . . . my dear, if you will forgive me, I hardly feel this is the time or place to discuss worldly affairs."

"Very well, then. What about affairs of the heart? Do you hold your faith in God as paramount?"

"I hold the Church in highest esteem, as should every decent British gentleman. But this has scarcely any place in our discussion this evening, my dear."

"If truth be known, Lord Harwick, you would prefer never to speak of such things with a woman, am I not correct?"

"Miss Nicole, please, we were discussing our courtship."

"Just answer my question, Lord Harwick. I beg you."

He gave an exasperated sigh. "All right, yes. I do feel there are certain matters which, if brought into a relationship, would only result in unnecessary hard feelings."

"With respect, sir, I must disagree."

"My dear, I can perfectly understand your sentiments, given your most remarkable heritage. But that hardly means we are not meant for each other."

"Again, with respect, I disagree." A faint

hint of desperation entered into Nicole's voice. "Lord Harwick, I don't mean to offend, but I fear if I say anything more, I will do just that."

"I came out here hoping you might consider me as a worthy prospect for marriage," Harwick protested. "Somehow we have entered the disagreeable fields of politics and religion and war. I must ask you to return to the matter at hand."

"Oh, very well. I suppose I shall have to speak plainly." Her tone was harder than Anne had ever heard Nicole use. "Lord Harwick, I would not marry you if you were the last person on Earth."

There was a moment of shocked silence. "Why would you say such a thing?"

"Because it's true." The words became a torrent, quietly spoken, yet heated nonetheless. "I don't wish to become some man's ornament. Nor do I intend to remain silent on issues I consider vital, merely because some men prefer women to have no opinions, or at least not to speak them. Lord Harwick, these issues are *vital* and must be a part of any relationship I might enter into. I desire a partner who respects me and wants to share his life with me. *All* his life."

"My dear—"

"Please allow me to finish, sir. I have a

duty to perform here. I have an obligation to my uncle Charles, to the position and wealth he intends to bestow upon me, and most especially to God. I must seek a husband with whom I might share this vision, someone who will treat me as a partner in this shared mission."

There was a long silence. When Lord Harwick spoke again, his voice turned bitterly cold. "I would not be the least bit surprised to learn that you die a lonely old maid."

"If that is God's will, then so be it," Nicole replied flatly.

"Your uncle must be behind this farce. Filling your head with idealistic nonsense. I must say it matches this ridiculous stance he has taken over the colonies."

"I must ask you to take your leave, Lord Harwick, before you say something we both shall regret."

"Very well."

Anne barely had time to back away before the man stormed from the balcony. He marched straight over to where Charles stood talking with Captain Madden and his wife, and then gave a curt bow. "I regret, Sir Charles, that common sense requires me to take my leave."

Charles started to speak, but then

happened to glance over toward Anne, who was watching the two of them. Something in her look caused Charles to alter his response. "We shall miss your presence, Lord Harwick, but will not insist that you remain."

"Before I depart," the gentleman said gruffly, "I must once again warn you to hold off on your plans for the morrow."

Charles's face turned to stone. "*Warn* me, sir?"

Lord Harwick held to his course. "It's a dangerous route you have chosen, one that will bring much harm and no good whatsoever. Those words, sir, are not my own."

"My mind is set."

"Then you will become an outcast, a pariah within your own class."

"I have no choice in the matter."

Still Harwick pushed on. "Not to mention the harm your would-be heiress is causing you. I should not be surprised if the Crown—"

"You have said enough!" Charles snapped. "And more besides. Now common decency *requires* that you depart at once."

"I shall look forward to your coming demise, sir." With that Harwick wheeled about and left the chamber without a backward glance.

Immediately Charles excused himself from the captain and Mrs. Madden, then hurried over to Anne. "Might I ask what was said here?"

Nicole came in from the balcony, her eyes glistening but her composure intact. "It was all my fault, Uncle. I humbly apologize."

"On the contrary," said an unexpected voice. A stranger stepped up from his station behind Anne. He bowed deeply to Nicole and said, "Your pardon, m'lady, I could not help but overhear." He looked at Charles. "All you need to know, m'lord, is that your niece has done you and the Harrow name great honor this night."

Anne saw the crimson blush rise from the collar of Nicole's dress. Anne reached over, grasped Nicole's white-gloved hand, and said quietly, "I agree."

The young man was perhaps an inch shorter than Nicole. He gazed at her with undisguised admiration, his dark eyes alight with awe. "Again, I beg your forgiveness, Miss Nicole. But I must tell you that your words have sparked my heart."

He bowed once more and then left them. Anne watched his passage through the room and quietly asked, "Who, pray tell, was that?"

"Percy's nephew and heir," Charles replied. "Thomas Crowley."

Nicole then demanded, "What was it Lord Harwick asked you about, Uncle? What dangerous course are you taking?"

The grimness returned to Charles's features. "I am to address the House of Lords tomorrow morning."

Nicole gathered herself and said, "I wish to come."

"My dear—"

"If this is a matter of such grave importance, I should be there." Her tone came close to matching her uncle's. "I wish to be coddled no longer, Uncle. I want to know. I want to help."

Chapter Twenty-seven

It was a somber assembly that set off for the Houses of Parliament the next morning. Twice Nicole started to ask her uncle what was about to happen, but Charles's stern look kept her questions trapped in her throat. They halted before the members' entrance, where Charles alighted and said, "I must bid you adieu here. One of the porters will show you to the visitors' gallery. Take the carriage when you wish to depart. I will make my own way home." Without another word or backward glance, Charles turned and entered the great stone edifice.

"I wonder what's happening," Anne said.

But before Nicole could respond, the young face from the previous night suddenly appeared in the carriage's open doorway. "Good morning to you, ladies. Thomas Crowley at your service. I could not help but overhear. Perhaps you will permit me to escort you upstairs?"

Nicole felt the flush return to her cheeks. "You seem to do a great deal of listening into others' conversations, sir."

"It's true, Miss Nicole. I cannot deny it." He smiled admiringly as he offered his hand to help her from the carriage. "My only defense is that I listen with the highest possible motives."

Thomas led them through the labyrinth of passageways and up a series of winding stairs. Parliament was far from the most ornate structure Nicole had visited, but certainly one of the most formidable. There was an austere look to the place, as though the frivolity of social exchange had no place here. The visitors' gallery was a long hall with a stone frieze that overlooked the House of Lords.

Nicole spotted Lord Charles seated on the more crowded side of the chamber, but speaking to no one. Unlike most of the members, her uncle did not usually wear a formal wig, preferring instead to powder his hair and gather it at the back in a black velvet ribbon that matched his black robe with purple borders. It seemed to Nicole that all those around her uncle deliberately avoided engaging him.

Anne recognized it, as well. "Why does Charles appear so alone?" she asked.

"I cannot say with any certainty, ma'am." Thomas Crowley's former air of excited ardor had vanished, and he now exhibited a grave expression and spoke in a solemn whisper. "But I have heard snippets of his discussions with my uncle Percy. All I can tell you is that Charles has decided to speak as his conscience dictates."

Nicole studied the young man for a moment, then said, "But you know what he intends?"

"I would rather not hazard to guess, Miss Nicole. Forgive me."

"Tell me what you can, then."

Her response must have gratified Thomas, for a glimmer of his earlier zeal returned. "The House of Lords is the king's chamber, as the saying goes. The House of Commons, the lower chamber of our Parliament, is far less predictable. Though, at the moment, the Tories control both houses. The Tories are the king's party and so are devoted to the Crown's cause. Of course, this is no surprise, since they're made up mostly of the landed gentry and therefore are the king's men."

"The Tories are in control of England's government, then?"

"Just so. But within the House of Commons, Miss Nicole, the balance is much more delicate than in the chamber you see here below. The Whigs are growing in force, especially now. The Whigs are the party of the merchants, you see, and they are being hurt mightily by the war with the American colonies."

Thomas pointed down beneath the frieze and continued, "The side where your uncle sits is occupied by the Tories. The other side, this one below us, is reserved for the Whigs and the independents. As you can see, the Whigs are much fewer in number."

Nicole took another moment to inspect the dark-haired man. Thomas Crowley was not a particularly handsome person. His head appeared too large for his frame, along with his hands and feet. But he was far from an ungainly figure, especially when he was in motion. And he was seldom still. He displayed a remarkable agility, even in the way he used his hands while speaking. His words revealed a scalpel-like mind.

"Are you yourself a Whig?" Nicole ventured.

"I am, as is my uncle Percy." Even when speaking softly, he showed a unique richness of voice, and fervor. "The Whigs represent the dissenter churches, as well. The Lutherans, the Methodists, the Congregationalists, the Protestants, the Quakers, the Anabaptists. These are the churches backing the American colonies' struggle for independence, you see."

"I did not know that," Nicole admitted.

"Oh yes. We have become most active in—"

His words broke off at the sound of a great booming from below and a voice intoning for Order. Nicole turned with him and Anne and watched as the Lords began the formal ceremony of session.

It was not long before the Speaker called on Charles. There was a general muttering among the Tories, and one older gentleman went so far as to pull on Charles's robe.

Nicole noticed that Lord Harwick was sitting in the row behind Charles. Harwick leaned forward to speak, his face tight as a clenched fist, but her uncle did not give any sign of acknowledging him. Instead, Charles lifted a handful of papers and said, "My Lord Speaker, Lords and Ladies of the House, three weeks and two days ago, the Continental Congress of the American States—"

"The American *colonies*!" Lord Harwick shouted loudly from behind him.

"Order!" The Speaker sat enthroned in the center of the room, with the golden chalice of office situated on a black velvet stand before him. He wore a wig whose sides curved downward like unfurled wings, resting on his shoulders. "Order, there! Lord Charles has the floor."

"Thank you, my lord." Charles raised his voice and continued, "The Continental Congress has issued a Declaration, of which I now have a copy. In this Declaration of Independence, they declare their intentions to secede from the Crown."

Again there was agitation among those seated on Charles's side of the chamber. Soon another call for order came bellowing from the Speaker. Charles waited for the room to quiet down, then said, "Our newspapers have been reporting on this development. It has even been mentioned in the Commons. Yet nothing has been said of this momentous event here in our august chambers—"

Lord Harwick shouted angrily, "That is because the entire colonial proceedings are illegal!"

"It is time a formal record be made," Charles went on, ignoring Harwick's comment. "My lords, you have known me for many years. My family and I have faithfully served the Crown for eight generations. I stand here upon my honor as a loyal British subject, and say . . ." Charles hefted the parchment in his hands and then raised his voice even more. "I say, let these former colonists have their freedom!"

Pandemonium erupted in the chamber below. There were shouts of treachery, of cowardice, of treason, of wordless fury. There were also a few cheers, mostly from those gathered on the opposite benches, though two among the Tories clearly agreed with Charles.

Nicole observed Thomas making hurried notes. "What are you writing?" she whispered.

Without looking up from his work, he said, "The names of those Tories supporting Charles. Up till now, none have had the courage to speak out."

"Why not?"

"Because the king has expressly forbade this debate from taking place. He wants the Lords to show a united front against the colonists and the Whigs both."

Anne's expression mirrored Nicole's concern. "What will happen to Charles?"

"With his power and name, hopefully nothing," Thomas replied, but his face was creased with concern, too.

Finally order was restored once more. The Speaker sounded outraged by what Charles had to say, for he exclaimed, "Lord Charles, this is not a debating society! You requested this time, claiming you wished to set forth a motion."

"I do indeed, my lord. I hereby propose that this Declaration of Independence be ratified by the House—"

"Sit down, sir!"

"I move that we vote to grant them the freedom they demand to follow their own God-given destiny!" Charles dropped the papers he held so that his hand could reach out toward the gathering. "These articles state very clearly that we have *failed* them. These people were once our friends and brethren. But they have now grown so outraged by the way they have been treated, by the failure of our governors to serve and protect, by the heavy-handedness of laws passed by this very body, that they demand their freedom. They have come to this decision through careful thought and prayer. They beseech God to be with them in this momentous decision. And I say, we must respect their . . ."

Whatever else Charles had to say was drowned out by the Speaker's hammering gavel and the vehement roar of those surrounding him. Charles stared around the room, trapped within a sea of black robes and angry faces. He said nothing more. Instead, he slid from his bench, marched across the aisle, accepted the handshake of one seated in the front row, and then joined himself to the Whigs. After sitting down, he bowed his head and began massaging his chest with his left hand. Heated debate and calls for Charles to be punished rose up from the chamber. The loudest voice of all belonged to Lord Harwick, who furiously declared that he spoke for the king and that the Crown demanded Charles be sternly censured. Charles neither spoke nor raised his head.

Chapter Twenty-eight

The journey to Wales began two days later. The road from London to Bristol was as straight and broad as the River Thames. Anne spent the trip seated across from two very glum figures: Charles, who had remained morosely silent since the confrontation in the House of Lords; and Nicole, who had been strangely shaken by her having witnessed the dreadful scene. Yet Anne felt herself invigorated, although she could not say precisely why. She had a hundred questions for Charles. But she was content to wait till Charles had recovered from what had happened. Then she would seek to learn more.

Anne surveyed the summer landscape rolling by outside the carriage and felt as though she were seeing it for the first time. Her tragic veil was gradually lifting. It was not that she had stopped missing Cyril; she would feel his absence the rest of her life. But Anne now realized she was learning to live with the wound. Here in this world, thousands of miles from her life with Cyril, she was discovering a new life beyond her beloved. But did this mean she would remain in England? Anne smiled toward the vista beyond the carriage window. Not all the questions rising within her were directed toward Charles. Nor did they all require immediate answers. For the moment she was content to observe within herself this gradual awakening, this leaving behind the long slumber of grief.

They passed through the bustling port of Bristol, ferried across the River Severn, and entered Wales. The Mann estate lay on the outskirts of Newport, not as large a town as Bristol but a burgeoning harbor nonetheless. The Mann family were prosperous flax and linen merchants. They were delighted to meet Anne and proved to be as warm and cordial in their greetings as they had been in their correspondence.

Judith Mann, Cyril's mother, was an ample woman dressed in black. She had lost her husband two years before Cyril's own passage and seemed content to remain permanently in her widow's weave. Despite her appearance of mourning, however, Judith Mann was a warm and intelligent woman. The first three nights after their arrival, Anne stayed behind long after the others had returned to the inn where Charles had taken rooms. She and Judith sat up till the wee hours, and she recounted the time of Cyril's illness and subsequent death. Anne talked till her throat grew raw and she could speak no more.

On the fourth morning, she slept late and came downstairs to find Nicole seated on the bench by the front garden. It was a sunny day, and already the coaching inn was comfortably warm. Newport had been erected within a series of narrow hills that fell in graceful waves down to the broad waters of the Severn. The town was built mostly of close-cut local stone, gray and harsh looking in the rain. But now, with the morning sun gleaming down, the entire village glowed yellow as fresh-churned butter. Slate-tile roofs shone like silver-black mirrors upon the slopes leading down to the port.

Anne smiled her greeting to Nicole and asked, "May I join you?"

Nicole made room for her on the bench, but said only, "Nanny left a few minutes ago, taking John for his morning walk. Charles is out meeting an ailing friend. We are to go together after lunch and survey more of his holdings."

Anne took note both of the news and the flat way Nicole had said it. "I've missed our mornings together," Anne said, wondering if her absence was what was causing Nicole distress. "But I confess the evenings spent with Judith Mann have done me a world of good. In the beginning I thought I was speaking for her, sharing Cyril's departure from this earth. But I think now it was more meant for me, a good purging of all the horrors of those days." Anne traced with her eyes the lane's passage as it wound down to the distant harbor and then said, "I believe she knew this all along. Judith is a truly remarkable lady."

Nicole sat with her face turned toward the sun, the bonnet's wide brim masking her features and her reaction. Anne was about to ask if she'd done something to offend her when Nicole said, "I've decided to formally accept Charles's offer to become his heir."

The sudden news sank in slowly. "What?"

"I have known it ever since hearing Charles speak in Parliament. I stood and watched him and knew there was my answer, and my challenge." Nicole spoke with the toneless quality of one recently bereaved. "Along with Andrew and Henri, Charles is one of the finest men I have ever known."

"He's most certainly that," Anne agreed. "But—"

"I watched Charles speak out that day, acting against his own best interests. He knew his words would cause tempers to flare and that it might hurt him. He also knew that he had no choice. Someone had to speak out for the colonists and their desire to gain religious and political freedom." Nicole finally turned to face her sister and her friend. "He did what he did because he felt called by God."

Anne studied Nicole's strong, beautiful features. She saw the tragic resignation, and her heart felt constricted by the woman's deep sadness. "Are you certain this is what God is calling you to do?"

Nicole's mouth worked for a moment before she calmed herself again by strength of will alone. Yet there was nothing she could do about her blank tone as she replied, "If not me, then who?"

The dappled mare Charles had hired from the Newport stables had a back wide as a table and gave a steady ride. As he climbed the hill leading out of town, the horse's neighing and the gentle *clip-clop* of the hooves on the cobblestones lulled him into comfortable thought. Then he sighted the dark-clad figure walking toward him, and he doffed his hat. "A good afternoon to you, Mrs. Mann. I hope you are well."

"It is a grand day indeed, Lord Charles."

"I was actually on my way to your home," Charles said. "I was delayed at a friend's house, and returned to the inn to find Nicole had left."

"She and Anne have gone into town. They will return directly." The woman had the gentle smile of one used to facing adversities. "Climb down from your great steed and take a walk with me."

"It would be an honor." He slid down from the saddle and tied the horse to a nearby gatepost. "Shall I carry your basket for you?"

"I thank you, but it holds nothing save an excuse for me to depart." She set a brisk pace over the lane's uneven stones. "I find it easier to maintain peace in the house if I am absent when it comes time to prepare dinner."

"I could not help but notice," Charles said delicately, "there were some frictions between you and your daughter."

"Daughter-in-law," Judith Mann corrected. "Cyril's two elder brothers have chosen good wives, with strong characters and hearts wedded firmly to God. But

Donald's wife is now the head of this house, as Donald is the head of the Mann trading house. And at times I fear she finds my presence wearying." They walked on for a while, then she added, "Of course, someone in your position might say that is a small price to pay. After all, I have children and grandchildren of my own, a strong and believing brood to carry on the family name."

Charles considered the woman next to him. She was perhaps six or seven years his junior, with attractive, even features. Rich brown hair with but a few strands of gray emerging from both sides of her small black cap. Despite the losses she had suffered, she carried herself with a calm strength. "You are a most perceptive woman."

"I am also perhaps too outspoken. You will forgive me if I say that word has arrived in Newport of your assertion in the House of Lords." When Charles did not reply, she said, "Might I ask why you spoke as you did?"

"I had no choice," Charles replied tersely. "I felt called to do so."

"It's remarkable to find a man in your position who feels so strongly about his God and his obligations to the colonies. Few of the other Tories share your concern about freedom for the colonies."

"I can speak for no man save myself," Charles answered. "And I am a Tory no longer. But that does not change the fact that the Americas were settled by people seeking a place where they might worship their God as they saw fit. And this tenet is firmly at the heart of their Declaration. I have no choice as a believer but to support their cause."

Judith gazed frankly at him. "I agree with you, Sir Charles. And I admire your fortitude."

They continued their walk, passing through a square with a fountain in its middle. Children were scampering and spraying one another with the water, while mothers and nannies watched from a safe distance. They rounded the square in silence, then turned back toward the house. When they were once again within the lane's relative quiet, Judith mentioned, "There is something else I have observed that is quite noteworthy. And that is how young Anne is settling into her position."

This halted Charles in his tracks. "You mean Nicole."

"No, I mean Anne," Judith said quietly. "Nicole acts out of duty. With Anne, the proper responses come more naturally."

Charles felt the familiar squeezing

pressure in his chest. "But Nicole—"

"Is to become your heir. I realize this, as does she."

"She has said nothing to me of her decision."

"Nor to me. But one can see it upon her face. Nicole's mind is made up. She will accept your proposition, and I have no doubt but that she will do you proud."

Charles massaged his chest until he noticed the way Judith was watching his hand. He drew his arm back to his side. "You are certain of this?"

"I am certain of nothing save my Master reigns in heaven, and that I shall one day go to join Him and my beloved husband and son." Her quiet voice rang with strength and dignity. "But I have watched the two young ladies for several days now. And I see in Nicole a woman who recognizes her duty and is determined to do it. Yet the decision is forcing her into a corset that I fear does not fit her well and will chafe all her life long."

Charles compressed the hand upon his heart once more. "And Anne?"

"Yes, Anne." Judith looked out over the sparkling water and the horizon beyond. "How long has she been in England?"

"Four months."

"And yet already she seems of the

manor born. She comports herself extremely well."

"Yet Anne bears the responsibility of position with ease," Charles said, giving voice to thoughts he had not allowed himself to entertain till now. He made a half bow to Judith and said, "Your husband was a very fortunate man to have such a wise woman at his side."

Her face folded into dispirited lines. "Perhaps that is why it's proving so hard to give my daughter-in-law the freedom to rule the house now as her own. It's not just my husband that I lost, but my place in life."

A thought occurred to him. "Why not come and stay with us at Harrow Hall for a time?"

The invitation obviously shocked her. "I beg your pardon?"

"Nothing would please Anne more, I am certain of that." Charles felt strangely lifted by his proposal. "She would dearly love the chance to have young John become more attached to his father's clan. And I am certain your presence in our household would do everyone a world of good."

Judith's brown eyes shone with a new light. "I see why the two ladies adore you so," she replied. "I thank you for the kind invitation, Sir Charles, and I promise to think upon what you have said."

Chapter Twenty-nine

On Sunday it seemed to Anne as though the entire town of Newport went to church. Every lane was filled with people on the move, the men in long dark cloaks, the women in fine dark jackets over dresses of gray or muted stripes. They were solemn yet comfortable in their greetings to the Mann family and their guests. Clearly the Harrows' desire to worship with the Manns went far toward establishing their place in society, as did news of Charles's stance before the Houses of Parliament. Conversations overheard in the market and at the table had revealed to Anne just how much the war against the American colonies was despised in Wales.

There were many reasons for this almost universal opposition. The Welsh had undergone two recent revivals and so sympathized greatly with the Americans' desire to worship in a church not tied to the king. Many families also had kin who had settled in the southern colonies, and most understood their relatives' need to forge their own course. And Newport, as all the trading ports of Britain, had suffered much by the enforced blockade of American trade. Thus the people of Newport went out of their way to tip their hats to Charles and the ladies, bidding them their Sabbath greetings.

Anne found the town's central church to be a great blessing. The English services, both in Charles's home village and in London, were coldly formal and often sparsely attended. This church, on the other hand, was packed. Every pew was full, and people crammed along the back and up both side aisles. The hymns were sung with great shouts of joy, so powerfully that they brought tears to Anne's eyes. Here was worship in the spirit she knew at home, people bonded together by generations of shared faith.

On their way home, she drew Charles to a slower pace, permitting the others to walk on ahead. "I cannot help but notice, Uncle, how you are holding your chest more often these days," Anne said.

Charles attempted to brush it off. "It is nothing. A mild ache that comes and goes."

Anne halted him with a gentle hand on his arm. "It's your heart, is it not?" When Charles responded by staring out over the cloud-draped harbor, she went on, "Have you seen a doctor?"

"I've been around enough to know there's nothing anyone can do about such things." For a moment he considered whether to continue, then added, "Besides, there's too much risk of word spreading of my eventual demise."

"Particularly at this point, after your address to the House of Lords," Anne finished for him. "You don't wish to reveal weakness to anyone."

This brought Charles around. Anne continued, "First you wish to have the issue of your legacy settled, is that not so?"

"Judith Mann was correct," Charles murmured, almost to himself. "You are a most remarkable young woman."

But Anne would not be swayed from her course. "There are in fact several things which might help your discomfort. With Nicole's help, I will prepare for you a cathartic."

"My dear, I assure you—"

"A mild one should suffice. I shall boil rhubarb with brimstone and figs, strain it, and serve you the soup. You should feel better with just a few doses."

Charles bristled. "You shall do no such thing."

"I assure you, Uncle, I am well used to dealing with those who dislike being instructed in matters of their own health. But I have studied under a truly gifted medical mind and so I know of what I speak. A cathartic is what you need, and a cathartic is what you shall have. Do I make myself clear?"

Charles focused more intently on her, seeing her anew. "The Lord our God saw fit to compress quite an impressive spirit into your small frame."

"Good, then that's settled." Anne suddenly felt uncomfortable under Charles's gaze. "I shall make the necessary purchases in tomorrow's market."

Nine days later, they bid their farewells to the Manns and to Wales and then traveled by coach back to Harrow Hall. John spent the journey trying to pull the tassels from the window shades and shouting made-up words to everyone they passed. Charles found the hours flowed most easily when John was in his lap. The lad pretended he rode a horse, using Charles's glittery waistcoat for reins. The longer Charles was in the company of the young child, the stronger grew his affections.

The first person they met as they passed through the gates was Will Days astride Charles's dappled mare. He grinned widely as he bounced up and down in an effort to stay abreast of the carriage. Will tipped his hat and said, "I've just gone to meet the post coach. There's mail and company both, Lord Charles!"

"Good day to you, Will," Charles said. He reached out the window and accepted the leather packet. "Is all well with the house?"

"Aye, your honor, sir. Could not be better. The hound had her litter yesterday, and I've got me seven new pups to play with!"

Charles laughed at the youth's simple delight with life. "Would the company awaiting us perhaps be Lord Percy?"

"That's right, your honor. Lord Percy and Thomas Crowley. Came in the day before yesterday. Said you had called for them."

"That I did. Ride ahead and tell them I wish to see Lord Percy as soon as I arrive." He fished out a silver farthing and passed it over. "A penny for the post, and more to give speed to your horse."

"I shall fly like the wind, m'lord!" Then

Will flapped his legs and reedy elbows and cried, "Hyah!"

John, who was sitting in Charles's lap, loved the sound Will made. The child shrieked his accompaniment, causing Charles and Anne to bend over in laughter.

Nicole's smile appeared strained. Charles started to say something about it, then decided it was better to leave things for a more private moment. Then he was struck by a thought from a different direction entirely. He asked Anne, "Do you think I might be permitted to carry John atop my saddle when I go for my morning rides?"

If Anne was startled by the request, she did not show it. "I should think he'd like nothing better in all the wide world."

Charles was therefore beaming with coming pleasure as the coach halted before the manor. He stepped down and looked up at the old house. He had seen Harrow Hall in many different lights, often thinking of it as little more than an anchor tied around his neck—all the egotistical, grandiose desires of his forebears piled one on top the other. But today the late afternoon sun struck the edifice full on, making the stone and glass shine as if lit from within. The air was replete with summer fragrances and the fields bright with various shades of green.

"What a beautiful, splendid mansion," a voice beside him said.

Charles turned around to find Nicole staring at Anne with utter astonishment. Anne did not notice, however, for her face was tilted up at the house.

The sun's rays shone gently on her refined features, giving Anne a look of strength she did not in truth possess. "Often have I walked around this house and thought, this is how the houses of heaven will look one day." Anne turned her open, happy expression toward Charles and added, "I would be so pleased to know Cyril lived in such a place right now."

For some reason, Charles found it necessary to clamp down on his jaw. His voice sounded strangled as he replied, "You are ever welcome here, my dear. Please do me the honor of considering this home your own."

Instead of offering a standard word of thanks, Anne said, "I have thought much upon this journey back from Wales. If I am to stay through the winter, there are some projects I would like to begin."

"Projects," Charles repeated dumbly.

"With your permission, I would like to begin work with the surrounding villages, offering medical help where I can. Your own villages are now in satisfactory condition, Uncle. But many of those beyond your borders, I am sorry to say, remain in a very dismal state."

Charles could not deny it. "The other landowners might object to your meddling," he said.

"Not if a local society of churchwomen was formed to help the country people in need."

Then Lord Percy descended the manor's front steps. "A most worthy thought, if I do say so myself, Lord Charles." Percy had obviously dressed with some haste. The buttons of his waistcoat were done up incorrectly, and his wig sat askew on his head. He bowed and said, "Your arrival caught me napping. Might I be the first to welcome you home."

"You may not," Anne said sweetly. "Since young Will has beat you to it. But your words are well received just the same." She moved toward the young man accompanying Lord Percy and said, "Good afternoon, Thomas."

The man's face showed a wild conflict of emotions. "Mrs. Mann, Miss Nicole, your lordship. Forgive me, I could not help but overhear . . . Your lordship, if I may say so, I think Mrs. Mann's idea is superb. Simply superb. Not only that, sir, but we could expand upon the idea. There are a great many people of merit about here, within the church, the courts, the trades, and some landowners besides who all stand mightily opposed to the war on religious and moral grounds. We could—"

"Thomas," Percy said mildly, "they have just arrived from a long journey."

"Of course. I do beg your pardon."

"Not at all, not at all." Charles hoped the tumult occurring in his chest was not apparent on his face. "Percy, perhaps you and I might retire to the library. There are several urgent matters to be discussed."

But before they started up the stairs, Nicole stepped up beside him and said tensely, "Uncle, the post packet."

"What?" He glanced down at the unopened leather pouch. "Good gracious, I utterly forgot." He untied the thongs, then grinned at the first letter revealed. "There you are, my dear."

"A letter from home!" Nicole broke into such a smile as Charles had not seen in many days. He watched thoughtfully as Nicole worked at the seal with fingers so eager they trembled. "Oh, there's a letter from Mama in Louisiana, as well!"

Anne switched the baby to her other side so she could move in closer. Soon their two heads were touching as they read the words together. Charles turned and made his way inside along with Percy.

He warmly greeted his staff at the front door, then said, "A large pot of coffee would do me wonders just now, Maisy."

"Aye, m'lord. And perhaps a little toasted cheese to see you through to dinnertime."

"I am a bit famished from the road." Charles nodded to her husband and asked, "Are there fresh candles in the library, Gaylord?"

"Been kept lit and tended since Lord Percy's arrival, your lordship. He's claimed the place as his own." Gaylord then bowed. "Always good to welcome your lordship back home."

"Thank you kindly. Come, Percy."

Charles climbed the stairs in impatient bounds, scarcely containing himself as he hurried to get safely behind the library's closed double doors. Percy had to work hard to stay with him. "Percy, I don't suppose you have noticed how well Anne is fitting in."

"I could hardly miss it." Percy settled into one of the leather settees by the huge side window. "I have watched her over the weeks in London. Her veil of sorrow has gradually lifted, revealing a woman of outstanding intelligence and ability. Not only that, she's extremely well suited to the life here."

"Well suited and happy both, with a disposition that is quite appropriate for English society. Much more so than . . ." Charles let the thought trail off as he paced to the room's other end. He clasped his hands behind his back and said to the back wall, "This idea of hers for the women's society is extraordinary."

"Brilliant." Percy remained seated, waiting.

Charles paced off three more routes from wall to wall. Finally he asked what had been growing in his mind ever since his conversation with Judith Mann. "Would there be any chance to name Anne as my heir?"

"At this point in time," Percy replied, without hesitation, "utterly impossible."

"But she was raised by my brother Andrew. She is his daughter."

"In all but name," Percy corrected. "If I understand what you have previously told me, your brother never formally adopted her."

"They lived in a village at the back of beyond," Charles protested. "There were no Crown registers there, nor any need of them."

"Such reasoning means nothing at the royal court and if presented would only serve those who oppose you. You must remember, Charles, if there is not a clear and documented bloodline between lord and heir, the Crown has every right to reclaim all your holdings." Percy hesitated a moment, then ventured, "Might I ask, if you seek another besides Nicole, why not approach your brother?"

"Because he would accept," Charles said simply.

"I beg your pardon?"

"You know the code of my legacy far better than I. The earl of Harrow must reside in Harrow Hall. Andrew would come if I asked. I know this for a fact. But he would be utterly miserable, and his wife would positively loathe the life here. Not to mention that they'd lose everything they have struggled so hard to build." He thought back to his brother and the visceral bond that Andrew shared with his people, with his church and village. "It would kill him stone-dead to return to England."

Percy nodded his acceptance. "Back to Anne, then. Her blood parents are still alive, are they not?"

"Yes," Charles grudgingly agreed.

"Then you have no hope of succeeding." Percy settled his hands across his ample girth. "My dear friend, at the best of times such an endeavor would be extremely difficult. There is no blood relation, nothing upon which a claim of legal heritage might be laid."

"Adoptions take place all the time!"

"Indeed they do, but not involving earls of the realm."

Charles rounded on the seated attorney. "I thought you were my ally in this!"

"That most certainly is the case. You can trust me to give you honest advice and counsel at all times." Percy seemed unaffected by Charles's rising ire. "May I explain myself?"

"Carry on then." Charles resumed his pacing.

"Any transfer of royal title and lands that does not follow the line of blood must be recognized by the Crown. Even in the best of circumstances, such permissions are rarely given. The truth is, the Crown is jealous of your wealth and property. Not to mention the fact that they are boiling over your recent public defection. They would be quite happy to see your holdings disbursed upon your demise."

Charles stopped in front of a window. "So my recent proclamation before Parliament has churned up continuing ire."

"You had little hope to begin with. Now you have none at all," Percy agreed. "You also have a new and formidable enemy."

Charles did not have to think long to hazard a guess. "Lord Harwick?"

Percy nodded solemnly. "He represents the Crown's interests, but he also acts with a vengeance that is all his own. Give him such a lever, and I assure you he'll pry loose both your titles and holdings. You would be left a pauper."

Charles peered out the window as the afternoon light gradually softened and the distant valley faded to russet shadows. "I suppose it was to be expected."

"To all who oppose the war, you are a hero," Percy added. "I include myself among those people, as does Thomas. He absolutely reveres you." But Charles remained silent, still facing the glass. So Percy continued, "You have a worthy heir in Nicole. She may not suit the place and the title so well as Anne, but I am certain she'll do her very best to make you proud."

"Of that I have no doubt," Charles replied quietly. "Life is strange, is it not?"

"Very strange indeed, old friend."

With his face pointed toward the dying day, he mused softly, "God has seen fit to grant me exactly what I requested. I have a beautiful, spirited young lady who will, if I ask, accept to carry on my lineage."

The leather settee creaked as Percy sat up straight. "If you ask?"

Charles did not turn from the window. "What . . . what am I to do?" he whispered.

Chapter Thirty

Nicole finished reading the letters a second time and then stepped away from Anne and the child. Most of the staff had returned indoors. Will and one of the footmen were unpacking the carriage hold. Only Anne was watching, and Nicole knew she needed to say something. "I think I shall go for a walk."

"But don't you wish to freshen up from the journey?" Anne asked.

"No, I shall just . . ." Not knowing what further to say, Nicole simply excused herself and left. She took the little path that led around the manor, being careful not to allow her feet to begin hastening until she was out of sight. Even then she did not run, though she wanted to race so fast her feet would grow wings and fly her far away from here. Someone might be watching. If not a maid on the back balcony, then a gardener or one of the visitors. Someone was always watching here.

The gardens were meticulously tended, laid out in checkerboard patterns of greenery and flowers and shrubs. Even the bushes were trained to grow in a certain manner, then cut to resemble a castle wall. Freestanding shrubs were trimmed to favor birds, rabbits, and squirrels. The trees had been planted and made to form orderly lines of shade. Nicole continued down the long path now leading away from the manor. Overhead, birds flitted and bees hummed, drawn by the fragrant fruit that pulled heavy on the branches. She finally reached the path's end and walked over the cattle guard—a trough with a narrow-planked bridge over which cattle would not pass. Beyond this began the first of the manor's fields. Only here did Nicole permit the first tears to fall.

It was not a longing for family that left her filled with such sorrow. Time and events had scattered those closest to her heart, so that there were as many of her loved ones in England as there were in Nova Scotia or Louisiana. And she did love her uncle Charles. He was a good man, with a fine heart and a great mind. She knew without a shadow of doubt that if she asked, he would release her. But she would not. Could not. Not even when her heart felt close to breaking with longing for a land so far away, so different from here in England.

Nicole followed the trail out beyond the first field, down through rushes and an ancient spread of wild oaks, finally coming to the banks of a swift-running stream. There she came upon a delightful scene, unspoiled by any taming hand. Yet even here she did not find what she truly sought. There was none of the wild vastness of the colonies. None of the challenges of great open vistas, nor the feeling that came from days of traveling from village to capital. Here the winters did not blast off the sea with raging fury, as she had known during the winters in Nova Scotia. Here the summers did not bake with the heat of the Louisiana bayou. Here the seasons were gentle. Even the foulest weather was milder.

Nicole wiped her face as she looked for a rock where she could sit and watch the bubbling stream. But as she sat and observed the speckled trout that lazed beneath the water's surface, her mind searched for a different scene. One that stared out from a cliffside and over far broader, bluer waters.

It was strange how Catherine's letter had affected her. Her mother had neither begged nor expressed any aching sorrow. Instead, she had merely related the daily events of their lives: working at the Acadian school, Andrew's ministry, helping new families settle in, and about their neighbors and friends in Georgetown. Yet the words had caused Nicole to feel transported, taken back to the harsher world of Nova Scotia. For a single instant she'd seen everything anew that she was giving up—all she was losing by becoming Charles's heir. Not just now, but for all time.

Nicole bowed her face over her knees and prayed as she wept. Why was it all so difficult? She knew her duty and was willing to do it. Why then did she know peace one moment and sorrow the next? Would it be her destiny always to feel torn in two? Was this a burden she had to carry all her life?

There came no answer, only birds singing and the music rising from the stream. After a while, Nicole gathered her skirts and went to the water's edge. She crouched down and splashed water on her face to erase the marks of her tears. Then she straightened, took a long, shaky breath, and began walking back to the manor.

For Anne the final weeks of summer and the beginning of autumn swept by quickly and with ease. Work and responsibility seemed to unfold to meet her, so that soon the women's society was rapidly growing. The two south-facing drawing rooms were converted into permanent gathering places, and the manor became an ever-increasing hive of activity.

Thomas Crowley was released temporarily from his uncle's London offices and took up residence in the manor's smaller gatehouse. From there he helped supervise many of their projects, especially those in which Charles had taken a personal interest. Coordinated efforts were applied to Charles's plans to modernize farming techniques, which were expanded to include neighboring landholdings. And a more unified position was established to oppose the enclosure of common lands that had resulted in an increasing number of small farmers losing their homes. They also started health programs in the local villages, putting into practice guidelines for sanitation and infant care.

Anne found she received comfort from

two sources. The first was her morning Bible studies with Nicole. For as the work occupied more of their time, so too grew the intensity of their study. It was here that Nicole shone, and her hungry delving into the Scriptures proved to be times filled with surprise and pleasure for Anne. Nicole threw herself into whatever work was at hand, giving the task all her energies. In most cases, though, she sought Anne's guidance. Nicole was not the leader type. This was something that came much more naturally to Anne. Yet Nicole was not resistant, nor did she resent Anne's guidance. Far from it. Nicole was the most willing worker, the most eager helper.

The second source of support was Thomas Crowley. He too proved to be a tireless advocate, who was constantly aiding and advising Anne. Anne's only regret was that during his time at Harrow Hall, his initial ardor for Nicole seemed to fade. They still enjoyed each other's company and worked well together, but the romance never developed. They remained friends, nothing more. Anne took small comfort in the fact that Thomas never declared any intention toward Nicole, which meant her sister had no reason for raised hopes. Besides, Nicole seemed to care little about romance these days. Since Charles's proclamation in Parliament, there had been no invitations from the landed gentry, nor any suitors come to call, yet neither seemed to bother Nicole at all.

Of Lord Reginald Harwick—the formidably powerful man Nicole had confronted on the balcony—there had been no sign. Occasionally Anne would hear Charles and Thomas speaking together in hushed tones, suggesting they did not wish for word to spread. She was fairly certain Harwick's name had come up on several such occasions. Always Charles would retreat from these discussions with his forehead creased in worry, his hand massaging his chest.

The final Thursday in September saw Anne with the first free moments in weeks. She escaped to the back garden and the bench among the sheltering shrubs. All about her, the world was cloaked in brilliant autumn hues. The neighboring trees had begun their annual transformation and glinted proudly in the afternoon light. The day remained warm, yet there was a faint hint of northerly breeze that spiced the air with a special scent. Anne knew the fine weather would not last.

"Mrs. Mann?"

She looked up from her bench and

smiled at Thomas Crowley's tentative approach. "I think it is high time you call me by my given name," she said.

"I hope I am not disturbing you."

"Not at all." She slid over to make room for him. "John is off riding with Charles and could be gone for days. The child has taken to the horse like no one I've ever seen. All he has to do is hear a horse whinny and he's beside himself with excitement."

"He's truly the bonniest child I have ever known," Thomas agreed. "And Charles is a devoted uncle."

A light gust of wind shivered the bush overhead, and the chill drifted down to where Anne sat. Even so, she felt sheltered, as if the world itself were protecting her. "I am so very happy here," she confessed.

"That is plain to all who know you," Thomas said. "The place agrees with you."

"Yes, it does." A myriad of thoughts came rushing into her mind. The same thoughts she'd had so often lately, as she wondered how long she might stay and whether she might ever feel this way again. She pushed them away and said, "Nicole has ridden out with Will to meet the doctor." This was yet another of their projects, arranging for a doctor to tend the illnesses among the outlying villages. "She promised to be back in time for tea."

After a moment of silence, Thomas mused, "It has often struck me that you two ladies share the same spirit, as though one person occupied two bodies."

"What a remarkable thing to say," Anne said.

"Miss Nicole loves you intensely, so much so that she does not seem to mind your having assumed her position as leader in the many activities here."

"I don't mean to take anything from her."

"Well do I know it." Thomas studied her, his dark eyes gleaming with the fervor that had become his trademark. "I hope you do not take offense at my speaking so openly."

"To be equally frank, you say things I've often wondered about myself," Anne said. "To call her *sister* does not seem a strong enough word for how I feel about Nicole. If only . . ."

Thomas watched her, then finished quietly for her, "If only she could be happy."

"Yes."

"At least she's at peace. At least she has her God."

Anne then gave voice to the concerns that had been disturbing her nights. "I wish she could find a group of like-minded folk here, people to support her and pray with her after I am gone. But the church here . . ."

Thomas nodded. "Any words I speak on this point would paint a fearful picture of this day and age. England, I regret, is a fallen land."

"So I have noticed," Anne said, hurting for Nicole.

"The churches here in Sutton parish are typical of our realm—low attendance, lazy vicars, and dull sermons. England has joined with France and others in what they like to call the 'enlightened age.' " A bitter, angry note entered his voice. "The elite consider it fashionable to treat matters of faith with skepticism. They claim that rational man stands at the center of creation. In response to the call of faith, they cry, 'I think, therefore I am!' "

Anne felt a chord being struck in her heart. This man's passion thrilled her. She leaned forward and listened more attentively.

"The only trinity that interests these so-called enlightened folk is the monarch, our Parliament, and scientific advancement," Thomas went on. "They claim that reading the so-called book of nature offers all one needs to know of God. And they reduce

Jesus Christ to an ethical figure, a worthy teacher of practical living. What a lonely and deceptive prison!" Thomas slapped the bench between them. "How it cages man's hopes! How it blinds us to the eternal bridge!"

Again Anne found herself exhilarated by his words. "But in Wales we saw just the opposite. The churches were full, and people were seeking to live a devout life."

"Yes, and were that only to happen here!" Thomas said. His eyes blazed with the zeal of finding someone who shared his concerns. "It is not merely an issue of which church one attends. What's needed is the same preparations in England that led to the revival in Wales. Door-to-door evangelism by women and open-air preaching. A recognition of what it means to live a religion of the heart."

Such an invitation caused Anne's heart to take flight. "That's a challenge worthy of dedicating one's lifetime to its success!"

"That's my great big lad!" Charles held the reins so that they ran through John's tiny fingers. The boy continued to bounce up and down long after Charles had reined in the mare. Charles smiled as the nanny hurried over. He greeted her and said, "An hour in the saddle and still the lad's eager for more."

"That's as may be," the nanny replied, reaching for the child, "but it is past his dinnertime, and the young master needs a rest."

John put up a pretty fuss as he was handed down, then wailed and reached two grasping hands woefully back toward Charles. Charles chuckled both at the boy's antics and his own continual pleasure in spending time with John.

Then the pain hit him, harder than it had in weeks. Charles would have gripped his chest with both hands had not Will chosen that moment to come racing around the side of the stables. Charles gritted his teeth against the pain, took a couple of tight breaths, and said with false joviality, "What says the glass, young Will?"

"Falling, sir. Falling fast, it is." He took hold of the reins. In the past year, Will had shot up such that his head now crested the stirrups. "Nasty weather ahead, sir. You mark my words."

"That's what must be troubling my joints, then." Charles raised and lowered his shoulders, willing the pain to ease.

"Do you need a hand coming down, sir? Shall I run and call for help?"

"Not a bit of it. Just give me half a moment." Gradually his chest seemed to unbind itself, and Charles was able to lift his leg over the horse and slide to the ground. He landed hard and leaned against the horse's flank. When he noticed Will's anxious look, he forced a smile. "A change of weather bothers me more these days, that's all. Price of growing older, I suppose."

"Aye, sir, it is the same with Mam. She's always going on about her back and her knees when the blows are coming on."

Charles patted the boy on the head and then headed for the manor. He entered through the side door and was pulling off his boots when Gaylord appeared with a steaming mug. "Thought you might use a cup, m'lord."

"Most thoughtful, Gaylord." Charles sat down and sipped the hot tea, grateful for the excuse to remain where he was. "Any news?"

"Aye, sir. The post is in. There's a note saying Mrs. Judith Mann is coming in on tomorrow's coach. And a court messenger from London, bringing papers under Lord Percy's instruction, and a message that the man himself will be coming this very after-noon as expected." Gaylord smiled. "And he's bringing a pianist, sir!"

"Is he, now? Music and a houseful of guests. Upon my word, that's good news." Charles did not play an instrument, nor did he sing, but he loved music all the same and enjoyed sitting and listening. He was kind to amateurs and deeply moved by perform-ances of real talent. Handel was a favorite, as were Bach and Haydn. Hymns and cho-rales and fugues brought him almost to tears. "Pass the news on to your dear wife."

"I've already done so, sir. Will you be having a bath now?"

"In time." With his chest expanding comfortably again, Charles handed back the empty mug and rose to his feet. "First there are a few things I must tend to. I shall be in the library if anyone wants me."

"Very good, sir. The post and Lord Percy's papers are all on the library desk as usual."

Charles mounted the stairs and entered the library, closing the door behind him. But he avoided the desk. He knew what lay there, tied with the purple ribbon and bearing the court seal. Under pressure from Percy, he had finally agreed to have the attorney draw up the documents that formally named

Nicole as his heir. There was no choice. This was not just because of his growing chest pains but also because of Lord Harwick, who had been relentlessly pressing the Crown for a review of Charles's right to select his successor. The things Charles heard spoken about Nicole left him panting with rage. No, there was no time to lose. Each day brought fresh word of Harwick's maneuvers.

All that was required now was his signature and that of a formal witness, which no doubt was why Percy was coming. And bringing the musician along for a celebratory tune was the sort of thoughtful gesture that made Percy such a good friend.

Charles had no interest in inspecting the documents. He was certain Percy had done his customary excellent work. Instead he moved to the library window and stood staring down at the back garden.

"Uncle?"

Charles spun around. "My dear Nicole, please come in."

"I knocked, but did not hear you respond." She stepped inside and shut the door. "Am I disturbing you?"

"Not in the slightest." Charles motioned to her. "Come over here, will you. There's something I should like you to see."

Nicole stepped into the window's light.

The afternoon sun revealed that she still wore her riding habit and outer cloak with a trailing of dust. She set her bonnet on a nearby settee, unfastened her cloak, then walked over to stand beside him.

Charles pointed at the couple seated on the bench within the surrounding shrubbery and said, "Now, what do you see there?"

Nicole looked down at where Anne and Thomas Crowley sat in intimate conversation, lost to all the world, caught up together in their shared thoughts. "If one did not know better, you would think they were in love."

"Indeed so." For an instant, Charles felt a sharp pain in wishing it were Nicole seated there rather than Anne. The flash of agony came and went so fast, he could not tell if it was physical or an inner longing. "Have a seat, my dear."

"Thank you, Uncle." But Nicole did not take the settee opposite his. She retrieved a high-backed chair from the corner and placed herself much nearer to him. Sitting with her back erect and her chin at a proper ladylike angle, she poised herself beautifully and said, "I have something I wish to say."

Charles surveyed her with deep fondness. "Upon my word, Nicole, I wish you could see yourself."

"Why?" As Nicole glanced down, her old hesitancy briefly resurfaced. "Forgive me for not changing from the road, Uncle. I've been busy in the village and I needed to speak with you before—"

"I did not mean to scrutinize. Quite the contrary. I simply found myself filled with pride over the wonderful woman you have become." He raised his hands in silent accolade. "My dear, you have become a lady. A viscountess in all but name."

Nicole settled once more, but now into a different stillness, as she quietly replied, "Thank you. That is precisely what I wished to speak with you about."

"Yes?"

"Perhaps I have delayed this too long, but I wanted to be absolutely certain. Not certain in the sense that I should stay here and do my duty to you and the Harrow name, but certain that I should be able to find a mission here and live out God's will in this station."

"Duty," Charles said softly. "Mission."

"Indeed. You are offering me a multitude of gifts. I wanted to be sure I could live up to the responsibility."

Charles marveled at the beauty of this poised woman, at the keening sorrow he felt in his heart. "And you feel you have done so?"

"I . . . I think so," Nicole said. "Yes. I may not be as much of a visionary as my sister Anne, but I shall always seek others' guidance." She lifted her chin a fraction more. "If you are still wishing to grant me the title and the honor, Uncle, then I am willing to be your heir."

"You are *willing*."

"Yes. I promise to do the very best I can, before you and before God. With all that I have within me and all that I am given."

"My dear, I am so proud of you. . . ." Then Charles stood and stepped back over to the window. He saw that Anne and Thomas were still on the bench, so engrossed in conversation they seemed unaware of the falling dusk. He said to the world beyond the manor, "I am moved beyond words by your offer, Nicole, and by the way you seek to fulfill your role."

"Thank you, Uncle."

Charles returned to his seat. "I find myself recalling the day of your arrival. Do you know, the first impression I had of you that day was not your stepping from the carriage, but rather your laughter drifting upon the wind."

Nicole gave a half smile. "James let me

help drive the horses."

"When we walked inside that day," Charles said, "I asked one thing of you. I asked you to bring laughter and joy into this house."

Nicole blinked, then twice more. "It has been very hard learning the lessons of this world. But I've found a certain happiness, which came again to me this very afternoon. I am doing the best I can and I am truly helping people. They need me."

Charles rose, reached out his hands, and drew Nicole to him. He gave her a tight embrace and whispered in her ear, "You are one of the most beautiful, remarkable women I have ever had the honor of knowing." He then released her, feeling his throat swelling closed. "You have enriched my days, my dear Nicole. You adorn my heart and my home."

He watched her curtsy and take her leave, and then he walked back to the window. In the ensuing moments, the two on the bench had left, so that now there was neither sound nor person to interrupt his reverie of the grounds. The sunset was made brilliant by a gathering of clouds on the horizon. The sky was burnished a magnificent gold, with flashes of crimson and copper streaking the coming storm. He looked out at the waning day and wondered what was right, what his own duty was here.

The pain struck him then, a force so strong it stripped the strength from his legs.

Charles crashed to his knees, both hands clenching his chest, as sweat burst from his forehead. But there was a difference this time: No longer did he feel fear or pressure to accomplish anything, to *change* anything. With the single thread of thought he could manage beyond the pain, he wondered if this was what it meant to die and relinquish all. To accept that no matter what he did, it would account to little in the face of heavenly perfection.

Soon the pain disappeared. So sudden and total was its departure, it was hard for Charles to believe he had ever been attacked at all. He clambered to his feet and wiped the perspiration from his face. "Thank God," he whispered.

For in that instant he knew what was to be done. Finally, after all the hesitation and wondering and struggle, he now knew. There was no longer any question. None.

Chapter Thirty-one

Charles remained standing at the head of the stairs as Gaylord opened the front door and greeted the guests. He stayed there and observed how Nicole moved to the center of the front hall. She gave the solemn nod of the head, like a queen receiving visitors. "I bid you welcome, Lord Percy," Charles heard Nicole say, with the quiet dignity of a woman twice her age. "It is always good to see you again. Was your journey pleasant?"

Percy seemed to recognize that, on some deeper level, the transition had been made. Her role had been accepted, and the transformation was now complete. He gave a bow as low as Charles had ever seen from the portly older gentleman, and replied, "All but the final hour, m'lady. We were struck by a great lashing of rain and such wind that I feared the carriage would be overturned."

Not one person walked in behind Percy, but two. The woman wore a mud-stained travel cloak and the weary expression of one who had had a trying journey. The man was hawk-faced and held a piercing gaze. He instantly recognized Charles leaning against the upper banister and gave him a single sharp nod.

"May I have the honor," Percy went on, "of presenting Samuel and Sylvia Blackthorne, of Philadelphia. And this is the lady of the house, Miss Nicole Harrow."

"It is always an honor to welcome friends of Lord Percy," Nicole said. To the woman she said, "You look all done in, madame."

"My wife has not been in the best of health," Mr. Blackthorne replied. His voice matched his expression—hard and clear.

"Then we must put you straight into bed, and I shall ask my sister Anne to have a look at you. She has a wondrous talent for medicine."

Sylvia responded weakly, "But I was told that I was to perform tonight."

"Nonsense." Nicole's voice, though quiet, brooked no argument. "Guest accommodations have already been prepared for you. Gaylord, please have the maid draw a bath and ask Maisy to prepare a bowl of her excellent marrow broth. Then see if Anne might take a moment to speak with Mrs. Blackthorne here."

"At once, m'lady."

Percy observed Nicole with a keen eye and, to Charles's surprise, offered her a second bow. "My lady, might I be the first to congratulate you." He rose back up. "Not merely for the position which is now yours, but for the way you have come to deserve it."

Nicole reached out her hand and touched the gentleman's arm. "It will only be with God's help and the wisdom of trusted friends such as yourself, Lord Percy, that I shall manage."

Charles's heart swelled with affection and pride as he watched his niece below.

It was obvious that Percy had also been deeply affected by Nicole's presence this night. "I am yours to command, my lady. And might I add that I am more than confident you will not merely manage, but thrive at it."

Charles retreated, leaving Nicole as hostess. Percy was right, of course. There was no question in Charles's mind but that she would thrive.

After dinner Charles invited the two gentlemen to join him in the library. Mr. Blackthorne entered the room, saying, "I must thank you once more for your niece's

kind ministrations, Lord Charles. I understand my dear wife is already feeling much
better. She asks that I extend her apologies
for not playing the piano tonight as she intended."

"She has graced the concert halls of
Philadelphia and New York, among others,"
Lord Percy added.

"Then I shall look forward to hearing
her upon another occasion," Charles said.
In truth, he was not of a mind for music just
then. "But at least it grants us an opportunity to speak together on other matters."

"Yes, of course," Samuel Blackthorne
agreed. "Lord Percy and others have related
to me the sacrifice you have made on behalf
of our efforts. And so on behalf of the Continental Congress, sir, I offer you our humble thanks."

"I did not see it as a sacrifice," Charles
said, "but as my duty." He leaned forward
in the settee and added, "My duty to my
king."

Responding with a somber nod, the colonial did not appear surprised. "Which
makes your actions all the more laudable,
sir."

Charles resisted the urge to wave aside
Blackthorne's comment. He had no intention of showing disrespect to his guest, yet

he had no desire to be praised either. Nor did Charles want to spare the time. Everything seemed to press down on him now. He felt both a growing sense of impatience and of peace, as though there was time left for only the essentials. Essentials such as the first formal dinner, where Nicole sat at the head opposite Charles and assumed her role as the manor's hostess, or riding his horse with John, and time for other matters . . . "Mr. Blackthorne, I would ask if you are willing to act on my behalf."

The gentleman shifted uncomfortably, caught now by his words of gratitude. He glanced at Lord Percy, who seemed mystified by Charles's request. "That . . . would depend, Lord Charles."

"As a loyal British subject, I cannot offer support to forces opposing my king. And yet I consider this war to be a tragic folly. I must do something. . . ." He stood up and walked over to his desk, sorted through some papers, and pulled from them a document. "I have prepared this. It is in rough form, so Percy will have to fancy it up. But the gist of it is that I wish to establish homes for women who have been widowed by this war. And homes for orphans, as well."

The man leaped to his feet. "My dear Lord Charles!"

"My desire is to see such houses of comfort established in all thirteen colonies. Perhaps it will help the weakest of those who now suffer the consequences of our folly."

Samuel Blackthorne grabbed Charles's hand and wrung his arm violently. "Lord Charles, this is a magnificent gesture! Truly it is."

"I must agree," Percy said from his perch on the settee. "You have done us all proud."

"You cannot imagine the number of people I've met on this journey who claim the best of intentions and yet are seeking their own selfish gain," Blackthorne continued.

"Yes, well . . ." Charles managed to extricate his hand. "I seek nothing for myself."

"Perhaps not, m'lord, but I have something for you nonetheless." Blackthorne reached into his coat pocket and withdrew a sealed parchment. "My voyage here was not just to thank you for your actions before Parliament, m'lord. It was also to gauge the man and his motives."

Percy stiffened. "You said nothing of this."

"Because I was instructed not to." His hawkish features did not waver. "The Continental Congress is now considering a motion whereby the property of our British opponents is to be seized and redistributed. This would include all the landholdings of absentee British landlords."

"What!" Percy sputtered and struggled to rise. "This is an outrage!"

"On the contrary," Charles admonished. "It is perfectly reasonable in time of war. England has done the very same on a number of occasions."

"Just so." Blackthorne handed over his carefully folded papers. "This document attests to your services to the new United States of America, m'lord. And confirms your rightful ownership of the property in Massachusetts."

As he accepted the document Charles felt an energy race up his fingers and straight to his heart. Instantly he knew this gift for what it was. "I am indeed grateful, sir."

"It is I who am thankful, both for your gift and for your hospitality." Blackthorne bowed and started across the room. He opened the door, then paused long enough to look back and add, "My only regret is that England does not have more men like you at her helm."

After the door had closed quietly behind Blackthorne, Percy turned to Charles and said, "I am absolutely thunderstruck!"

Charles smiled down at his old friend. "Let me call for Nicole. I believe the evening might yet hold more surprises."

Chapter Thirty-two

Nicole and Anne were seated in the antechamber, seeing duty now as baby John's nursery. Anne had drawn her chair close enough to reach out and rock the cradle with her foot. If she and Nicole kept their voices down, there was no need to worry over disturbing the sleeping child. The older John became, the deeper grew his sleep. The nanny had remarked on this as well, saying that in another year or so the child would nap through heaven's trumpets.

A single candle burned from the side table, casting the room into a smaller and more intimate space. It was a place for secrets, made cozier still by the baby's peaceful slumber. But the girls were silent for a time, at peace with each other and the night. Finally Anne spoke, confessing softly, "I had a most wondrous talk with Thomas Crowley today."

"I saw," Nicole replied. "Charles and I spied upon you from the library window."

"I thought I saw a head appear, but I did not wish to draw Thomas away from his talk." Anne still felt a thrill of excitement from their words. "I was so very moved by what he had to say, Nicole."

"I saw," she repeated. "I am so happy for you."

Anne felt a slight blush rise to her cheeks. "Does it show?"

"Not so much from you. But the way Thomas watched you across the table to-night at dinner, I thought he would scorch the linen."

The blush grew stronger. "Now you jest."

Nicole smiled slightly. "Only a little. He's positively smitten, you know."

"You shouldn't talk so."

"Whyever not?"

"Because . . . I feel as though I am being untrue to Cyril's memory."

Instead of offering the expected comfort of reassuring words, Nicole asked, "So you care for Thomas?"

"I . . ." Anne swallowed. It was hard to confess such things, not so much to Nicole but to herself. "I fear I do."

Again there was Nicole's quiet assessment. "Have you prayed on this?"

"I have. In fact, I feel as if God's hand is upon our quest."

Nicole's head tilted downward, causing her rich auburn hair to spill over one shoulder. "That's an odd word to describe a relationship."

"Well, it is far more than that. I sensed God speaking to me through Thomas this afternoon, outlining a work I might do here for Him—work I would be suited to perform."

"Like a calling," Nicole whispered.

"Yes, perhaps even that," Anne said.

Nicole turned and stared at the candle. Anne was again struck all over again by the aura of strength and beauty that emanated from Nicole. The strong lines of her face were heightened by the candle's shading, as were the depths to her eyes. "I should think," Nicole said, "Cyril would be more than happy to see you returning to life and the future with such a sense of dedication to our God."

The power of those quietly spoken words was enough to bring tears to Anne's eyes. Impatiently she brushed her vision clear and said, "Might I stay with you in

Harrow Hall a while longer?"

"What a question," Nicole chided. "This is your home for as long as you wish."

"Thank you, dear sister." Anne hesitated a moment, then said, "I only wish you would find a man and a love for yourself."

Again the gaze returned to the candle. "First I must find my place," Nicole said.

"What are you saying? Your place is here. All know it to be so."

Nicole's eyes remained locked on the flame. "A calling, then. A purpose of my own. A direction and a—"

The words were cut off by a soft knock on the door. Gaylord opened and said, "Forgive me, ladies, but Lord Charles asks if Miss Nicole might join him and Lord Percy in the library."

A faint shudder ran through Nicole's body, which she quickly suppressed. "Of course." She then rose up and crossed to the door, only pausing there long enough to whisper back to Anne, "Pray for me. Please pray."

Nicole stood motionless outside the library doors. All the determination and resolve in the world were not enough to hold back the single tear now rolling down her cheek. She wiped it away and in the same motion knocked on the door. Instantly a voice called from within for her to enter. Still she hesitated as she struggled with herself.

The hardest thing she had ever done was to reach down and turn the handle.

Charles smiled at his niece as he welcomed her. "My dear Nicole, please do join us."

She stepped inside and softly closed the door. Nicole immediately spied the sealed documents on the table beside Percy. Charles noticed her trembling and also the way she stifled it. Nicole lifted her chin, gathered the folds of her dress, walked over and settled onto the edge of the settee—graceful and dignified as a queen. "It is growing rather late, Uncle. Should this not perhaps wait until tomorrow?"

"No, it should not." He saw how Percy's smile of anticipation gradually disappeared in the face of Nicole's solemnity. Charles sat down in the chair opposite them and could not help but take a moment to wish for things to be different. But he pushed this aside with the strength given him by the afternoon's realization and the evening's gift. "You look beautiful tonight, my dear."

"Stunning," Percy agreed.

"Thank you, Uncle." Nicole folded her hands in her lap and waited, forcing herself not to look at the papers on the table.

"I've asked you to join us here, Nicole, because there are matters of great import to be settled," Charles said.

"Here, here," Percy said.

Charles continued. "I've decided that I shall not ask you to become my heiress after all."

"And may I be the first to congratulate . . ." Percy's mind caught up with what his ears just heard, and his jaw flopped open.

But Nicole was swifter to respond. She stiffened and said, "Have I offended you in some way, Uncle?"

"No, not at all. Far from it, my dear." Charles smiled sadly. "You have made me proud in every possible way. You have gone so far beyond my greatest hopes that I could do nothing but see God's hand in the woman you have become."

"Then why. . . ?"

"Yes, by all the stars! Why?" Percy sputtered. "I must insist, m'lord, that you think carefully—"

"Hold there," Charles ordered. When he was assured Percy would remain in his place, he turned back to Nicole and said, "It is difficult to explain, but I want you to know that I find myself utterly at peace with this. And peace is what I wish for you."

"I am, Uncle. I've found God's peace sustaining me here."

"Peace and something more, my dear. I wish for you also the blessing of *joy*. My own destination is set. For the first time, I can truly leave all my worldly affairs in God's hands. I am defeated and yet on the other hand I feel triumphant."

Nicole looked at him intently, and it seemed to Charles that her eyes held the clarity of precious jewels. "Is it your heart?" she asked.

He decided not to answer directly. "God has helped me to focus upon the *true* goal that lies ahead. I am beaten and yet I am victorious."

"I understand," Nicole whispered, her words trembling with the effort to maintain control.

"It is the least I can do," Charles said. Then he reached and took hold of her hand. "To reward you for the trials you have overcome, for the sacrifices you were willing to make."

"But I still am . . ." Nicole said and then took a shaky breath. "I *am* willing."

Charles smiled again. "But I don't ask this of you, Nicole."

Percy looked to be foundering on the settee as he struggled to collect himself from the shock. "M'lord, this . . . this is scandalous!"

"On the contrary," Charles said, not removing his eyes from Nicole. "Of all my decisions, of all my actions, this one has the feeling of being the most correct."

"You must realize that with the enemy you face . . . sir, you could lose your lands, your title, everything!" Percy protested.

"What I have," Charles replied softly, "in truth is not mine at all."

"Uncle, I must refuse."

"I beg you not to. I am releasing you from your obligations. In fact, I *want* you to return to the New World."

Percy stared at them openmouthed. "You want. . . ?"

"That's right." Charles then stood and walked over to his desk. "But there is something I would ask you to do for me."

Nicole was no longer able to hold back the tears. "Anything."

"I want you to live a full and joyous life. I want you to find your *own* destiny. I want you to become the woman we've all seen beginning to blossom these past months."

Nicole raised her hand to her lips to stifle the sobs.

Charles picked up the documents that were handed him that evening by Samuel Blackthorne. "These papers confirm my landholdings in Massachusetts. Percy, I want you to draft a deed that will transfer ownership to Nicole and then add sufficient funds to enable her to do with the land whatever she pleases. No matter what the Crown might do to me here, at least she'll be safe and well taken care of in America." He gave them both a grand and satisfied smile. "And transfer to Nicole ownership of the painting that graces the wall of her bedchamber. May it always remind you, my dear, of one man who will be praying for you the rest of his life."

Percy was unable to lift a hand to accept the packet. He just sat and watched as Charles laid the documents on the settee beside him. "But . . . what of your titles? Your home? Your holdings here, m'lord?"

"That's all in God's hands. As is everything upon this earth." Charles felt the burden of a lifetime suddenly lifted from his shoulders and his heart. He smiled with deepest affection at the quietly weeping Nicole and said, "My dear, I beg you to agree to my request."

Chapter Thirty-three

Over the following days, Harrow Hall became a hive of activity. Captain James Madden had responded promptly to Charles's letter of inquiry, stating there was a ship leaving in two weeks for Halifax from which they hoped to learn whether or not the New York port was still in British hands. The captain also mentioned that he'd be commanding the foredeck. This news was taken as a sign by all, and so the entire manor threw itself into preparations. For Charles, these days took on a breathless quality.

Even Lord Percy, indignant as he had been at the outset, could not hold himself back from becoming caught up in all the excitement. He finally left for London, where the newly drafted documents for the Massachusetts property were to be formally deeded and sealed. Percy had shouted from the carriage window as he pulled away that they were mad, the entire lot of them. Yet he was smiling, and, earlier, he had embraced Nicole, promising to pray for her every day. Furthermore, Percy had taken Charles aside and vowed to do everything in his power to arrange for Anne to be appointed his heir. The key, he said more than once, was to strike before Charles's foes could marshal their forces.

To everyone's amazement, the stabilizing force in the household had turned out to be their latest visitor, Judith Mann. Cyril's mother had arrived the day after Charles's surprising announcement. Immediately Judith set about helping Nicole prepare for the upcoming voyage. And there was not a moment to lose, that is, if the ship was to sail before the first of the winter storms arrived. For the weather seemed to emphasize the sense of urgency. The days were now marked by blustering showers and wind enough to toss the trees violently back and forth. Their world now lay littered with the parchment of a passing season.

Eleven days later they set out together for Portsmouth harbor. They traveled in Charles's carriage and a hired coach that trailed behind, both piled high with trunks and bundles. It was not a penniless colonial lass returning home, but rather a fine lady traveling in the style which befitted her station. Their departure was graced with the fairest weather in weeks, chilly yet filled with sunshine accompanied by a light breeze.

Charles had risen early that morning and gone downstairs for breakfast, finding Anne and Judith sitting together near the fire. He was about to greet them when Judith said, "I could not help noticing the affection you hold for Thomas Crowley."

Charles took a step back and listened as Anne replied, "I do hope you believe me that I mean your son's memory no disrespect."

"Which is precisely why I decided to mention this at all." Judith's chair creaked as she leaned forward, closer to her daughter-in-law. "My dear, you are young and alive with passion and potential. From everything I have seen, Thomas is a fine and upstanding gentleman."

"Oh, he is!" Anne cried. "He holds the Lord in his heart's central place and seeks ever to do His will."

"Of that I have no doubt. Nor do I question that His hand is upon your relationship."

"Mrs. Mann, to hear you say these words . . ." Anne stopped and composed herself. "I confess that with Thomas I find myself able to dream again. His hopes and plans for the future absolutely thrill me."

"I am very happy for you, then. Would you accept an old woman's advice?"

"Words from you are always welcome."

"Thank you, my dear. If the experience of years has taught me anything, it would be that in the matters of the heart, especially when one has endured such rough times as you, it is vital to move slowly and with caution. There's no need for rushing into anything. Take time to heal fully. Take time to come to know the man as well as his mission. Therein lies your greatest hope for lifelong happiness."

Charles turned and walked silently away. His breakfast could wait a while longer.

Though the morning brought the first autumn chill, Anne and Nicole elected to ride together in the hired coach, leaving John with Charles and Judith riding in Charles's carriage ahead. Some of the bundles that would not fit on the roofs of the carriage and coach had to be placed on the seats alongside the two women. One of the coach's windows stubbornly refused to close, so that the brisk weather hustled inside, carrying occasional leaves and the sounds of the road—clopping horses, creaking wheels, and the intermittent cracking of the driver's whip. Anne and Nicole nestled together beneath a large woolen travel wrap to stay warm.

It was all a distinct reversal as to how things had been expected to be, with Anne remaining behind in Harrow Hall and Nicole preparing for yet another seaborne adventure. At first they traveled in silence. Now and then a trivial word was passed back and forth, but the immensity of the occasion seemed to have stilled their tongues. Then Nicole finally spoke to the feelings of her heart. "I wish you were sailing with me. The voyage would be much more pleasant with you and little John along."

"I wish you were staying," Anne said. "I shall miss you so." She hesitated for a moment and then continued. "No, that's not quite honest. Deep inside, I know what you are doing is right. You would never have been truly happy here."

Nicole breathed deep, finding release in

Anne's forming the words she had so avoided speaking herself. "No."

"Duty bound, yes. I've no doubt you would have performed your duty well. But I fear that true happiness would have eluded you." Anne glanced at the world beyond the coach's window and then turned back to Nicole. "I've watched you. You have come to wear the social graces like a well-sewn garment. However, your eyes have never lost their restless longing. Often I have looked your way and found a hunger and a thirst."

"I was not aware that it showed. I tried so hard to mask it."

"I know you did, and I admired that about you. You would have set your chin and gone about what you considered your duty to Uncle Charles without a thought to your own happiness. I am so glad that Uncle Charles saw what I saw and was willing to free you from your sense of obligation."

Again there was silence.

"That does not mean I shall miss you any less," added Anne with a sigh. She reached over and clasped her sister's hand under the heavy blanket. "I cannot imagine what it will be like without you."

Nicole had to blink back tears. She

asked in a subdued voice, "Will you ever return to the colonies?"

Anne took a moment before answering. "I cannot say," she said at last. "I thought when I first left that I could not travel back soon enough. On the ship over, I was wishing to turn around and head back to the safety and security of home. But now... life keeps moving forward. I still long for family and the village. And I ache for the life I knew with Cyril. We had such a wonderful marriage. I had not fully realized how blessed I was until he departed." She paused then, gathered herself once more, and continued on, "But that's gone now, and I shall never have it again. There was a time when I thought I could not bear to live without Cyril. But God has sustained me. I am still here, still alive. At first I felt dead inside, yet how can one be dead if the pain is so sharp? And I had John. He gave me reason to keep on fighting, to hold on to sanity in an insane world.

"I believe God knew how much I should need my little lad. At least he was there with me... when Cyril died. And how I thank Him that Cyril was alive to see his son. That's something I can share with John. I can say to him, 'Your father held you in his arms. He prayed for you with his dying breath. He loved you greatly.' I tell him these things every night when I tuck him into bed. I want John to know and feel the love of the good man who was his father.

"I was befogged from medications during the birthing, so I did not realize at the time just how great a gift God had given me in allowing John to be born before Cyril passed away. But God had my good, my future peace and happiness well in mind when He planned as He did. I thank Him daily for that blessing."

Nicole stirred restlessly. It was still hard for her to hear Anne talk of her loss. She tucked the blanket close under her chin. Anne released her hand to wipe the corners of her eyes.

"So you see, I still don't know what God's plans are for me in the future," Anne continued. "I do hope I have enough discernment to hear and enough obedience to follow His will, whatever it may be. For now, in a way I cannot express, I feel His presence. His peace. His gentle assurance that I am where He intends me to be. I cannot explain it. I don't even understand it. Perhaps . . . perhaps He's led me here more for John than for me. I have this . . . this inner sense that this is right, though I cannot tell you why. I feel there's something ahead that will show me without a doubt why He's brought me here—what He has in mind for me and John."

She paused, drew a deep breath, and half-turned to Nicole. "Now and then I dare to hope that Father and Mother might decide to return to England. Perhaps bring Grandfather Price back to the land of his birth. But I will not press for that. It must be of God if it is to be at all."

Nicole felt her heart lurch. She wanted to cry aloud that she needed them there with her. Whatever would she do if Anne were to find some way to hold them here? But she halted the words before they formed, in time to hear Anne say, "And then I stop and remind myself that such thoughts are, well . . ."

Nicole murmured. "I confess to such selfishness myself."

Anne pressed firmly down upon Nicole's hand. "They are happy in Georgetown. Mother has never known any other life. She would be so distressed, lolling about a morning room. She has to be active, involved, helping those in need. And Father would find it impossible to return to life as a country squire. And Grandfather . . . I doubt he even claims England as his homeland any longer."

Nicole felt herself relax.

"And what of you?" Anne asked. "Will you return to Louisiana?"

Nicole shook her head. "Not unless I feel a very clear and direct leading from the Lord," she answered. "Some days I long for the bayous and the village. And especially for my folks. But I know I would not fit there now. Things have changed. I have changed." She remained thoughtful for a while as the face of Jean Dupree flashed momentarily in her memory. She had not thought of him for many months. She soon dismissed the thought and went on. "Life does not stay the same for very long, and one cannot go back to how it used to be. No, I don't suppose I shall ever return to Louisiana—at least not to stay. But as to my future, I expect there will be many changes ahead for me, things I cannot now sort through nor plan. Only God knows what they are to be."

They sat in silence as the carriage jostled over the rutted roadway. They both knew that when the journey ended there would still be so much that had not been said. Yet it was becoming harder to find the words to express their feelings.

"You will give them my love?" Anne asked softly.

"Right along with my own," Nicole replied.

"I do miss them."

Nicole gave Anne a look of sisterly understanding. "I know that," she whispered. "So do they."

Anne nodded, willing to take to heart this spoken truth.

Chapter Thirty-four

Portsmouth was a town filled with clamor, sailors, and the briny taste of the sea. Charles sat with Judith and pointed out the great houses built by trade with the far-flung world, the ships at anchor, the bales and bundles of newly imported goods. A convoy had recently arrived from the Orient, signaled by tall stacks of cedar chests which gave off pungent fragrances of spice and tea.

The carriage clattered along the cobblestone quayside, halting by a group of seamen tying up a ship's longboat. As Charles stepped from the carriage, a uniformed gentleman with bushy sideburns came forward and bowed. "A good afternoon to you, Lord Charles. Captain James Madden at your service."

Charles grasped the man's hand and wrung it gratefully. "What a pleasure it is to see you again, sir." He turned to the woman emerging from the carriage. "May I present Mrs. Judith Mann, a relative by marriage and, I am delighted to say, a dear family friend."

"An honor, Mrs. Mann." Captain Madden bowed a second time, then gestured and said, "You remember my wife, perhaps."

"Of course. A delight to greet you, madame." Charles took note of her heavy travel garb and the bundles at her feet. "You don't mean—"

"My younger daughter is with child, m'lord," she explained proudly. "Word arrived with the same post as your request for a ship and formal escort for your niece. I intend to travel with my husband."

Charles clapped the captain on the shoulder. "What glorious news! A finer escort for my niece I could not imagine."

"If we make the tide this day and have a strong wind in our quarter, we might be there for the wondrous event," Captain Madden declared.

"Give you joy!" Charles cried. "Give you great joy, and myself besides. I am positively delighted Nicole will be in such company for her voyage home." He spun around at Nicole's approach and said, "My dear, have you heard the wonderful news?"

Nicole curtsied. "It is indeed grand. I cannot think of a greater blessing upon the journey than to share it with such friends."

Captain Madden doffed his hat again and said, "It is we who are honored, m'lady."

"Indeed, ma'am." Emily Madden's smile was bright as the day. "I warrant I shall be offering you no more advice upon how to be a lady."

"Advice such as yours will always be welcome," Nicole said. "Always."

The captain then signaled for his men to begin loading the trunks and bundles aboard the longboat. "We have less than an hour before the tide changes, m'lord. Best say your farewells now."

Charles drifted back and observed as Nicole and Anne bid their tearful good-bye, fiercely embracing each other. The trip into Portsmouth and now the departure itself was proving a remarkable experience for Charles. All the emotions he would have expected to feel—anger, bitterness over his future, futility, defeat, disappointment with Nicole—none of these were present. Instead there was a peace so overpowering he wondered if it was a presage to his own death.

Judith moved alongside him and whispered, "Look how they cling together. It is hard to see where one girl ends and the other begins."

"And not just here and now," Charles murmured. "Young Crowley mentioned how they seemed as one spirit dwelling in two bodies. I could not agree more."

Then Judith looked up at Charles. "Anne has shared with me what you have done. I was moved to tears."

Charles glanced back at the woman and said, "Kind of you to say so."

"I am not the one who is kind here, Lord Charles." Her smile was so great and warm it revealed all the freshness that still resided in her, all the youth. "It is the gesture of a good man, the sort of which ballads should be sung and tales told for generations to hear and learn from."

Charles felt his face get warm. "My lady, I am deeply touched."

"As am I." She started to reach for his arm, but stopped, for others were watching. "You make me feel as though there might yet be years left to live."

He understood her words all too clearly. "I confess to having had the same thoughts upon our journey here."

From beneath her bonnet, she cast him a gaze of such warmth Charles felt it in his boots. "Indeed," she whispered.

"My lady, I have been married twice. Great unfortunate errors, the both of them. Done strictly for earthly gain, and the shame of these acts I shall carry all my days." He grimaced. "And now, when the Lord has opened my eyes as to what a true union might hold, I find I am barred from knowing such gain."

"Barred . . ." Judith realized her voice carried loudly. Softening her tone, she asked, "Barred how?"

"By ill health—my heart."

To his astonishment, Judith laughed out loud. "My dear sir, please forgive me, but you are a fine figure of a man, with none of the signs one might expect of a coming demise."

"Nonetheless, my lady, I could never ask anyone to take such a risk."

This time the hand did indeed reach and rest on his arm. "Ah," Judith said, smiling with her words, "but perhaps this lady is not asking."

Nicole released Anne only so she might pick up John. She held the baby as long as she could. Baby John clearly realized something was happening, something that would leave him unhappy. So when Nicole handed him back to Anne, he expressed his disapproval in the loudest possible way. Finally Anne took him and her own tears back to the waiting coach.

Nicole felt hesitant about approaching her uncle. Her emotions were in such a topsy-turvy state, she had not an idea what she was feeling or why she was crying.

Captain Madden could not contain his impatience any longer. From his position at the head of the longboat, he called, "Your pardon, m'lady, but the tide waits for no man!"

So Nicole stepped forward and said, "Uncle, I cannot begin . . ."

"Don't even try, my dear Nicole." Then Charles held her so close she could hear the irregular thumping of his heart. "All that lies between us goes far beyond the realm of words."

Nicole placed her hand on his chest. "I leave my heart here with you, Uncle, so that it might help give strength and comfort to your own."

"And I in turn offer you but one wish,"

Charles said, taking her hand and walking her toward the waiting longboat. "That you live well. Live well and enjoy God's many blessings."

As soon as she was safely on board, the captain barked, "Shove off, there! Bosun, have the men lay heavy on the oars!"

Nicole remained standing at her seat amidships, watching as the rowers pulled them ever further from the quayside where the gathering was waving her off. She waved back and cried out her farewells till the longboat passed around another ship at anchor, when Nicole had no choice but to turn and look ahead. Yet she gazed past the vessel to which they were rowing and focused on the horizon instead.

Out beyond the harbor walls, dazzling pillars of sunlight broke through the clouds to settle on the white-capped sea. Nicole searched further still, wondering at what she was leaving behind, at what now lay ahead.

They made swift progress across the waves. As they pulled up alongside the waiting ship, the bosun's chair was lowered. Emily Madden was the first to be lifted to the main deck. Scrambling up and down the rope ladders, the seamen were busy hefting bales and barrels and chests. Their actions were propelled by the rough cries coming from the captain and the officers on the quarterdeck. Even before Nicole set foot on deck, the sails were being unfurled, the anchor raised, the longboat secured. She stood as the ship gave way before the wind, heard the sails snap taut with the first press of the breeze, and watched as the people and houses lining the quayside turned gray as they intermingled with the sea mist and the distance.

To the wind and the future, Nicole whispered the question, "What is my destiny now?"

But there was no answer except the crying of gulls circling overhead. It seemed to Nicole that they sung the chant of her life, a voyage without end, bound by mystery and questions that would be answered only in God's holy presence.

Then heavy feet marched across the foredeck and descended the stairs near where Nicole held the railing. She knew the sound meant an officer approached, for only officers wore leather boots. She dried her eyes and prepared herself to speak with Captain Madden.

But when she turned, instead of facing the captain, she stared blankly at a tall, dashing officer with copper-blond hair and a slash mark under his right eye. He doffed his hat, bowed deeply, and said, "Forgive me for not being here to greet you upon your arrival, my lady. But all haste was required to make the tide."

"Captain Goodwind," she said, "what a nice surprise."

"Captain Madden requested that I accompany him on this voyage," Gordon Goodwind explained. "He and his wife are uncertain how long they will remain in the colonies, and such a ship as this must be kept busy." He hesitated, then added, "When I learned who was to accompany us, I was genuinely delighted."

Nicole felt a warmness spreading over her cheeks and neck. She could not recall feeling thus for ages, not since departing from Louisiana. It left her feeling almost shy as she said, "I shall eagerly await your company at dinner, sir."

For some reason, her words brought a similar flush to Goodwind's strong features. He bowed again, lower this time, and said, "Your servant, my lady."

Nicole watched him as he returned to his station on the foredeck. She then turned back toward the sea, while the ship passed the harbor's final rocky promontory on which rose a tall, white watchtower. Behind her, Captain Goodwind bellowed a string of orders. The ship made a graceful turning about, beating upwind. Footsteps raced across the main deck, and more sails opened with snapping force.

Nicole used her hand to brush the hair from her face, then lowered the hand to rest it on her chest. Strange that her heart would trip in time to the racing sailors. Stranger still was how she could stand there, so full of sorrow over having just left her loved ones behind, yet now thrilled by what lay ahead.

Chapter Thirty-five

The same startling peace followed Charles throughout the journey home. And although the questions that had carried him across the Atlantic in search of his brother still remained unanswered, somehow it did not matter any longer. The questions that mattered to him now had changed beyond all recognition.

He sat alone on his side of the carriage, with Anne and John and Judith sitting across from him. They sensed his thoughtful isolation and granted him as much silence as John would allow. For if there was anything the youngster loved as much as horses, it was Charles's carriage. John stood by the open window, bouncing up and down in Anne's careful grasp, blurting out in his own language at everything that caught his eye. The boy's excitement filled the carriage. Charles watched him with a smile, sighing contentedly as he reflected on how he'd reached a very special juncture. For even though nothing had been resolved, still everything was settled. Though he might face the dissolution of his estate and titles following his imminent demise, he honestly felt he could finally let go and die in peace. Whatever the future held, however short his remaining days, Charles felt he was ready. He welcomed the future as never before.

Judith looked over at him, and his smile tinged with a fond regret. It would have been so wonderful to come to know this fine woman better. Indeed, for the first time in many years he could consider the prospect of marriage with some genuine desire. But he turned away from her playful eyes as he reminded himself there was not sufficient time left for a budding romance.

Despite this, Judith was unwilling to release him so easily. "It is remarkable, Sir Charles, how the bonds of generations have brought us together."

"Indeed so, ma'am." Charles was glad for the reason to turn back to her. Judith Mann was not only pleasant to look at, he also found in her countenance all that his two earlier marriages had lacked. He was then hit with piercing regret over the many mistakes he'd made during his lost and wandering years. The neglected opportunities, the false paths. "Yes, I count it a great blessing that my niece had the wisdom to marry herself into your family."

Anne glanced over from her dutiful attending of the bouncing John long enough to reward Charles with a look from the heart. Then she turned back to the boy and said, "Yes, that's right, John. Many, many birds."

"I count it a godsend to call Anne my friend and daughter," Judith replied. "But that is not of what I speak."

"No?"

Her smile turned anxious. "I hope you will forgive me for divulging secrets, Sir Charles."

He felt a sudden drumming through his body, as if the road had risen to shake his very soul. "I am not certain I follow you, ma'am."

"There is in fact a *second* miracle that intertwines our families." She then looked at

Anne and said, "Ever since our first meeting I have wondered if I should mention this, and now I find I can withhold the secret no longer."

Charles leaned forward slightly. For some reason, he was finding it hard to breathe now. "What secret is that, ma'am?"

"The secret of our shared heritage," Judith said. "You see, my mother was your father's half sister."

Charles felt as though he'd been blasted back into his seat. He worked his mouth, yet could not speak.

It was Anne, wide-eyed with shock, who managed to ask, "They were what?"

"Siblings," she confirmed, looking pleased over the response to her words. "Sir Charles, your grandfather had two wives. The first died young, giving birth to my mother. The old earl then remarried, and eleven years later, his second wife gave birth to your father. My mother had long before this time fallen in love with a Welshman, a gentleman far below her station. Your grandfather was by all accounts a most domineering man and vengeful when crossed. My mother ran away to wed the man of her heart, and your grandfather never permitted her name to be spoken of again."

In reflex to his thundering heart, Charles reached up to massage his chest. It only added to his astonishment to discover that his heart was not hurting him.

"I fear my mother carried a good deal of your grandfather's same force of character," Judith continued, "for it was only when my mother lay on her deathbed that she shared with me the secret. How we were related by marriage to one of England's wealthiest scions. She asked me to guard this mystery well—which I have."

"Good woman!" Charles finally managed to gasp. "Do you have any idea what you are saying?"

In reply, Judith turned to Anne and said, "Naturally, when you and Cyril wed, I had no earthly idea who was your adoptive father's brother. It would not have occurred to me in a dozen centuries. Only when you wrote and told me of your visit and where you were staying did I then realize. It gave me such a start, I cannot begin to tell you."

"Gave you a start!" Charles laughed out loud. He lifted his cane and hammered hard on the wall that separated them from the driver. "My dear Mrs. Mann, gave *you* a start!"

As the carriage slowed down, Judith's expression showed her worry. "Oh, I do hope I haven't done anything wrong in sharing this secret with you both."

"Wrong? Wrong!" Charles leaned out the window and shouted up to the driver, "Is there a lay-by ahead?"

"We're at the outskirts of a village, m'lord. There must be a place for watering."

"Then pull in and turn this carriage around!"

The driver bent over so that his astounded face showed through the open window. "Around, sir?"

"You heard me! Now make all possible haste!"

"Oh, oh, dear me," Judith moaned. "I have ruined a perfectly splendid day with words I should never have uttered."

"My good woman, nothing could be further from the truth." Charles wanted to stop the carriage, fling open the door, and race around dancing a jig. But there was no time to waste. None. "Nothing whatsoever could be further from the truth!" he repeated.

Both women were alarmed as they stared at him. "I-I fear I don't understand," Judith said.

"My dear Mrs. Mann, you have made this day perfect!" He reached over and grasped her hand with both of his. "Do you have any idea, any idea at all the miracle you have just revealed to us here this very day?"

Anne gasped with the shock of realization. Her eyes grew round again as she looked from Charles to Judith.

The carriage swung wide and made the turn around, then the driver's head appeared once more. "Begging your pardon, sir, but what is to be our new destination?"

"London!" Charles laughed as the shock spread to Judith's features, as well. A blood relation, Percy had demanded. Someone who was linked to the Harrow name by blood would be the only assured heir, the only indisputable link to an earthly legacy. And now it was his. "Make all possible haste!"

"London it is, m'lord."

Judith whispered, "Do you mean . . ."

"I do indeed, my lady. I do indeed!" John chose this moment to turn and give them his widest grin. Charles laughed in reply. "Hold fast to the lad there, my dear Anne. For in your hands rests the Viscount John Harrow, ninth earl of Sutton, and the coming heir to Harrow Hall!"

The Promise of Hope
From Lancaster County

Beverly Lewis's compelling, dramatic fiction brings to life the rolling hills and quiet towns of Lancaster County. Whether exploring the effects a long-held secret might have on a closed Amish community or showing the clash of cultures between a New Order Amish woman and a city-born journalist, she creates unforgettable characters and explores vital spiritual themes in each one of her novels.

THE HERITAGE OF LANCASTER COUNTY

An emotional and poignant trilogy of novels is the series that marked Beverly Lewis's entrance into Christian fiction. In the quaint Amish community of Hickory Hollow, time stands still while cherished traditions and heartfelt beliefs continue to flourish. When Katie Lapp uncovers a satin baby gown buried deep in her mamma's attic trunk, the tranquillity of her life is shattered. Will her community bring her to redemption or will her world unravel, leaving in its wake a hopeless furrow of pain?
The Shunning, The Confession, The Reckoning

The Postcard and *The Crossroad*

Growing up Amish, Rachel Yoder dreamed of becoming a woman of confidence, but as a young widow she is shadowed by grief and trapped in a lonely solitude. Philip Bradley, a world-weary journalist, meets Rachel while on assignment in Lancaster County. His discovery of a postcard leads them to the bedside of a woman with a tale of dark secrets and lost love.

The Redemption of Sarah Cain

Lydia Cottrell, eldest of five Amish orphans, makes a promise to her dying mother—to "keep the family together." But custody has been granted to her aunt, a businesswoman who cares little for Mamma's last wish. Sarah Cain is stunned by the news that she is to be the children's guardian. Can she sacrifice her career and her modern ways to raise the children? And what of the man in her life? Riveting and dramatic, this novel examines the balance between prevalent values and those of tradition.

◊ BETHANYHOUSE
11400 Hampshire Ave. S.
Minneapolis, MN 55438
www.bethanyhouse.com
1-800-328-6109